Pao

By the Same Author

The Art of Youth Work

A Novel

Kerry Young

BLOOMSBURY
NEW YORK · BERLIN · LONDON · SYDNEY

Published by Bloomsbury USA, New York

All papers used by Bloomsbury USA are natural, recyclable products made from
wood grown in well-managed forests. The manufacturing processes conform to
the environmental regulations of the country of origin.

Every reasonable effort has been made to contact copyright holders of material
reproduced in this book, but if any have been inadvertently overlooked the
publishers would be glad to hear from them and to make good in future
editions any errors or omissions brought to their attention.

LIBRARY OF CONGRESS CATALOGING-IN-PUBLICATION DATA

Young, Kerry, 1955–
Pao : a novel / Kerry Young. —1st U.S. ed.
p. cm.
ISBN-13: 978-1-60819-507-7 (pbk.)
ISBN-10: 1-60819-507-4 (pbk.)
1. Chinese–Jamaica–Fiction. 2. Organized crime–Jamaica–Fiction.
3. Social classes–Jamaica–Fiction. 4. Jamaica–Fiction. 5. Jamaica–Race
relations–Fiction. 6. Jamaica–History–20th century–Fiction.
I. Title.
PR6125.O86P36 2011
823'.92–dc22
2010040733

First U.S. Edition 2011

1 3 5 7 9 10 8 6 4 2

Typeset by Hewer Text UK Ltd, Edinburgh
Printed in the U.S.A. by Quad/Graphics, Fairfield, Pennsylvania

For my father, Alfred Anthony Young (1924–69).
My mother, Joyce Young.
And Jamaica, land we love.

People 'make their own history, but they do not make it as they please; they do not make it under self-selected circumstances, but under circumstances existing already, given and transmitted from the past'.

Karl Marx

1

1945

Me and the boys was sitting in the shop talking 'bout how good business was and how we need to go hire up some help and that is when she show up. She just appear in the doorway like she come outta nowhere. She was standing there with the sun shining on her showing off this hat, well it was more a kind of turban, like the Indians wear, only it look ten times better than that. Or maybe it just look ten times better on her.

She got on this blue dress that look like it must sew up with her already inside of it, it so tight, and a pair of high-heel shoes I never before seen the like of. I almost feel embarrassed that she come here and find me like this, sitting on a empty orange crate, in my vest with the beer bottle in my hand.

So we all three of us quickly jump up and ask her how we can help. And what she want is for me to go visit her sister in the hospital so I can see what some white sailor boy do to her.

'What he do to her?' Hampton ask.

'He beat her. He beat her so bad I can hardly recognise her, my own sister.'

'So what he beat her for?'

'Just go see her. That is all I am asking of you.' And then she look directly at me and say, 'Can you do that?'

And I just say yes even though I don't know why.

Then she say, 'Thank you,' and hand me a piece of paper with the details of the hospital where the sister at. The sister name Marcia Campbell. Then she say, 'Marcia will tell you how you can contact me if you decide you want to help.' And she turn and walk outta the shop.

No sooner than she gone Hampton start, 'The sister a whore, man.'

'How you know that?'

'Sure, man, sure. What you think she doing with the sailor boy? They most likely arguing over money. And this one, she probably a whore as well even though she look so good and I bet she taste good too, but she a whore, man, sure.'

'So what you saying, if she a whore it don't matter if she get beat?'

'It come with the territory. Like should I get vex if somebody try my patience? No, man, it come with the territory.'

I ask Judge Finley, 'You think she just a whore as well?'

'Yes. I think most likely Hampton right. But if this white boy really beat her like the sister say then you have to ask yourself what kinda man this is and if it OK for a white man to beat a Jamaican woman and it pass just like that.'

'Cho, man, white men been beating Jamaican women for three hundred years.'

'That is true,' I say to Hampton, 'but this is the first time anybody come ask us to do something 'bout it.'

The next day I go up the hospital to see Marcia Campbell, and she is in a state. The boy break her arm and two ribs and he mash up her face so bad her own mother wouldn't recognise her. Then she show me the bruises and fingerprints he leave all over her body, and her back where him kick her. Is a wonder the girl still alive.

I ask her, 'You know the name of the man who do this to you?' And she tell me, and I say, 'How can I get hold of your sister?' I didn't ask her nothing 'bout what happen because I reckon no kind of argument could justify the condition this woman was in.

When I catch up with the sister she tell me her name Gloria

and she ask me what I going to do. So I say to her, 'You don't need bother yourself 'bout that. You just leave it with me.' And afterwards I tell Hampton to go sort it out.

A week later Gloria Campbell come down the shop with money to pay me. She hear 'bout what happen to the sailor boy and how him in the naval hospital. I say to her, 'I don't need no money for that. The bwoy had it coming.' So she put the money back in her purse.

Then she say to me, 'You know what happen with all of that?'

And I say, 'No, and I don't need to neither.'

'But you know the business we in?'

'I can have a damn good guess.'

'We have a house in East Kingston. We got four girls living there. Men think that just because we a house of women they can come there and do whatever they want. That's how come what happen to Marcia.'

So I tell her, 'This got nothing to do with me. Yu ask me to help yu and now it done. Yu don't need to come here to talk 'bout it or explain nothing to me.'

'I wanted to ask you if you would keep an eye on us. You know like you watch over Chinatown.'

This is the first time I look at this woman properly. Look her in the face because it suddenly strike me that she is a serious businesswoman. And when I look at her she catch me the same way she did that first day. And even though my head is telling me not to get involved with her, my mouth is moving and I hear myself saying, 'What do you have in mind?'

When I tell Zhang he say, 'They have a name for that.'

'I am not pimping these girls. They running their own business. All I am doing is trying to make sure what happen to Marcia Campbell don't happen again. They paying me the same as Mr Chin and Mr Lee and all the rest of them.'

'Chin and Lee run honourable business. What these girls do not honourable.'

3

'They making a living. You want me not do it?'

'Is your business now, I tell you that the day I retire. You must run it way you see fit.'

The first time I go over to the East Kingston house Gloria invite me to dinner to celebrate Marcia coming home from the hospital. They make a traditional Jamaican dinner, stew chicken and rice and peas with coleslaw and cho-cho that Gloria cook herself. The only people that is there is me and these four women. And what I discover is that these women are just ordinary people who talk 'bout everything from the price of rice to how Bustamante come outta jail and go set up his own political party and win the election from Manley. And that was after a year and a half detention at Up Park Camp because his union call so much strike him nearly bring the country to a standstill and Governor Richards couldn't take it no more.

To me the whole thing was a joke because after three hundred years of British rule the Queen decide she going let us go vote but the House of Representatives we elect didn't have no power to do nothing. All it could do was talk, and make decisions that the Governor have the last say over anyway. They call it a partnership between the Colonial Office and the ministers. I call it a stupid waste of time.

But these women take it all serious, like they think all this going actually make a difference to something. Then just the same way they want set the country to right, the next thing is they laughing and joking and getting up and dancing with one another when the mood take them.

What I discover 'bout Gloria is that she got a edge but she also kind and gentle. And when she walk with me out to the car I notice how her arms look like black satin in the moonlight, and my nose catch the sweet, spicy smell coming off of her. Afterwards I discover it a perfume called Khus Khus.

After that I find I am going over there almost every other day. I take something with me, like a hat or a newspaper or something like that, and I leave it there on purpose so I have to go back and fetch

4

it. Then it seem that every errand I am running take me by the house and I step inside because I am passing. It get so bad the rest of the girls just start laughing when they see me coming. So then even I know how it must look. And all I am doing there is drinking tea with Gloria Campbell. I am sipping Lipton's Yellow Label at ten o'clock in the morning and ten o'clock at night. And I am talking about god knows what because half the time I can't remember.

Then one day Gloria smile at me and say, 'You know when I ask you to watch over us I didn't mean for you to be sitting down here every day looking at me. I already broadcast the news that we under your wing so everything is fine.'

I rest the cup in the saucer, and I put the saucer on the table, and I stand up and say, 'That is good,' and I walk out.

Some days she have to tell me to go away because the poor woman can't get no work done. Every day I promise myself that I will stop going there, and that last maybe two or three days.

Next thing you know I become a odd-job man, fixing up the cupboard door, sawing and hammering even though I don't know a damn thing 'bout what I am doing. I swear every time I fix something and leave they must have to call a carpenter to come sort it out.

Then one day me and Judge Finley sitting alone in the shop and him say to me, 'What you doing with Gloria Campbell?'

And I say, 'Nothing.'

'Well you better make up your mind to do something or stop going over there. You got things to do and I'm damn sure she got plenty to keep herself busy as well.'

So I say to him, 'What yu think of Gloria?'

'What you asking me this for?'

'I just asking yu, that's all.'

'Well now you asking me to give an opinion about a woman I hardly know, a woman I seen maybe five or six times when I happen to take a envelope from her. She beautiful, I give you that. And she got style. She carry herself well. And I think she have some brains as well running all them girls and turning a profit.

Well, I reckon a man wouldn't mind to be seen out with a woman looking that good on his arm. But he wouldn't marry her.'

'Who is talking 'bout marrying?'

'Well maybe it time you thinking 'bout it at least.'

'So what you know 'bout it? You not even married yourself.'

'Oh yes, I get married last year.'

'You get married and you don't tell nobody 'bout it?'

'Her people from St Thomas, we go over there and we do it.'

'And you don't invite nobody to come join in the celebration?'

'Marriage is not for celebrating. It is something you do to give your children a name.'

After that I stop going to see Gloria, but it don't stop me from thinking 'bout her. I am thinking about her so much it like I am in a daze. I drive the wrong way from Half Way Tree to Red Hills and have to turn 'round. I count out the pai-ke-p'iao money two, three times but I can't make it add up. I have to keep asking Hampton and Finley what they say to me because I can't remember.

Then one evening me and Zhang sitting at the table in Matthews Lane. Ma at temple and Hampton out on the prowl. Zhang ask me, 'You sick?'

And I tell him no.

'So it must be a woman.'

What Zhang know about women I don't know. He and my father was just boys when they busy fighting for Dr Sun Yat-sen and the Republic and when that was done he leave China and come to Jamaica and live like a hermit, until my father get killed and Zhang save up the passage and send for us. And in all that time I don't think he even talked to a woman.

'How you feel?' he ask me.

'I feel like I am under water and everything is just out of reach. Everything is muffled. I can't quite hear. And I can't touch or feel anything, my arms just waving about in the air. Except when I am with her and then it is like my feet are on the ground. Everything is sharp and focused and when I put my hand on the table like this, I can feel the wood under my fingers. And it feel like it matters. That it matters that I am sitting there with her. That it mean something. I feel happy just to watch her pour the tea and stir in the milk.'

'This is the whore in East Kingston?'

That word hit me so hard because it don't seem to describe anything about Gloria. It don't seem to be associated with her in any way. But I know what Zhang mean and I say, 'Yes.'

And he just get up from the table and walk away up the yard.

The next Friday night when I go to make the weekly pick-up everything seem different. I don't know what. The music is playing, the liquor is flowing, the women is busy. The place look exactly the same. So I decide that it must be me that is different. Maybe it because I decide to harden my heart against her.

So now it seem like this is the place that is under water. Like I am inside some invisible bubble and I am just looking out. And when I reach out to take the envelope from her I not even sure that my hand is going make it outside of the bubble to pull in the money. But somehow I manage to do it, and she just stand there and look at me like she know something is different as well. But she don't say nothing 'bout it.

After that I can't stand to go over there so Hampton is doing the weekly pick-up on his own. And then one Friday morning I bump into her, just like that, standing up in King Street after I finish drop off some cigarettes.

It seem rude not to even say hello so we standing up there passing the time of day when she say to me, 'You keep thinking all the time about what I am. But maybe you should concentrate on who I am, the sort of person I am, and maybe that way you might get to know how you feel. I see the way you look at me. And how you stand far from me in case you might touch me by accident. And how when you have to come close to me you hold your breath like you think something bad about to happen. Well maybe you just need to let yourself breathe.'

I don't say nothing to her. I just stand there feeling like it is me and her now trapped inside this bubble and the whole of

King Street is going past us 'bout its business like it can't even see we there.

Then she say, 'Next Monday and Tuesday the rest of the girls are taking themselves up to the north coast to Ocho Rios. They reckon we not so busy then and they can spare the time to have a break. But I am not going with them. I am just going to close up the house so I can get some time to myself. So Monday night I will be there in the house on my own. And what I am saying to you is you can come over for the night if you want to.'

All of this time she is talking to the side of my head because I can't bring myself to look at her. I am staring out into the street watching the cars fight with the buggies and pushcarts for road space while I feel her eyes burning a hole into my temple.

'You don't seem to think that maybe I have some feelings as well.' And then she stop.

And then she start again, 'But I have to tell you that this is a one-time offer. If you decide not to come then it will be strictly business between you and me from that point on because we can't carry on like this.' And she step out into the noise of horns and cross the street and walk away into the crowd.

I don't go do the pick-up that Friday night but all weekend I think about what Gloria say to me. And what Hampton say about whores. And what Judge Finley say about marriage. And how Zhang just get up and walk away. And I know they is all right. No matter how you feel, you can't marry a woman like that. So I think on it, and I think on it. And when Monday night come, I take a shower and go to her house in East Kingston.

Next morning when I set foot inside the gate at Matthews Lane I see Ma up the top of the yard feeding the ducks, and Zhang sitting at the table finishing his tea. So I walk past him and I head to my room. But just as I put my foot on the step with my back to him, and him sitting at the table with his back to me, he say, 'Your mother start to fret last night when you don't come home, but I told her it was alright because I knew where you were.'

And I say, 'Thank you,' and step into my room.

2

Moral Influence

But Zhang don't like it. First of all he just ignore it like maybe I going get over it, sorta grow outta Gloria. Then when this no happen he start make comments 'bout what sorta thing a honourable woman do, what kinda life she have, and how she act and suchlike; and how a dishonourable woman will bring a man down. According to Zhang a shameful and disloyal woman is the one single source of a man's ruination. Then after that no work him start talk 'bout how I need to meet a nice Chinese girl and now every day he is mentioning to me the name of every man in China-town who has a daughter. He can't see that I am not interested, that the time is going by and my life is full. Because apart from seeing Gloria three times a week, I am busy driving US navy surplus all over Kingston and double counting eggs because I discover that the Chinaman on the chicken farm in Red Hills can't be trusted. Plus Gloria introduce me to two of her friends so now I have three houses to look after. The last thing I need to be thinking about is getting a wife.

But Zhang don't care. He is on and on at me morning, noon and night and he is beginning to vex me now. So I agree to go up the Chinese Athletic Club and see what going on. I reckon that will shut him up. When I get there I find a bunch of kids playing ping-pong and drinking lemonade.

Then them tell me they organising a garden party. Zhang, and now Ma, very excited. It seem like this is the best thing to happen since Mao Zedong win the war and they set up the People's Republic of China. Zhang and Ma fuss me so much that Sunday morning I barely make it outta the house on time, with Zhang looking at me all expectant like, and Ma waving me goodbye, and Hampton stand up in the yard with his hands on his hips laughing like him witnessing a clown show.

She was there though, with her dark wavy hair pin in a neat bun at the back of her head, and hips, and lips, and hands that she wave about all the time she talking, and throwing her head back and squeezing her eyes tight shut when she laugh. I ask somebody who she is.

'That is Fay Wong.'

'You mean Henry Wong daughter?'

'That's the one.'

So then I know there is no point me even going up to her because most likely she wouldn't even talk to me. Henry Wong is one of the richest Chinese men in Jamaica. He own supermarkets, wholesalers and wine merchants all over Kingston, Ocho Rios and Montego Bay, and he have a big house uptown busting with servants. And I think well if Zhang reckon Gloria not good enough for me what is he going make of Fay Wong? So right from that moment I had her in my sights.

When I go back to Matthews Lane Judge Finley tell me that Henry Wong is a regular player at the mah-jongg tables in Barry Street. So the next time Henry Wong come down to Chinatown I get a professional to lift his wallet, and that give me a chance to go uptown to return it.

The Wongs' house on Lady Musgrave Road got a semi-circular driveway, and between the two entrances a grass tennis court with a big red hibiscus hedge. The house sit on top of a flight of concrete steps with a wide tiled veranda, and a low white-concrete balustrade. And all over it there is wicker armchairs and little tables. The flower bed under the veranda crammed with all sorta colours and shapes, pinks and purples and reds, and to the side there is a twelve-foot-tall angel's trumpet, which I know, come evening, is going to put out a real strong, sweet, heavy scent.

When I get on this veranda I see they got a swimming pool 'round the side with some nice little almond trees for shade. Then I see a black woman filling up one of them big wicker armchair. So I introduce myself and she say she is Cicely Wong, who I know is Henry Wong's wife.

I tell her what my business is and I reach out with Henry Wong's wallet in my hand but she don't take it from me. Instead she call out, 'Ethyl,' and this girl come running outta the house like Miss Cicely just call out 'Fire', and it turn out that she is the one that is going to take the wallet from me, and then pass it directly to Miss Cicely.

Then Miss Cicely ask me if I want to join her for afternoon tea. Well, this I know about, so I say, 'Thank you.' And she tell me to sit down. She move her embroidery so that I can sit on the chair right next to her.

But no sooner than I sit down she stand up and sorta march over to the edge of the veranda and start shouting, 'Edmond, gather up those mangoes from under the tree, I don't want them turning to pulp on the grass there around the swing. You need to sweep up all that rubbish from 'round the back as well, all sort of rotten fruit and things 'round there. And when you done that cut back that poinsettia, can't you see it getting too big for that corner.' And she come back and sit down again. Edmond standing up under the tree look like him tired. But I don't know if it from overwork or from Miss Cicely yelling at him.

Before Ethyl finish pour the tea Miss Cicely is on her feet again. 'Lord, Edmond, what is it you think we paying you for? Every other garden down the road look better than this one. The garden next door look like it belong to a palace and their gardener is only part-time and a old man at that, not a young sap like you. Make me wonder if I should ask him to come over here and see what he can do to help us out. I keep praying to the good Lord to see if he can send you some inspiration, but He don't seem to be paying me no mind. When the ecumenical women's group come here next week I want the place looking spick and span and beautiful, you understand me? I don't want it looking like this while you leaning up under a tree shading yourself and acting like you sweating from exhaustion.'

Miss Cicely take a liking to me though, and after that day a week didn't go by without her inviting me for afternoon tea. So week after week I was sitting there drinking tea while I watch her instruct the butler, and arrange the menu with the housekeeper, and check the grocery bill, and dish out household chores to the maids; all of the time Ethyl keeping us cool with ice-cold lemonade, and at four pm precisely, Earl Grey tea with tin salmon and cucumber sandwiches, and a slice of Victoria sponge cake. Well this bit I never did with Gloria, so I wait and watch and make sure that I do everything just exactly the same way Miss Cicely do it, and that seem to work out fine.

I find out a lot about Miss Cicely. First of all that she like chocolates and grapenut ice cream, so I always make sure to bring plenty of that. Also, she like Chinese men.

'A Chinese man,' she say to me, 'is hardworking and diligent. He is prudent and steadfast in his resolve to make a better future for himself and his family. A Chinese man hunts out prosperity. Not like the Africans. The Africans are irresponsible and unreliable; indolent and slipshod. They squander every penny. That is why I married a Chinese man. And why my daughters will also marry Chinese men.'

Another time she tell me, 'I can see you have money in your pocket, Philip. You are well dressed, and well mannered and charming. Yes, quite charming, and quite good looking if you will excuse my impertinence. I understand you have a shop in downtown Kingston. When I married my husband, Mr Henry, he had only the one shop as well.'

Every now and again she tell Fay to come sit on the veranda with us and Fay do it, but she don't seem that interested and after a while she get up and go back inside, or she make an excuse that she have to go somewhere and she leave the house. I keep thinking I should try to say something to her. If I could get her talking 'bout something she might sit there for longer than five minute. But every time I open my mouth she just look at me like she thinking 'bout something else, and she don't even seem to care that it rude to just sit there and nuh say nothing to me.

After my visiting with Miss Cicely I say to Finley, 'Cicely Wong, she talk one way to the help and a completely different way to me. When she talk to me she sound like a proper Englishwoman and every afternoon she serve Earl Grey tea and Victoria sponge cake.'

'The story I hear 'bout her is that she grow up on a banana plantation outside of Ocho Rios with her father, but her education come from missionaries. The first thing she learn to read was the Bible and that how come she such a staunch Wesleyan but I also hear tell that she convert to Catholicism because she think that Catholics are a better class of person.'

So one Wednesday afternoon after months of swallowing gallons of Earl Grey tea and carting quart after quart of grapenut ice cream to Lady Musgrave Road I finally say to Miss Cicely, 'I was wondering if you and Mr Wong would consider me marrying Fay.'

And she say, 'Yes.' Just like that, like she was expecting it.

'You don't have to ask Fay or check with Mr Wong or anything like that?'

'I already took the liberty of asking my husband about you, Philip. He tells me your father is an honourable man. A man greatly respected by the Chinese merchants in Kingston. Henry says you have a family business and have served the Chinatown community for many years. I understand your father is retired now, is that correct?'

I so shocked I dunno what to say. I can't figure out why Henry Wong no tell her the truth about me.

Then she say, 'Anyway, you are a charming young man and Fay will do as she is told. Mr Henry doesn't involve himself in this sort of thing, the household, marriage, children, this is the domain of women as far as he is concerned.'

So it was done. I was busy the next two days but Friday evening I realise I need to go tell Gloria before she find out from somebody else. But when I get there she already know.

'Is it true what I hear 'bout you marrying Fay Wong?'

I feel that bad about it I dunno what to say to her. After all me and Gloria been going well over four years now, so I say, 'I can't marry you, Gloria, you know that.'

'I didn't expect you to marry me.'

'So what you expect?'

She think on it and then she say, 'I didn't expect you to go marry somebody else.'

I can see she have a point so I say to her, 'I have to give my children a name.'

She turn her back to me and I can tell she crying from the way her shoulders heaving up and down. So I go over to her and put my hand on her shoulder, but she just shrug it off and say to me, 'Get out, Pao, I don't want to look at you.'

The wedding at Holy Trinity Cathedral, with its big stained-glass window and white dome roof. I just invite Ma, Zhang, Hampton, Finley and his wife, a nice straight schoolteacher-looking woman, and Hampton's sister, Tilly, and McKenzie the old ragamuffin that Zhang nearly kill that day years back and who turn out to be his best friend. McKenzie come in them same tartan socks him been wearing day in day out ever since I know him that him tell me is the tartan for the McKenzie clan in Scotland. Why a man like him should be proud of a thing like that I don't know. You would think he would want to forget that he not even got no name apart from the one he get from the old slave master, not be parading it round on his feet every single day like that.

When I get inside the church it look like Miss Cicely invite half of Kingston, all of them dress up like they attending some royal coronation. Miss Cicely herself got on a big bright yellow frock and a even bigger hat all decorate with feathers and whatnot. Afterwards, when we step through the front door into the noon-day sun, it seem like the other half of Kingston and the whole of Chinatown turn up as well to witness the spectacle. Or maybe they just come to see if it was really true. That a boy from Matthews Lane could marry a woman like Fay Wong.

We drive up to Ocho Rios for a week because that is the place Gloria and her friends always talking 'bout. Finley tell me they open a new hotel up there called the Jamaica Inn and Marilyn Monroe and Henry Miller just done staying there. Maybe it true 'bout Marilyn Monroe, I dunno, and in truth it don't mean nothing to me but I reckon if it good enough for any kinda movie star then it sound like the sort of place Fay will think is alright for a honeymoon.

But the moment I clap eyes on the place, I fall in love with it. It got it own white sandy cove with the breeze coming off the sea, and banana trees, blushing jacaranda, coconut palms, bougainvillaea. It was like a piece of heaven right here on earth. Elegant, that is what it was. I almost couldn't believe I was in the same country.

But if I think it was the scenery that was captivating me I was wrong because the thing that I find myself staring at all week was Fay. And what I realise was that I go marry this woman but I didn't know nothing about her. I seen her two or three times at the Chinese Athletic Club and I seen her back plenty of times as she leaving Lady Musgrave Road, but I didn't know her. I hardly even talk to her. All I knew about Fay Wong was that she light-skin and her papa rich.

But this week now I wasn't doing nothing but sitting and watching. Watching how she take the napkin and dab the corner of her mouth, gentle like, before she drink from the glass. And how she look at the waiter direct and smile at him when he come to take her order. And how she touch him lightly on the arm just after he put down the plate in a way like it seem the whole of him melt under her fingertips. And how the maids dance round her picking up everything she put down, and fetching this and carrying that, and all the time asking her if there is anything else she want them to do for her, like there is nothing they wouldn't do to please her just because they want to. And when she look at them and say thank you it as if they think she give them a gift that maybe they should be thanking her for.

They flocking to her and it not just the help. When she go to breakfast or dinner, or pass the afternoon on the beach, there is people she is greeting. And she know them by name. She can ask them questions 'bout their day because she remember what they tell her the day before. She even know the names of the children back home in New York or Washington or Baltimore. She chat with them maybe two or three minutes and after she move on I look at them and see how they sorta sink deeper into their chair, like they can rest easy now because Fay recognise them.

Then one morning this man is walking 'cross the veranda and outta all of the people sitting there it is Fay that he stop to talk to and ask if she is having a good time and if everything in the hotel is to her liking. It turn out Mr Charlie own the place and him and Fay sit down there some long time talking and laughing and ordering up rum punch.

I sitting and watching from across the terrace because most of the time she keep her distance from me. But it don't bother me none because what I see is something I have never ever seen before in my whole life. What I see is somebody who know they belong. She know it for sure. One hundred per cent. Fay not got, not even in the smallest corner of her mind, any doubt whatsoever 'bout her place in this world. She not got one question 'bout who she is or what people going make of her. She just take it for granted that they going love her and that she going take them in her stride, whoever they are.

To me, that is rare. So I sit there all week and look at her knowing that I couldn't even begin to imagine what it would feel like to be that certain.

I look at her, this wife of mine, and I look out across the veranda at the white sand and the croquet lawn, and the shrimp plant and red ginger filling up the flower bed, and I think to myself, you sure come a long way, bwoy.

3

Command

I was just a boy when I come to Jamaica. It was 1938 and all sorts of mayhem was going on with strikes and disturbances because the workers wanted better wages and conditions. It didn't seem too bad to me. I just come from Guangzhou where the Japanese was raising hell trying to take over the place.

First time I see Kingston I couldn't believe what a mess it was. Piles of wood and corrugated zinc just like it heap up in every direction, all brown and grey and zinc-sheet flat. Not like China with the yellow and the red, and the sloping roofs that peak to heaven. No, the only bit of colour I could see was this blue mountain way off yonder.

Kingston look like the worst kind of shanty town I ever did see. But then I never see anything from the top deck of a cargo ship before, so most likely Guangzhou look just the same. I didn't know. When I left there all I saw was the Japanese lighting up the night.

The wharf look like it a sea of black ants heaving and humping and sweating. They got crates pile up this way and that, and a big zinc shed that they must burn up inside on a hot day, and a little concrete building stand next to it.

And that is when I see the two of them standing on the dock. The little Round One look excited and waving his arm in the air, but the other one don't look too interested. That is the one I think I recognise from the way Ma describe him to me, tall and straight, proud and strong. I think this is Zhang, Zhang Xiuquan, my father's best friend from China. My older brother name after him, Yang Xiuquan. Zhang is the one that send passage for us after my father get murdered by British and French soldiers at Shaji. But what with the war and everything it take a long time for us to get here.

When we get inside the little concrete building Round One is there arguing with a white man in a uniform. The white man sitting at the desk and Round One is standing next to him nodding his head, 'Yes, yes.' White man shaking his head, 'No, no.' Then Round One go away and come back a bit later with a brown envelope and put it on the desk. Him sort of pat it with his hand and step back. White man pick up the envelope and look inside it. Then him put the envelope in his pocket and wave his hand to tell us to come forward.

When him ask my name I tell him Yang Pao, but he have me tell him again two more times and then him write on a piece of light brown paper and thump down heavy on it with a big red rubber stamp. Him hold out the paper to me and I take it. I was going to bow and say, 'Xièxie, thank you', but him don't look at me, him just keep on looking down at his little desk. Later on I find out that the paper say my name is Philip Young.

Outside on the dock we get introduced. There is me, Ma and Xiuquan just come off the boat; and Zhang and Round One who come to meet us. Round One turn out to be called Mr Chin. He is the chairman of the Kingston Chinatown Committee. He is Zhang's employer.

When Zhang and Ma come face to face they just stand there and look. I was thinking they would say something after not seeing each other for such a long time, but Zhang just bow his head and Ma bow as well. Zhang look just like Ma say but older than I had him fix in my mind. He even starting to get grey on his head.

Mr Chin got a buggy waiting for him. It got one horse and two big wheels and a black canvas canopy to keep the sun off. He tell Ma she must come ride with him, but is only two people can fit in the buggy so then he say to Zhang that maybe they should have bring another one. But Zhang say no, boys can walk. And Mr Chin say OK because Matthews Lane not too far, turn left and right and straight up. Then Mr Chin call over a barefoot boy with a pushcart and Zhang put the bags on it.

All the time we walking my legs wobbly from so long at sea. And then I realise I must be some kind of curiosity because every corner and doorway got people hanging there just to look at us. Plus, little pushcart boy cannot take his eyes off me. I try not look at him, but every now and again I let my eyes wander to see if him still staring at me, and sure enough him looking straight back, even though every time I catch him he lower his eyes or look away to pretend him not watching me. The thing I notice 'bout pushcart boy is how dark his skin is. And how his hair tight on his head, and how his eyes round. And how he don't look nothing like me.

When we get to the house it is a concrete yard behind a door in a fence. To the left, Mr Chin say, is a storeroom. It have a deep red wooden door with a big galvanised metal padlock on it. A little further in on the right, there is a row of five single rooms, each with its own door and two small steps into the yard. The shower cubicle is on the opposite side to the rooms and made from corrugated zinc, and between the shower and the first two rooms is a piece of zinc over the top of the open space, to keep out the weather. Underneath it is a oblong wooden table and a little stove. Up the top of the yard there is a dugout pond, and ducks. And beyond that, the toilet shed.

The first room is for Ma to sleep in, Zhang say, then the next door me and Xiuquan to share, and him at the far end. Two empty rooms between him and us, to show respect. Mr Chin say, 'Hope you and family happy in house.'

Zhang say, '*Xièxie*, thank you. I am full of gratitude.' So it seem like Mr Chin give us this house.

Then Madame Chin come with all the Chinatown Committee and them wives. They bring food for everybody to share, like a celebration, and all of them saying welcome, welcome.

After they gone Zhang say for us boys to take a shower and go to bed and him go to his room. The shower cold and refreshing, and afterwards when I lay in the crisp cotton sheets I think to myself this is no Chinese farm. No green rice fields or gold rape carpet. But it is all we need. Best thing, no Japanese soldiers outside. And then I close my eyes. I so tired all I want to do is sleep the rest of my life, but all I do instead is listen to dogs bark and people making a ruckus somewhere off in the distance.

Next morning Zhang say me and Xiuquan must put on our best clothes and come with him. The best we have is our changshan. We both got them, in black. They old fashion we know, and even in China people hardly wear them now except for a special occasion when some people still like you to wear a gown. But it is what we have. When Zhang see us he shake his head and mutter something to himself 'bout men and changshan, and pigtails and the revolution, but he march us outta the gate anyway into the blistering heat and the stench of the drains.

We walk up Matthews Lane till we get to Barry Street and as we turn the corner all I see is the buggies. One after another, line up in one long, neat row, all the way up the street. With their little black canopies and the horses, and the drivers cleaning up the stinking piles that dropping from under their tails because, Zhang say, they going sell the manure to the Indians for growing the vegetables. When we get to the post office we turn into King Street and into a shop call Issa's that sell everything, including what Zhang want us to have – underpants, vests, socks and shirts. Then he march us outta there and into a shop where they sell sturdy lace-up shoes, which we have to try on wearing the new socks; and then he put us in a buggy, where he sit up front with the driver, and go to another place where he choose some material, and buy the whole bolt; and then to a tailor who got a little cap on his head and who measure us for trousers, after we put on a pair of the new underpants. Two pairs of trousers each outta the same fabric, which Zhang want in a hurry so the man promise that the trousers soon come. And then the buggy take us back to Matthews Lane and Zhang seem satisfied with that.

He sit us down in the yard and cut our hair himself, which Xiuquan not too happy about, I don't know why. Maybe because he used to Ma doing it. Maybe he think Zhang taking too much liberty taking charge of us like this. Because the hair not that long, it just too long for Zhang's liking. But when I look at Ma she sitting there and she smiling, and she putting her palm flat against her cheek and leaning her head to one side like she enjoying watching what going on. So I reckon if it alright with her then it alright with me.

The thing that strike me all the time we going about is not just how the streets and the buildings look different from China, or how the place smell different, more sorta salty than earthy. What strike me is how different the people look. There was ones with dark, dark skin and the broad nose and thick lips and tight hair. And even the ones that got lighter skin still got the nose and the hair. They got every shade from blue-black to all sorts of brown. They even got some with ginger hair. Then they got some with skin sorta smooth and sallow, and they got straight nose and straight hair. And they got ones with white, white skin, and yellow-white hair and red eyes. I never know there was so many different ways a person could look. All I knew about was the straight black hair and the flat nose and the eyes.

The next day I find out why Zhang in such a hurry for the trousers. We have to go to a banquet. So when the tailor come in the yard with one pair for each of us, Zhang relieved. And he tell us to go get dressed. When Xiuquan ready Zhang tell him to run up to Barry Street and fetch two buggies and when he come back we leave with Ma wearing a traditional cheongsam in deep red with white plum blossom, and Zhang dressed in a dark blue Zhong-shan suit, with its turndown collar and four symmetrically placed pockets, named after Dr Sun Yat-sen and now the army uniform for Mao Zedong.

The place they have the banquet got a big room with wooden tables and benches and a veranda all the way 'round outside. And then it got that same thing again upstairs. The stairs go up straight out of the middle of the room. Every inch of this place is packed so I reckon the whole of Chinatown must be here. Mr Chin at the door to welcome us and escort us to his family table where Madame Chin sitting with their three daughters and two sons and one daughter-in-law and one son-in-law and the children. Everybody bow and happy to see us.

All 'round the corners of the room there is big barrels full of rice, and a lid to keep it warm. So when you need to you can just go up there and fill up your bowl. The meat and vegetables come on a big wooden tray that it take two people to carry and they unload it all on to the table because that is the food for our family. There is everything. Just like home. Preserved salted fish and pork; char siu, roast pork, roast duck and white cut chicken; duck gizzard and beef stew; ginger lobster, steam fish, boiled shrimp, stir-fry vegetables, choi sum, pak choi, steam eggs, wanton noodles. And we just eat, in the noise and the heat, and with the little ceiling fans whirling round and round.

All the time we eating I see them moving a little wicker basket from one table to the next. All 'round downstairs, and out on to the veranda and then someone take it upstairs. And a long time after when they bring it back down they go in the yard with it. Then after that they come back inside and bring it to Mr Chin.

Mr Chin stand up and Zhang stand up, and Mr Chin give the basket to Zhang and they bow. And then Zhang turn 'round and he bow to Ma and I think to myself well this thing getting on like a wedding banquet. So I don't understand what is happening, except I know for sure that the basket full of money.

After the dinner over, Madame Chin get out a basket with four shut pans and give it to Ma so that she can take home some of the leftover food.

Two days later when Zhang think we well enough rested him say, 'You boys save from death. You come make new life. Time you turn your hand to something.' And him walk towards the gate expecting us to follow. He open the gate and stop, and turn to us and say, 'The Jamaicans angry. They causing a stink because of bad wages and unemployment, so you boys mind how you act. They don't need no aggravation from you.' And we step into the lane and the dry morning heat together.

We walk up Matthews Lane till we get to Barry Street, where Zhang know every man and woman in sight, every shopkeeper and market trader. People in grocery stores, laundries, hardware stores, bakeries, dry goods; people who happy to see him; people who just stand up on the street and talk to him and smile and bow their heads.

We visit every shop, and from every one Zhang collect a small brown paper bag, with smiles and bowing heads; and wishes for him to have good health and a long life. Shopkeepers offer 'Perhaps a small gift for your young charges?' but Zhang refuse and bow his head in respect. This is how we travel the length and breadth of Chinatown.

Afterwards, Zhang say we must go get something to eat. So we go down a little alley off Barry Street and open a gate into a yard with a lot of Chinamen just standing there, and we go up a couple of wooden steps on to a narrow veranda and open a door where this big room is full of men playing mah-jongg, and shuffling the tiles and making a racket. We walk 'cross the room and Zhang open another door, and that is when the smell hit me. This heavy, sweet, pungent smell.

The room big like the mah-jongg room, and it got a lot of plat-forms that them laying on with the wooden pillow under their head. There is Chinese men and white men as well. Well-dressed white men, some of them even in the Queen's uniform. And the little lamps is burning, and they laying on their side with the long pipe puffing over it. Or they just laying there on their back with their eyes wide open. I hear plenty of stories about opium but I never actually see anybody smoking it before. And what I notice is how all of the smokers look half dead and sweaty, and how the men preparing the pipes and serving the tea wearing the changshan that Zhang don't like, and how quiet the place is. Quiet.

Then we go through into the next room and that is where they got the food. Wooden tables and benches, and steaming rice and a red-hot wok, and steamed pork buns and pickled cabbage. And a open window looking out on to the back of the yard with a wooden shutter prop up with a long piece of old wood. And catching that bit of air is nice because the other two rooms don't have no windows.

After we finish eating and walking back to Matthews Lane I notice how Zhang look sorta proud the way him coming through Chinatown, puffing out his chest and holding his head high. He say, 'Back in old days the Negroes steal and burn and loot Chinese shops. But things get better. Chinatown get safe and happy.'

After that it was just one thing after another. Do this, do that. Go here, go there. Ma do this, Xiuquan do that. Me run and fetch, help this man, collect from that shop. It was like Zhang was settling everybody into their place. Fixing them into their routine.

Every day, except Sunday, Ma make saltfish fritters with the help of a girl named Tilly. Then Tilly take the fritters for sale in Chinatown. Later she come back, and she and Ma pick duck feathers to make pillows to sell.

Zhang teach us tai chi although Xiuquan already know some from our father. We do it every morning. From the beginning – Grasp Bird's Tail, White Stork Cools Its Wings, Brush Knee and Twist Step, Carry Tiger to Mountain. To the end – Shoot Tiger with Bow, Strike, Parry, Punch, Apparent Close-up and Conclusion.

Zhang tell us 'bout Sun Tzu and how more than two thousand years ago he formulate a strategy to plan and conduct military operations. And how Mao Zedong still take lessons from Sun Tzu's writing, and how important it is for us to learn the 'Art of War'.

Every evening after dinner, Zhang teach us English.

And what we have to do is just help him. Just help Zhang look after Chinatown.

Then one day I doing my chores and meet pushcart boy. I recognise him from that first day when we land. Him follow me all up

Barry Street, every stop I make. I go in the shop, him there. I come out, him there, leaning up against some post, or examining piece of old wood, or just kicking the dirt with his hands in him pocket. Not look at me. But I know is me him waiting for. I help Mr Chin and Mr Chung and Mr Lee. I shift barrels, sweep floors, collect Zhang's pai-ke-p'iao gambling money, but no matter how long I in the shop when I come out pushcart boy still there. In the end I can't take it no more so I go up to him and say, 'You following me, bwoy?'

Him look surprise. 'Me, sah? No, sah.'

'Yes, you follow me. You come all up Barry Street. I think you go all 'round Orange Street and back again.' I wave my arm in the air pointing in the direction we been walking all morning. 'You think you going follow me all day?'

'Uncle Zhang, 'im fi yu papa?'

'None of yu business.'

I turn. Walk off. Him follow. Then I spin 'round real sudden and I scream right in his face, 'Ahhhhhh!' But him just stand there. Not even flinch. Not even bat an eye. So I turn 'round and carry on walk and him follow.

Later on, is me look out for him. Is me dawdling so him can catch up. Is me bring him glass of lemonade I get from Mr Fung. Is me give him rice and sausage I get from Madame Leung. When we get back to Matthews Lane I stop at the gate and say, 'What your name?'

'Hampton Stokes. Tilly me big sista.'

So that was Hampton, and after that him come 'round with me most days excepting when him sister need him to go do something for her. All the time him keep asking me 'How old you is?' and I tell him it don't matter. But it seem to matter to him because him keep asking and asking. So one day I tell him, 'I was born on the second moon of gui-you, jia-zi in the year of the rat,' but it don't mean nothing to him. So I say, 'How old is you?' and him tell me fourteen. So I say, 'Same as me, fourteen.'

Then one day Hampton tell me him got a cousin little older

25

than him name Neville Finley that want to meet me. 'What for?' I ask him.

'Him just want to meet you, man. Any crime in that?'

So one Sunday Hampton take me over to East Kingston to the house where it turn out him live with him sister, Tilly. Miss Tilly seem like she sweet on me already and I don't hardly know her. All I do every day is say, 'Good morning, Miss Tilly, and how are you this morning?' or 'Good evening, Miss Tilly, have a good night.' That is it, but all of a sudden she wrapping herself 'round the porch post and giving me some half-toothless smile I ain't never seen the like of before. Hampton start grinning to himself, so I lean over to him and whisper, 'She too old for me, man,' and him laugh out loud so god knows what Miss Tilly think I say to him.

Then him take me by the hand and lead me 'round the back to some old shack of a outhouse he say is his palace. Well it is nothing but a rickety old shed, with a creaking door and open rafters in the ceiling. So I look up and I say to him, 'Yu nuh, if we fix up the door and put some boarding up there we can use it to store things.'

'Store what things?'

'I dunno.'

Right then the door fling open and this tall wiry thing is standing there. Hampton go over to him and give him a hug. I look at the two of them standing there together and I think, well Hampton got a baby face but him not bad looking and him broad and strong. But the other one, him face look like a horse. I don't say nothing but Hampton see the look on me and him start jumping and screaming like a jackass. Him laugh so much the tears running down his face. 'Go on,' him say to me. 'What you think me cousin look like?'

Well a thing like that wasn't for me to say. But Hampton keep going, 'Go on, go on,' till in the end I say, 'He look like he could judge a good horse.' This send Hampton spinning and turning and holding on to him belly like it going to bust.

'Horse judge! Man, that is good. What you think of that, Neville?'

And Neville Finley just say, 'I think your friend can recognise a man of wisdom.'

So after that me, Hampton and Judge Finley start go 'round together. Xiuquan not interested, in fact Xiuquan not interested in anything. He don't hardly even want to leave the house. He don't want to do the chores Zhang give him to do, and sometimes it seem like he don't even like Zhang that much. Him got some big problem 'bout being in Jamaica. All he talk about is how he going leave, which Zhang don't want to hear, so not that much pass between them.

When I ask him 'bout it he just say nobody ask him if he want to come to Jamaica. Nobody ask him if he want Zhang to replace his father or take over his life, treating him like a child when he is already a man. A man capable of looking after his own mother. Nobody ask him if he want to become some two-bit hoodlum.

'Zhang not no two-bit hoodlum. What make you want to talk 'bout him like that? He done nothing but look out for us and look after Ma.'

'Yu think he looking out for us or yu think he looking out for himself? Looking out for who going look after him when he get too old to be lord of the street.'

I can't believe Xiuquan saying this to me.

'If we stayed in China you would most likely be dead by now.'

'Well maybe I would be better off dead than having to watch every day while my mother run after some man she hardly know, and feel grateful to him for bringing us here to this country where the only decent job a Chinese man can have is to become a shop-keeper and where the black man only look at you when he want something and kiss his teeth as soon as he turn his back.'

'They not all like that.'

'They not all like that? Yu busy defending yu little friends? Well you wait and see what your friends do when the trouble really get bad.'

But I not paying Xiuquan no mind. Me and Finley and Hampton still just carry on go everywhere together. Up and down every street in Chinatown like we own it. Into any shop or bar or any kind of place, barber's, grocer's, baker's. We eat for free and we take what we want. People step aside when them see us coming. We big men now. It feel good but Zhang say, 'You boys make sure you don't wear out these people's patience'; and another time him say to me, 'Don't think more of yourself than a decent man ought to.'

Then one day the three of us take some bicycles and go over Rockfort way for a swim. Coming back we riding nice and fine till we turn into North Parade and run into some big protest gone bad. There was people running every which way and a whole load of screaming and hollering, and police and soldiers. I even think I hear some gunshot. It get so dangerous we just have to get off the bicycles and leave them.

Later on when I see Zhang him say to me, 'See you ride bicycle today. Turn corner but not put out hand. And because you not put out hand, truck get into trouble and run up on sidewalk and kill baby. And mother so shock she scream and cry and fall down in the street. So husband get worried and pick her up to shake her. But policeman think man beating wife so he arrest him and take him to the police station.'

'All that happen?'

'No, but it better if you put out your hand.'

4

Doctrine

So what with all him bicycle talk I never get a chance to tell Zhang 'bout the commotion, and how the dockworkers bring the whole of downtown to a standstill. But it no matter. Next day it all over town 'bout how Alexander Bustamante get arrested because they think he the one leading the strike, and how the English government probably going send a commissioner to *look into the disturbances*, that is how they say it, even though nobody can see no point in that because everybody already know what the trouble is – no work, no food, and no hope that anything going get any better.

Zhang say it not the Jamaicans' fault, they just hungry. He say the British set the slaves free but they didn't give them no education or training or any jobs other than the same ones they was doing on the plantation all them years for nothing. Plus after emancipation the British plantation owners go get themselves thousands of Indian and Chinese labourers so the ex-slaves not got no jobs and now all of them just trying to scratch a living outta nothing.

And even though a lot of the *disturbance* is against the Chinese, Zhang say it not about them and us. Zhang say Marcus Garvey is only concerned about the African, but the African's plight is the plight of the poor man everywhere. He like that word 'plight'. Just like it is the plight of the Chinese peasant 'who is right now fighting for liberty, equality and fraternity'. Zhang say Garvey right

29

'bout one thing though: 'the people will never be free as long as they are colonised by a foreign power.' Zhang say the Jamaicans same as the Chinese, poor and exploited and oppressed. He say we are 'brothers in arms'.

Every night Zhang tell us 'bout the revolution. How the British smuggle opium into China, and how the Chinese fight to stop it, but the British send armed forces and warships, and we lose. And then afterwards we have to pay them everything we got in war indemnities, and they still carry on with the opium anyway. Zhang say the revolution is a war between 'an army of workers and peasants determined to overthrow the feudal warlords and foreign powers; and the imperialists and counter-revolutionaries who wish to suppress them'. That is how Zhang talk.

Then one day me and the boys sitting on some empty orange crate on the corner of Barry Street trying to catch some shade when Hampton look across the street and say, 'That bwoy well out of his jurisdiction,' which start me and Judge Finley laughing.

Finley say, 'Where you get a word like that, bwoy?'

And Hampton lean over to him and say, 'Is the wrong word?' which set me and Finley off laughing even more.

I look over and see some skinny white boy standing outside the post office trying to look mean.

'Is a white boy?'

'No,' Hampton say, 'him just like to think so. Him papa white, but his mama just some whore from West Kingston.'

'What, a real whore?'

'They all whores, man.'

'So who he is?'

'Him called Louis DeFreitas, fancy himself a big-time gangster, but him nothing but a punk.'

I turn to Judge Finley, 'You know him?'

'Not as such. I know about him. I know him got a gang in West Kingston.'

Then Hampton jump in, 'Him got a gang alright, but him don't have no inheritance.'

I look at Finley but him don't say nothing, so I say to Hampton, 'What you talking 'bout *inheritance*?'

'God will forgive me for saying this, but when Uncle Zhang gone all of this is yours, man.' And him extend both arms, palms turned up to the sky. 'Your brother don't have it in him. Yu going to be the man. Everybody know it. I know it the first time I clapped eyes on your scrawny ass that day yu land at the dock. Uncle know it too. I can tell from the way he always putting yu right like him got yu in training for something, and how him look so gentle at yu even when him giving yu a dressing down.'

'What everybody call him Uncle for anyway?'

'Because he is not your papa but him look after you, man. Everybody got a uncle, or them know what a uncle is anyway. Them know yu can go to your uncle with your troubles and he will do right by yu. Them know Uncle Zhang tough, but them also know him fair.'

'Them know all that?'

'Yah, man. It all got to do with McKenzie.'

'What, that McKenzie that come to my house every day play cards and dominoes with Zhang?'

'That same one. That same McKenzie with the tartan socks. I swear every time I see that man him wearing them socks. I don't know how many pair he got or if he rinsing out the same ones every night but he always got them. You must have checked the socks, man. Don't tell me yu no notice.'

'I know the socks. I know what you mean.'

'And you never hear the story 'bout McKenzie?'

So Hampton tell me the story.

'When Uncle come from China he sort out everything in Chinatown good because the people could see him could fight and him frighten them to hell with it. All this Chinese fighting him busy teaching you every day. People didn't want to mess with him. But him was also kind to them showing some understanding for them situation. So after that everything was running smooth and fine till one night somebody burn down Mr Lee's shop. And that was bad because Mr Lee been good to the people since all the trouble stop.

'Uncle was mad so after that him go 'round asking everybody, "Who burn down Mr Lee's shop?" Every man, woman and child; every African, Indian, Chinese and Lebanese, every Syrian, every Jew, he was asking them. Him go everywhere, every shop, every street, every bar, every yard he was there, asking "Who burn down Mr Lee's shop?" It go on for days, man, till somebody tell him it was McKenzie and Uncle go and drag McKenzie outta a bar, with McKenzie kicking and screaming and Uncle pulling him by the arm or foot or hair or whatever him could get a hold of, all the way from the bottom of Rum Lane and all the way down Barry Street to King Street. And right here, right out in the middle of this street right here in front of yu, Uncle strip off McKenzie old shoes and tartan socks and hang him up by him feet, his feet you get that, on a wooden scaffold Uncle put up there for the purpose. And him leave McKenzie hanging there just like that for the whole day. Just hanging there, man, in this heat. I don't know how come the man didn't die. And all that time nobody go do nothing 'bout it because them was scared of Uncle and them wasn't going cross him.

'And when Uncle get to the bottom of it, it turn out that McKenzie burn down the shop because Mr Lee stop him from talking to his daughter. Talking to his daughter, you get that. Though McKenzie say he didn't mean for the shop to burn down completely like it did.

'When Uncle finally cut him down, McKenzie was in a bad way and Uncle pick him up and carry him all the way to his own room in Luke Lane where he look after McKenzie and nurse him better.

'So after that, that was it. Uncle law was in force. Martial law, man. Tough justice that was, but kindness too. And I swear I think McKenzie the only friend Uncle got because him the only person on earth that don't want nothing from him.' And then Hampton stop and look at me, and say, 'Apart from him family that is, if you get what I mean. Well, Uncle already give him life back, so

32

now all McKenzie want to do is give back some friendship. That's how I see it anyway.'

By the time Hampton finish all this chat and we look 'round DeFreitas gone but what we see instead is two white men stand up on the corner talk to one another. Then one of them turn 'round and hawk and spit right on top of the fruit on a nearby handcart. Just as casual and careless as you like. And then the two of them carry on talk like nothing happen.

The higgler turn 'round mad as hell when he see his business spoil up like that, but when him see it is a white man him stop dead in his tracks. Too late though. The white man see the look on his face and slap him down. The white man shout, 'Who you looking at, Nigger?' and then start take off him belt to give the man a hiding. Him so irate he don't even care that his panama hat fall off his head and float into the gutter.

We run 'cross the street and Hampton cover up the higgler with his own body and I jump on the white man. Before he could even lean back to swing the belt, he fall on the ground with me on top of him punching him in the face. Him friend drag me up, just when I hear Panama saying something 'bout teaching the Chink and his Nigger friends a lesson. That is when Judge Finley step in.

'I wouldn't do that, mister. That boy, his papa is Uncle Zhang, Chinatown Zhang.'

Panama hesitate for just long enough for me get the strength for a roundhouse kick just like Zhang teach me. Then I punch to the throat with my forearm, and when Panama on the ground I stand back and say, 'I am not a Chink and these boys are not Niggers. We are Jamaicans. We are brothers.'

When Zhang hear 'bout it him send for me. Him listen to me tell what happen then him say to me, 'When I was a young boy in China the country was run by warlords. These men made very high demands on the people in terms of taxes and provisions and suchlike. They were unjust and cruel men. One day the warlord came to our village to collect his due but the peasants could not pay him. So he selected a man at random from the crowd and he beheaded him. And then he urinated on the decapitated body. And got on his horse and left. I learned two things from this. The first thing I learned is that the masses have the right to live without the fear of being robbed or exploited or abused, especially by the authorities. The second thing I learned is that one man can do only so much. I could have thrown myself at the warlord and battered him with my child's fists. Or you can beat one white man in the middle of a Kingston street. But this does not change the way things are. And it will not make him behave any better in the future. To change things the masses must rise up. They must seize their ideal and take back their land. For it is the masses who will shake off the yoke of oppression, not individual men like you and me. That is what your papa died for, the right of the ordinary woman and man to live a decent life free from the tyranny of warlords and the domination of foreigners.'

5

Appreciation of the Situation

After they arrest Bustamante for the mayhem up in North Parade they keep him in jail for four days and then them let him go. A month after that him set up a trade union, the Bustamante Industrial Trade Union. And three months after that, in September 1938, his cousin Norman Manley, a barrister educated at Oxford University in England, who represented the strikers, set up the first national political party in Jamaica, the People's National Party.

Manley was interested in people getting the vote and Jamaican self-government. Bustamante wanted higher wages for workers. But to me, neither of them mean much. Sure enough Manley was a true gentleman and I believe he was right that we should all see Jamaica as our country; and see the life and destiny of Jamaica as being bound to our own lives and our own destiny. But it seem to me like him think freedom was something to debate over rather than something to fight for. So maybe he was too much of a gentleman.

Busta had spirit, I give him that. And he could command a crowd. But there was always something 'bout that man I never did like. He had a kind of smugness about him. A kind of arrogance that come from him believing that he alone control the masses. Maybe it was that same thing Zhang warn me against when him say to me, 'Don't think more of yourself than a decent man ought to.'

When war break out in Europe, being a British colony Jamaica get placed under the Defence of the Realm Act, so there was all sorts of regulations and controls over the price of goods and foreign exchange, and censorship of the press, mail and telegraph.

Then in 1940 Britain tell the Americans they can come set up military and naval bases in Jamaica. Next thing we know there was US sailors all over the place, parading up and down Harbour Street and King Street as bold as you like all clean and sharp in them navy whites. It turn out the women like bees to a honey pot, because the honey they could smell was some crisp US dollar bills and that was surely worth the time of day. And they didn't feel no shame 'bout it neither.

There was girls from Spanish Town and May Pen, Kingston and Linstead, and Bull Bay, all in them favourite colour. Red dress. Red shoes. Red fingernails. Red lips. Red hibiscus in them hair. And there was boys from New York and Baltimore, Washington and Detroit and Milwaukee. All of them laughing and dancing, and smooching and drinking right there in the street. Right there in the doorways of bars that got their ground-floor windows painted white on the inside.

I think to myself what I wouldn't do to see inside one of them places, but it wasn't no good me even thinking 'bout it. Zhang would have box my ear if him find out I been in there. But then business is business.

So one evening when I think him open to suggestion I try soften up Zhang with a nice ripe Bombay mango. With any other man you would get him a drink but Zhang never touch no liquor, never seen a drop pass his lips. So when him busy peeling the mango I say, 'These Yanks sure spend a lot of money on women.' But him just look at me and carry on with the mango.

Then him say, 'What we do here?'

'Look after Chinatown.'

'That is right. Look after Chinatown. Not look after American sailor want use Chinatown. You see Chinese girls do this? You see Chinese fathers want daughter do this?'

'In the old days . . .'

'In old days emperor have concubine, and rich man have

wife number one and number two and number three. And what was that?'

I know the answer he expecting from me so I just say it. 'That was imperialism, and the exploitation of the peasant and the subjugation of the Chinese woman.'

'That is right. So now, what you ask me?'

So that then was the end of the conversation and I had to think to myself what else these American sailors could be good for, because Sun Tzu's first lesson is to use the terrain.

I send Judge Finley on a mission to loiter 'round the bars and places these boys frequent to find out what they into. It was a kind of fishing trip. And within the week Finley come back to me saying him think he catch something but it might be just a sprat. So I say, 'Never mind. What you got?'

It turn out some sergeant down the naval base approach him to say he have American cigarettes and liquor and suchlike. The suchlike turn out to be navy surplus, which is just about everything Uncle Sam give this man to run his business, this sergeant is willing to sell to us, from cook pots to boots and T-shirts.

Me and Finley go meet him way over Windward Road in a lounge called the Blue Lagoon, a favourite of mine because everybody in there is up to something so you don't have to worry 'bout anyone reporting them see you in there. The sergeant is called Bill, a stocky, shifty-looking white boy with a little bit of blond fluff on his head. Bill come in civvies, but you would have to be a blind man not to know from a hundred yards away that him just step fresh off of the USS *Farmboy*. Well even a blind man would have smell him when all that washedness and scrubbedness step through the door.

Finley stand up so Bill can see him, and then Bill come over to the table and sit down opposite me. I order up some Red Stripe and we get started. We talking maybe five minutes before Bill get himself all agitated.

'Gasoline!'

'Bill, calm yourself nuh. And keep your voice down, man, this is a public place.' Bill ease back in the chair half inch but him looking red in the face and worried.

'Bill, you want me to take your cigarettes and liquor and all them other things and I do that for you. No problem. I not complaining 'bout that. In fact, I happy for the liquor because even though we got so much beautiful rum on the island rich people still pay hefty for that Scotch whisky. But I need things as well, Bill. There is a war on. We got shortages. And what I need you to do for me is rice and gas. After all, I need gas to drive your stuff all over town. And then I will need a little extra. And China-town is . . . well, Chinatown. We need rice. And that is all I am asking you for.'

So then him settle down, but now Bill want a fifty-fifty split and I am saying no way, we taking all the risk here. And he say, 'You think I'm not taking any risk?' And all the time he looking 'round like anybody care what him doing there. He don't seem to realise how many times men been knifed in that bar in broad daylight and nobody ever see anything. Not that there is much daylight in there anyway.

But I see he have a point and I say to him, 'I have expenses, you know, Bill, you only dealing with me, I am dealing with the whole of Chinatown. I have to negotiate. I have to transport. I have to distribute. I have to provide protection.'

So then we talk some more and I send for more beer till in the end we settle for seventy-thirty and him seem happy enough with that. And that is good with me especially since I have no intention of giving Bill any account books so he will just have to take my word for it 'bout how much this stuff is fetching.

So next thing we busy fixing up the door and boarding the rafters in Miss Tilly's outhouse just like I say to Hampton the very first time him take me there almost three years ago. And we getting a truck to move all this surplus.

Everybody at Matthews Lane very happy 'bout the rice, because up to then it was noodles, noodles and more noodles. We even hear tales 'bout people breaking up spaghetti into little pieces and cooking it like it was rice. Though I don't even know where they get the spaghetti from. And then there was some man uptown that was selling rice off a cart at three o'clock in the morning. Knocking on people's door to wake them up, which was his idea of a joke, but the rice got all sorta brown bits in it so I dunno where that was coming from.

Bill's rice was good though, and it go well with Ma's recipes. Like instead of duck and orange it was chicken and orange juice with tin garden peas. Or curry chicken with scallion and Irish potato. Or pork with butter beans. Or mince pork balls in cabbage leaves. She even take to curing her own ham choi, and it turn out that Ma's ham choi taste better than anything you could buy in the shop.

Plus I was selling the extra rice, like I was selling the extra gas to one or two special customers who didn't feel like they wanted to go take the engine outta their car and turn it into a horsedrawn vehicle like all them others you see 'round the place. And what a sorry sight that was, horsedrawn cars riding down the street next to them buggies that decorate up so fancy with all sorta tassel and lace and net all over it, and all over the horse as well. So that is when you realise how little there was for rich people to spend their money on.

This little arrangement with Bill turn out good for me, but how he was getting away with this every month I didn't know. I reckon sooner or later somebody going catch up with him, at which point I hope he know how to keep him mouth shut. So just as a sort of insurance I say to him one day, 'Bill, you know who I am?' And him nod his head, and I say, 'We making good money together. We good partners. But if you cross me I kill you, you know that?' I just say it, even though I never kill nobody in my life, and him just nod his head. Him look so frighten I wouldn't have been surprised to see a puddle under the chair him sitting on.

The funny thing was Bill never seem to realise that I was only a boy. But then him never really look at me. He only look at the idea of me, and see Fu Manchu.

6

Advantages of the Ground

So one day Bill say to me that the American navy going send a truckload of liquor and fancy food for some big shindig the British army having at Up Park Camp. Bill say it a goodwill gesture. I don't even know what half of this stuff is but Bill say it really nice and it going fetch a price, so that is OK with me.

The truck going leave the naval base and then turn up South Camp Road and head up to the camp. Bill going make sure that the escort that the truck got to have going leave late and travel slow. So we have to stop the truck and wave it 'round the corner at Hope Street and unload the things fast before the escort jeep catch up with us. And because everything got to happen so quick I decide to ask Xiuquan to come help us. But he don't want to do it.

'It no mean nothing to yu, man. A few minutes of yu time, that is all.'

'Yu asking me to go get involved in daylight robbery.'

'This not no robbery. This all fix-up. The truck driver expecting us. The escort expecting us. The whole thing organised, man. All we have to do is lift out the boxes and put them in the van and take off. That is all there is to it.'

But Xiuquan don't seem like him convinced and I don't want to just go get some stranger to come do this. People talk too much. Next thing yu know yu go turn the corner at Hope Street and find every Tom, Dick and Harry waiting there to come snatch their slice and make a run for it. No, man, I not going stand by and watch that happen. So the day before when me and Xiuquan walking up Barry Street to the post office I say to him, 'I never ask yu for nothing before. Everything me and the boys do we do it on our own. You all righteous 'bout not doing no robbery but I don't notice yu complaining every time Ma put food on the table that she pay for with the money that Zhang get from the pai-ke-p'iao or I get from the navy surplus.'

Him no say nothing to me. Him just keep on walking with his hand in his pocket like he not even intending to give me no answer. Maybe like he can't even hear me a talking to him.

'Everything that yu don't like is what is keeping a roof over your head and clothes on your back and food in your belly.'

And then he suddenly stop and turn and say to me, 'Yu think I don't know that?' And just then some rude man push past between us and almost shove me off the sidewalk so I crash into the juicy and nearly knock him and his shave ice into the street. When I look 'round Xiuquan walk off so I have to run to catch up with him.

'I dunno why we have to keep going up the post office to check some box that not got no letters in it anyway. Who the hell Zhang think writing to us?'

I don't even bother answer him because Xiuquan don't want no answer. He just want to complain and walk fast and vex with himself.

'What is it yu want, Xiuquan?'

'I want to get up every morning and know that I'm going to go do something honest. I want to stop choking on my food because I know where the money come from. I want to stop worrying every time somebody knock at the gate that maybe it the police that come to take you or Zhang or the whole lot of us to lock us up in some stinking Jamaican jail and never again see the light of day. I want to stop thinking that maybe one day the blacks going raise up and just come murder every one of us as we sleeping in our bed at night. The Indians, the Chinese, the Jews, the whites. Every

41

single person that come here thinking they going make themselves a home. I want to see my mother happy because she got some meaning in her life, because there is something she believe in like when she and my father was working the land doing something worthwhile and producing something wholesome. Something that made a better life, not just for them, but for every single person in that village that get to eat the vegetables they grow. The vegetables they planted and tended with their own hands, on their knees in the dry earth and in the mud when it rained.' And then he stop talk, and draw breath and say, 'I call that honest. What do you call this?'

The two of us look 'round as we standing there outside the post office where Barry Street cross King Street. The whole world is out here, with their hooting and honking and hollering. Every inch of the street is jam up with pushcarts and buggies and the country bus that pack up so much it actually leaning over and god help anything or anybody that standing next to it when the thing fall down on top of them; and cars that somebody should have put a hammer to rather than taking it out so all the pieces can drop off on the public road. And the fumes that is coming outta them is something else, which is why the pushcart boys is bobbing and weaving so them don't have to sit behind there breathing it all in. Never mind trying to miss the trail that the buggies and them cars powered by real live horsepower is leaving. And when them ease past, the pushcart boys got some words to give the driver 'bout the condition of his car or how he driving it and what he think the driver ought to be doing instead of just sitting there in the road with him hand on the horn. And because it so hot and nothing is moving one inch the driver is leaning outta the window shouting at the higgler on the corner to come bring him a cold beer or a soda or maybe he want a sweet mango from the woman that squat down on the kerb with the big basket she just take down from her head with the banana and mango and pineapple and sweetsop and June plum and a few guinep. Or maybe he want some shave ice with a bit of strawberry syrup pour over it. But the higgler not paying him no mind so maybe he got to shout some more or maybe stop a boy riding a bicycle past the car or just walking in the street and tell him to go get the drink or fruit or whatever it is he want. So he is reaching for the change with his left hand in his pocket and pointing with the finger on his right hand, and hoping that he can trust this boy to come back to him with his goods so as to collect the tip he is offering. And he got to do all of this because he can't get outta the car in case as soon as he leave it to walk to the corner it become occupied by any of the dozen of men just standing there in the street or leaning up against a post flicking through some dirty magazine.

So I look 'round at all of this and I say, 'I call it life.'

When Hampton ask me if Xiuquan going come help us boost the truck the next day I say I dunno.

'It no matter. If it four of us we do it and if it three of us we do it same way. And Finley going have to help not just sit there in the van waiting to be the getaway man. We don't need no lookout anyway. This whole thing ain't nothing more than shifting a few boxes.'

Next day when I ready to go I look at Xiuquan like to say 'well, what you going to do, man?' but he just sit there at the table and no say nothing so I walk out the gate and shut it behind me.

I walking up to the post office where I going meet Hampton and Finley with the van but halfway up Barry Street I hear Xiuquan shouting my name and when I turn 'round is him chasing after me. I wait there for him to catch up and then I say, 'What yu want?'

'I'm coming with you.'

'Yu coming with me? What for?'

'Because yu my brother.'

'What happen to wanting to do something honest? This thing here not honest, yu know.'

But him no say nothing. We just carry on walking and get into the van and head out on East Queen Street to South Camp Road. We park up and a little while later everything happen just like Bill say it going to. The truck come up the road. We wave it 'round the corner. Bill say we must rough up the driver and the other sailor boy with him. So I tell Hampton to hit them. Not too hard, just enough to leave a good bruise and maybe a split lip and a little blood. And he do it. So afterwards the two of them sit down on the kerb and smoke a cigarette while they watch us unload the truck.

And right in the middle of all of this I hear this deep voice say, 'What you bwoys so busy doing with this truck?' And when I look 'round it is some tall, scrawny policeman with big feet and a bicycle. Next thing Xiuquan push past me, jump down outta the truck and take off down the road. He don't even stop to look back. He just got his head down and he is going.

I standing in the back of the truck and I look at the policeman. And then I look at the boxes and I say to him, 'Yu see all this stuff in here, it belong to the United States navy and we taking it and putting it in that van over there. If you want to help us yu can pick out two or three boxes for yourself and afterwards we can drop you off with the boxes and the bicycle anywhere yu want.'

The policeman don't say a word but he get off the bicycle and go lean it up real careful with the pedal resting on the kerb and then he take off his hat and rest it on the saddle and walk over to the back of the truck and reach out his hand for me to haul him up.

When we done packing up the van with the boxes and the policeman and the bicycle we say goodbye to the sailors and pull out into South Camp Road. I look down the street and I see the navy jeep park up down there waiting for us to finish so I just wave to them outta the window and Finley turn left and we take off.

We go drop off the policeman and help him inside with his boxes and then we go pile up the stuff in Miss Tilly's outhouse and after all of that was done we open some Red Stripe and ease back.

When I get back to Matthews Lane Xiuquan is sitting there and when I take one look at Zhang I can see him vex with me.

'Your mother and me fret that maybe they have you down police station.'

I don't say nothing because I know this not a time for me to talk. This is a time for Zhang to talk.

'You not think that maybe this dangerous thing what you do? You steal from American navy. You get catch. They put you in jail. You no care what worry you give your mother? You think this some kind of game you play with your friends? You think Sun Tzu so reckless and stupid? This thing not make you honourable. It make you thief.'

And he turn 'round and walk off up the yard to his room. I look at Xiuquan sitting there so frighten while all of this is going on. And I think to myself you weak and you betray me and I don't feel like I want to say nothing to you. I don't want to tell you what happen with the policeman and I don't want to ask you what you say to Zhang. So I just walk off and I go take a cool shower and go to my bed.

Towards the end of 1943 Xiuquan announce that him leaving Jamaica. We all shocked because the first thing we hear 'bout it is the night him packing to go get on the boat the next day. Him say the US hiring farm workers for temporary employment to meet wartime needs.

I say to him, 'So what happen about wanting to see Ma happy like her life have some meaning? Yu think you leaving us is going make her happy? Yu just going go to America and forget about us?'

'I never said I was going forget about yu, but I can't live like this. I want something better. Something better than being a Chinaman in Chinatown.'

Xiuquan got the suitcase resting on the bed and him walking backward and forward between the bed and dresser with his things. But every time he put something in the suitcase Ma grab it out and put it back in the drawer, so the two of them just keep passing one another in the room. I stand up in the corner and say to him, 'Yu should have talk to somebody, yu know.'

'Yu mean yu never know how I feel?'

'I don't mean how yu chat to me. I mean serious talk. I mean like saying to somebody that yu was seriously thinking 'bout leaving.'

'Yu mean like in between you talking 'bout cigarettes and navy surplus, and him talking 'bout the glorious revolution? Well I am sick of his glorious revolution. Sick to my stomach with it.'

Then Xiuquan stop Ma in the middle of the room, snatch the shirt from her and throw it back into the suitcase. After that she just launch herself at him beating her fists into his chest and shouting something, I don't even know what it was.

I grab her from behind, not because she hurting him, because she only a little woman, but I think she need to calm herself down for her own sake. I put both my arms 'round the top half of her body to pin her arms to her side. This is when Xiuquan start. Him looking straight at me and Ma with him back turn to the door.

'Morning, noon and night all I hear about is the glorious Communist revolution, and the Uprising of the Righteous Fists, and how China and its people have been subjugated by foreign imperialists, and British opium smugglers, and how my own father was murdered by foreign soldiers while on a peaceful march supporting Guangzhou strikers, and how I share my name with the great Zhang Xiuquan and the poor schoolteacher, Hong Xiuquan, the leader of the Taiping Uprising.

'And how Zhang Xiuquan is the big man who rescued the livelihood of the Kingston Chinese merchants; and how poverty in Jamaica is the direct result of slavery and so, even to this day, the responsibility of the British.

'Well maybe the Chinese peasants are not all heroes, maybe they are nothing more than a bunch of murdering barbarians who think that life is cheap. Who kill Westerners when they can, and turn on each other when they no longer have the throats of white men and missionaries to slash. Didn't Chiang Kai-shek turn against his own allies ordering the arrest of Communist Party members and massacring the Communists in Shanghai? Killing, that is all it is. What is so glorious about that? And why should I feel guilty because I no longer want to listen to it?'

When I look over, I see Zhang standing there in the doorway. When Xiuquan stop, Zhang just turn 'round and walk out. By the time I let go of Ma and run to the door I see Zhang already halfway up the yard heading towards his room. The rain is coming down so heavy the drops is hopping off the concrete but Zhang don't even have a newspaper to cover his head the way he like to. He just let the rain soak into him so by the time he put his foot on the first step of his room his shirt is stuck to him like it been glued on with paste.

Next morning me and Ma walk Xiuquan to the dock. Zhang get up early and leave the house, so is nowhere to be found. The three of us walk the whole way in silence. Just as him ready to board the boat Xiuquan give Ma a hug, and then him hug me and I say to him, 'You will write when you get settled?'

And him say, 'Yah, man.'

7

Responsibility

As I watch the ship sail away I realise that I would never leave Jamaica. Never. I was committed to her, for good or bad, rich or poor, in sickness and in health. I stand there and I remember the day at Matthews Lane when I ask Zhang how come he leave China and come to Jamaica. And just the same way him do everything direct, Zhang get up from the table and march me up to the top of the yard and into his room. I never step foot inside that room before so I just stand there in the doorway and look inside. It was dark, because although it have a door the room don't have no window. Then what I realise is, is only the first four rooms got windows. The last one only got a door. Zhang give himself a storeroom to sleep in.

The first thing that hit me was the smell of clean cotton. Then when my eyes get accustomed, I see that the place look like him must scrub it from top to bottom every day. And it sparse, a canvas cot to sleep on, a camphor chest, and a old rocking chair. And hanging on the wall next to his bed, a narrow-blade sword with a brass hand-guard.

Him tell me to sit, so I ease into the rocking chair. Then him open the chest and dig into it like he looking for something. When he turn 'round he got three letters in his hand. He come over and squat down next to me, and hand me the first letter. It was from Mr Chin and the Kingston Chinese merchants.

我們聽說你是個勇猛的兵士. We hear you are a fierce and coura-geous soldier, loyal to the Chinese people. An expert in the martial arts, a crack shot with a gun. We have trouble in Jamaica and ask you to come as swiftly as possible. You will be generously rewarded. We will pay your credit-ticket on arrival. Do not bother with the coolie crimps. Those despicable Chinese gangsters will sell you by the head to a barracoon agent. Just go straight to the British Emigration House right there in Guangzhou. Let us know when you are leaving. We will be there to meet your ship in Kingston.

Zhang lean toward me and sorta whisper, 'I don't know how they come to settle their sights on me. I had heard of such things and I knew that if they were not there the ship's captain would sell me on the docks of Kingston to recoup the passage. He would sell me to the highest bidder, most likely stark naked for them to judge my full worth. So I was in no hurry to meet such a fate.'

Him whispering to me in the semi-dark like this give me a feeling that he was telling me something he never tell nobody before. It fill me with honour, and fear that maybe one day I go let him down. Then he carry on.

'China was ruined by the foreigners with their war indemnities and taxes and imported goods. We had become a country that was half feudal and half colonised. That is why your father and I partic-ipated in the fighting. We wanted to create a China that was free from foreign control, and a country in which the ordinary man and woman could have a decent life. That is what it was all about.'

I done heard this whole story a hundred times before. But something about him telling it to me right here in his room, with this long-off look in his eye, make it seem like there was something special 'bout it this time, so I just let him carry on and I listen to him with a keenness like it was all news to me.

'I took no notice of Chin's letter because I was busy fighting a war. But after such great victory and the founding of the Republic, everything came to nothing when Sun Yat-sen gave way to the warlord Yuan Shikai. The foreigners loved Yuan Shikai. He had their confidence so nothing would change as long as he was in power. The Chinese people would remain oppressed and impoverished and under the rule of the warlords and the foreigners. So that was when I decided to leave. I thought that maybe I could serve a better purpose helping these Chinese in Kingston.'

Zhang stood up in the middle of the room, straight and proud. 'Your father was my best friend from boyhood so when he married your mother I thought that was good for him. He was settled. Your mother was a hardworking girl from an honourable family; a believer in the Republic; a supporter of Dr Sun Yat-sen. He could not have made a better match.'

Just then I turn 'round and see one of the ducks making to come into the room so I get up and go shoo it away. When I come back Zhang got the second letter in his hand. By now the light was fading, so he walk over to the door and stand there in the open space.

'I wrote to Yang Tzu, your father, a little while after I settled in Jamaica but I did not get a reply. It was three years before your mother wrote back to me.' And then he start to read.

'Yang Tzu is well. We have been working very hard in the fields so that we have enough. But times are hard. The warlords are relentless. They keep increasing the land rent and other taxes are high and numerous as ever. Yuan Shikai has even tried to have himself crowned as Emperor. Tzu continues to support the struggle of the revolutionary forces, but it is difficult. Many of the bourgeoisie seem happy to follow the warlords, and although Sun Yat-sen is still committed to the salvation of China the revolution seems to have lost its way. At the moment Tzu is deeply concerned about the Japanese who have taken control of Shandong and Manchuria and whose enterprises are expanding greatly in China. He is convinced that they are set on turning China into a colony for their exclusive exploitation while the Western imperialists are busy with their war in Europe. We have a son. Tzu insisted that he should be named Yang Xiuquan. So he too is thinking of you.'

'Then in 1925 she sent me another letter.

'Yang Tzu is dead. Shot by British and French soldiers at Shaji supporting Guangzhou-Hongkong strikers. We have a second son, Yang Pao. Your sister by affection. Meiling.

'So that was when I went to Chin and the Chinatown Committee and asked them to pay me because in all the years I had never received a penny, I was just given whatever food or supplies I needed from the stores, and Chin paid my rent in Luke Lane so I had no need. But now I needed cash money for your passage. I also asked Chin to let me start up a little pai-ke-p'iao business. We Chinese like to gamble, so I thought I could make something there and he agreed.

'Chin said to me, "You get woman and boys from China? Good. Time you married and have family." So he was keen but he had the wrong idea, and I did not feel like I wanted to explain anything to him. I just wrote to Meiling and told her I would send the passage for the three of you to come to Jamaica.'

Next day I ask Ma why my father never reply to Zhang's letter. She say, 'He tried many times, but his tears soaked into the paper.'

After that I just do what Zhang tell me to do, and hope that maybe one day I become like him, a man that believe in something. A man that is loyal to a cause. A man that people can count on. Sun Tzu say, '*The wrong person cannot be appointed to command. This is like gluing the pegs of a lute and then trying to tune it.*'

8

Confirmation of the Ground

The year after Xiuquan gone to America Zhang tell me he want to stop.

'I have lost two Yangs. Yang Tzu to glory and the revolution and Yang Xiuquan to the Americans and their war. I am tired, Pao. This business is not for old men like me.'

I reckon he think it was a new era because in 1944 Jamaica get a new constitution giving us representative government and they decide to call a general election so everybody was running round excited to go vote for the first time. So maybe Zhang think it was my time as well. My time to come of age. I take over little bit by bit, so that by the time the war end in 1945, and they say I turn twenty-one, I had complete control of Chinatown. And that was when it hit me. That after all these years I wasn't playing at this thing no more. I was responsible.

Next thing Miss Tilly get herself a man and she want Hampton to move outta the house. Zhang say it OK Hampton can come live at Matthews Lane, so he move into the room next to Zhang. And this is when I discover how come Hampton so big and strong because when him move in him bring a tiny little bag with his things and a whole heap a iron that he set up in the yard so that every day he is busy doing bench and curl, and clean and jerk.

But then Tilly say she want all the surplus move outta her outhouse as well, and even though we have the storeroom at Matthews Lane Zhang say he don't want the surplus in the yard. So me and Hampton have to go find somewhere to put it.

We rent a shop in West Street. It is a dark, rundown wreck of a place but it cheap and it have a big, dry storeroom out the back. We got no intention of turning our hand to shopkeeping but we reckon with a little fix-up and a lick of paint we can make a nice office away from Matthews Lane.

The only problem is we have to put something on the shelves to make it at least look like we in business. So we have to go buy some things because the surplus we have in the storeroom we can't put out on the shelf like that in broad daylight. Well that is OK but we don't want to put out so much stuff so we actually start attract business, not that there is much likelihood of that in a place like West Street. So we balance it out. Every now and again we get a vagrant come by and we have to give him something to scram. The whole thing work out right in the end.

Now me and Hampton and the Judge down there most days eating oysters and drinking beer. We still have Zhang's weekly pick-up 'round Chinatown, and his pai-ke-p'iao business, which is good because Chin and the Chinatown Committee not looking after us like the way they do with Zhang in the beginning. Chin say that was a long time ago and a different sort of arrangement. Now we have to make our own way. So we got Bill, and now we have a Chinaman at a chicken farm in Red Hills telling his boss the chickens weigh four pounds when they weigh six and doing all sort of calculations over how many eggs he got; and we driving chickens and eggs all over town and taking our cut.

So business is good and we just beginning to think that maybe we should be hiring up some help, and that was when she turn up. Gloria. And everything that start with her start.

9

Humanity

The thing that play on my mind right after that night I go to tell
Gloria about the wedding was how come she already know 'bout
me marrying Fay. There wasn't but three days between me asking
Miss Cicely and me going to tell Gloria, but when I get there she
already know all about it, I think it curious as is only me and Miss
Cicely in the picture, apart from maybe Fay if Miss Cicely bother
to mention it to her and I couldn't see Fay going to Gloria with
the news. So anyway I decide I going go ask Gloria but I dunno
how to do it. I reckon I wait till Tuesday come round. That way
she have the whole of the weekend to think on it and Tuesday is
my regular day anyway. So I just bide my time and think that when
Tuesday afternoon come I will just turn up on the doorstep like
I do every week because my time with Gloria is Tuesday, Thursday
and Friday afternoon, and then Friday evening when I go make
my collection but that is just business.

I dunno why it like that. It seem to me that Monday, Wednesday and Friday would make better sense. But it no matter what I
think. My days is fixed just the way Gloria want it so that is how
it is.

So Tuesday coming and I can't decide whether to go over there
or not. I don't want to go in case she don't want to see me. But I
don't want to not go in case she think I not interested. I don't
want her to start think that now I going marry Fay being with her,

54

Gloria, don't mean nothing to me. I hope she know that she mean more to me than that even though I can't marry her. And then I start think what do I mean to her? She got so many men coming and going maybe she just think I one of them. One of them stupid, clumsy, good-for-nothing oaf that she and the girls always joking and laughing about when they gone. But I don't think she see me that way. After all she even tell me I didn't have to pay if I didn't want to, but that no seem right to me. It would seem like I was taking advantage because I think she only say it to me because of the protection we providing. But then I think I must mean something more than that to her because if I didn't she wouldn't have react the way she done when I tell her 'bout Fay. She would have just shrug her shoulder and say pour a drink so I can make you a toast. But she didn't do that, so that must tell me something.

When Tuesday come, I go. I knock at the door and after some long time she finally turn up and open it. She look at me, sorta up and down, and she just shut the door. She never even say a word to me. She just leave me standing there on the porch when she turn back and go inside. And looking at the closed door like that, I realise I wasn't going ask her nothing that day.

When Thursday come I can't make up my mind what to do. Is she testing me? Is she wanting me to show her how sorry I am? Maybe she want to teach me a lesson or maybe she just nuh ready. But the last thing I can afford to do is look like I don't care, so I go.

Gloria open the door and step back inside. And she just stand there looking at me. So I ease past her and step into the living room. And after a little while she walk out. I reckon she gone go make the tea so I sit down on the sofa and make myself look as prim and sorrowful as I can. I keep both my feet on the ground with my knees together and my hands in my lap so I don't take up too much space even though I am the only one sitting there. Then I start look 'round the room and I think how masculine it look considering there is only four women a live here. So I try figure out what make it look that way, and I realise that there isn't one single ornament in the place. Not a picture on the wall.

Nothing. It like the place strip down apart from the two sofas and a coffee table, and some Venetian blind at the window and the bar in the corner. And I think how different this look from the back room that I have dinner in that very first time I come here. And how the spirit of this room sorta still and empty apart from the little breeze that is coming through the window. And how different it feel compared to that night in the back room when the four of them was singing and dancing and talking 'bout Busta-mante setting up the Jamaica Labour Party. And how the life in them and their energy and their spirit lift up the place. Sitting here in this stagnant room it didn't seem like that other thing could even be possible. I start to wonder how come I never notice before what this room was like. Never notice before the sadness in it. And I realise that every other time I was in the room it was full of men and music and liquor. And when it wasn't that it was me and tea and Gloria. And right then I wasn't looking at no wall to see they not got no picture on. All I was looking at was her.

I am sitting there this long while and she nuh come back. So I start examine the floor and make my own patterns outta how the white colour swirling through the dark grey tiles and then after a while I get the feeling of someone standing there in the doorway. When I look up it is Marcia. She say to me, 'Gloria not here, yu know.'

'She not here?'

'No. She gone into town.'

'She gone into town?'

'Yu going repeat everything I say?'

I just stop and I look at Marcia because I can't believe Gloria do this to me. This thing gone beyond a joke now.

'I dunno what time she coming back, so I can't say nothing to yu 'bout how long yu should spend your time waiting here.'

I don't bother go there the next afternoon like I supposed to. But come evening I go pick up the money and she is there dress in a tight red frock that show off every curve of every inch of her body. And I can see that every man in that room want to reach out and touch her, but him know that you can't just grab a woman like that, all you can do is maybe brush up against her like it a accident, or pat her arm as you talking, or maybe take her hand like you playing with her or swinging into a little dance, but just when your other arm want to reach 'round her waist and pull her in you have to check yourself. It like Gloria got a big notice hanging 'round her neck and it say, 'Watch yourself, man.'

When she finally decide to come give me the money she don't say nothing to me. She just walk over to the door where I am standing, but when she get close to me I step outside. So she follow me, and when it just the two of us on the porch I say to her, 'I know I not got no place complaining 'bout how you treat me this week. I just wondering how much longer you going carry on like this.'

She staring out into the dark yard and after some long while she say to me in this calm, cold voice, 'I only ever ask you for one thing and you do it, and that was a piece of business for both of us. That is how it started. It didn't start out as personal, but I dunno what happen. Maybe it was because of how patient you was, sitting there drinking tea and doing your handiwork, till in the end it was me that had to give you permission to make a move. You are the only man I ever know like that. Every other man I know just want to jump me the minute he clap eyes on me. That is how it been for me my whole life.'

All that is there in the silence between us is the click of a cricket here and there. So I just wait because I can feel that she got more to say.

'When I find out you going marry Fay Wong I almost couldn't believe it. It was like I must have dreamed it when I thought you had some feeling and respect for me. Not that a woman in my position can have much to say 'bout respect. But it hurt. It hurt bad because the worst thing about it was it put me in my place. It told me who I really am to you. Your three-time-a-week whore.'

I grab her shoulder and turn her 'round.

'Gloria, it not like that. It not like that at all.'

And she look me in the face and say, 'How is it then, Pao? What is it like?'

'It is like –' and I stop because I really have to think what I am going to say to her. 'It is like every day you go out and you see this independent, strong, beautiful animal. Maybe something like a tiger, and you happy with that, but everybody tell you that a grown man got to have him something to keep at home. He can't be out every day chasing after some tiger that is going about her own business. And you think yes, so you go get yourself a cage and you get the tiger and you put it in there. And maybe you happy for a while but it not long before you start to think well this tiger just sitting there every day now, waiting for me to feed it, and clean out the cage, and entertain it and tend to it when it sick. It don't do nothing for itself no more. And after a while it start to vex you because it nothing like the animal that you used to see running free and full of life. Now it just lazy and dead. Yu no get no pleasure from it no more, but you have to live with that because is you that kill it.'

'That is all about you. You ever think that maybe the tiger, as well as wanting to be free, also sometimes want some security and some rest so maybe it don't have to fret every day 'bout where the next meal coming from or how it going defend itself against everything out there that want to hunt it down? That maybe the tiger want to be able to look forward to some support and company, especially when it getting older and it not so independent, or strong, or beautiful? That maybe the tiger just want some day to find some peace?'

'You can have all of that, Gloria, and yu don't need no cage to get it.'

She just look at me like maybe she believe me or maybe she don't. And then she say, 'You spend too much time listening to what everybody tell you.'

Well after we done say all of that I realise I can't go ask her now how she hear 'bout me marrying Fay. So I miss my chance. And that was that.

After I leave Gloria, Hampton is waiting for me outside in the car and I say to him, 'Come on, man, let us go walk back to town.'

'Is ten o'clock at night, man, you mad? Don't you know it dangerous?'

'What, you 'fraid duppy going get you? And anyway, who you think foolish enough to go jump you and me? Come on, leave the car, you can come get it in the morning.' And we start walking.

When we nearly reach into town we hear a commotion in a alley, like a barrel knock over or something like that. And we follow the noise because we think maybe somebody in trouble. When we get down there, there is the two of them. One of them stand up with his pants open and the other one kneel down in front of him. When the one on him knees turn 'round we see him young, and him get up and run. The other one is a grown man. Him do up him pants and disappear 'round the next corner. Me and Hampton just look at one another and carry on walk back to town.

10

Compassion

So I marry Fay, and we do the church and we do the party that Miss Cicely organise up Lady Musgrave Road with pink champagne and a little orchestra in the garden and a whole heap a people I never see before and never had nothing to say to, and who had nothing to say to me. And we drive up to Ocho Rios.

The whole week me and Fay having the honeymoon she say hardly two words to me. She busy with her hair, she fixing her face, she straightening her dress. She instructing the maid and telling the waiter what she want to eat, and she chatting with these complete strangers that she meet here and there every day. Me, she don't say nothing to. She can barely even bring herself to look at me. We got the double bed right there inside the room and I am sleeping so far over my side I nearly falling out. Is just the sheet tuck in there under the mattress that saving me from hitting the cold tile floor every night.

And then the last night before we go home we do everything just the same way we been doing it all week. Fay take her shower and fix up herself and when she finish in the bathroom then it my turn to go take a shower and get ready for dinner. They serve dinner the same time every evening. Seven thirty for drinks and the little snack things on the terrace, and the band playing some gentle calypso. Eight pm you seated and working yu way through these five courses that they serve you every night. Not that I am complaining. The food is good, and every night is something else that I never see before. Like to me callaloo was callaloo but here they got it pile up in a little sandwich tower with some thin fried bread in between each layer and some strips of saltfish on top lay out like a star. And what they doing with the lobster I don't know, but it cheesy and good, and the steak and the cream and the pork and the apple, and a whole heap a green and purple vegetable I can't even recognise. But it good. It all good. It beautiful too under the clear Caribbean sky with the stars, and the music and the white linen tablecloth and the ice cubes clinking in the big water glass and the candles flickering on a little evening breeze. It nice. It civilised. They know how to look after you in this place.

To me it is a miracle. It is not a dream come true because I couldn't have dreamed this. Fay, she take it like she take everything else, like she was expecting it. She in her element.

So this evening I shower and put on a nice pale blue Sea Island cotton shirt and some grey slacks and I stick a clean handkerchief in my pocket and I step out on to the veranda, and she is sitting there looking out to sea. She got the rocking chair pull up right to the veranda edge with her legs stretch out in front of her and her feet on the little white wall crossed at the ankles. She quiet. So I sit down on the sofa behind her where I can just catch sight of the sun setting. We nuh say nothing. We just stay there like that. Fay looking at the lawn and the sand and the hammock strung up between the coconut trees and me watching a blaze of orange sinking into the sea.

And then after a while I hear a little sniff and a snivel. A little snivel like she crying. I dunno what to do so I just sit there. But then the sound carry on so I get up and I walk over to where she sitting and I look at her. I look at her in the face and is true, she crying. So I take the kerchief outta my pocket and I hand it to her and she take it. She mop her eye gentle like she don't want spoil her make-up, but she nuh say nothing. So I go back and sit down on the sofa.

By this time now it is getting dark and I see the lamps on the other verandas switching on one by one. But neither me nor Fay make no move to go switch on any lamp. We just sit there in the fading light and the silence.

Then she say to me, 'My father told me it was better for me to marry you than to spend the rest of my life fighting with my mother.'

'You didn't have to marry me. You could have wait until somebody more suitable come along.'

'What, after Cicely had set her sights on you?'

'I'm sure Miss Cicely not so stubborn to stick to her own view if maybe you happier with somebody else.'

Fay just laugh. She just throw her head back and laugh with the tears still rolling down her face. And then she turn 'round and look at me. And looking at her like that it seem like for the first time ever since I set eyes on her that morning at the Chinese Athletic Club, her guard was down.

'You think so?'

I just sit there because I dunno what to say to her. She look at me and she sorta smile and then she get up and start walk back inside. But just as she going pass me I stand up and reach out. And I grab her and hug her to me. I dunno what make me think it would be alright to go do a thing like that. I never take any liberty like that with her before. I suppose it was just instinct, even though the only other time I ever touch her was when I take her hand in the church to put the ring on it. And just now with us standing there I realise that we even miss the bit in the wedding when the priest tell you to kiss the bride, so I reckon either Fay or Miss Cicely must have tell him to leave that part out.

So the two of us entwined in the dark on the veranda and that is when she start to cry. Really sob like her whole body was heaving and it was taking all my strength to hold her up and stop the two of us from falling on the ground. It was like a little kindness turn the key to a floodgate that open up and let everything pour out. So I reckon it was some heavy burden that she was carrying there, but I didn't say nothing. Truth is I didn't know what to say to her. So I just carry on holding her tight and hoping that would be enough.

This is how we stay while I am looking over her shoulder and seeing the waiters in their white uniform with the big wooden tray on their shoulder carrying the food to the guests that want room service. And as they coming and going I know it time, so eventually after she calm herself down I say to her, 'You want go get some dinner?' When she ease back I see she was looking at me with a tenderness that almost make my heart bust. Then she mop her face and blow her nose on the kerchief I give her.

I look at Fay standing there on the veranda and I think well I dunno who Fay Wong is but maybe Fay dunno who Fay Wong is neither because that face that she put on for everybody just seem like a mask to me now.

That night when we go to sleep she crawl over to me and pull me off the edge into the middle of the bed, and then she rest her head on my shoulder and wrap my arm 'round her, just as I was listening to the tree frogs picking up their song.

When me and Fay finish the honeymoon and come home she take one look at Matthews Lane and she start to cry. The next day she go to her father's and the day after that she come back. And then she start cry again.

I ask her what the matter, but Fay can't even look at me. All I seeing is her back as she laying down or sitting on the edge of the bed.

'I know this house not what you used to but it not so bad. We can do something fix it up.' She no say nothing to me and I can't make out if she angry or if she sad so I say, 'It better than fighting with Miss Cicely.' And that is when she turn 'round and look at me.

'What on earth made you think I could come here to Matthews Lane and live in a place like this?'

'It's my home, Fay. This is my family with Ma and Zhang. What do you want me to do, leave them? Look at them, the two of them old. I can't go leave them just like that. And I don't want to. I am the son, they my responsibility. You forget you Chinese?'

'You think I am Chinese?'

'What you talking 'bout?'

And she just get up and walk out the room.

I think maybe I go buy something to cheer Fay up, like some nice silk blouse and silk stocking and some vase to brighten up the bedroom. And every night when we go to bed I talk to her. I tell 'bout everything happening 'round Chinatown and I ask her what kinda day she have. But all I see is her back and all I hear is the constant snivel and the blow of her nose. I never know a person could cry so much. I thought maybe eventually they would run outta water but not Fay. She keep it up day and night till it really start to vex everybody.

I can't take it. It get so bad I start sleeping down the shop but Zhang say it not fair on everybody else in the house, I have to try do something with her. So eventually three weeks later I sit her down and I say to her, 'Fay, nobody in the house can take your crying no more. You have to tell me what we going do to put an end to it.' And I really look at her while she sitting on the edge of the bed and me kneeling on the hard wooden floor in front of her.

I take a finger and I wipe a few strands of hair away from her eyes because they wet and stuck to her face. And she let me do it which I know is a good sign. So I say, 'What we going to do, eh?'

'Why did you marry me, Pao?' And that is when the wave of shame wash over me because I didn't have no proper answer for her.

'You married me because my father is Henry Wong. Isn't that the truth? Honestly?'

I reckon the least I can do is face how ugly my own intention was so I say, 'Yes. Yes it the truth. That is how it start, Fay, but that not how it is now, not since the honeymoon. When we was at the hotel I see a different side of you. You must admit yourself we cross a bridge that week you and me. Don't tell me it didn't mean nothing to you.' And I take her hands in mine.

64

She let me stay there kneeling down holding her hand and then she say to me, 'I can't live like this, Pao. Can't you see that you and this house are the punishment my mother picked out for me? This is the suffering she wants me to have for the rest of my life.'

'What suffering?'

'The same suffering that I had as a child when she used to beat and starve me and lock me in the music room and take the key with her when she went to church.'

I can't believe what Fay is saying to me. Not that I think she lying but I can't believe that Miss Cicely carry on like this.

'What she beat you for?'

'For always being too much of one thing and never enough of another.'

I can't understand what she saying to me so I just kneel there and look at her, how serious she is 'bout this like she under some kinda obeah spell that she can't do nothing 'bout.

'It don't have to be like that, you know. We don't have to just sit back and let Miss Cicely decide what kinda life we going have together.'

Fay don't say nothing to me, but the next day she stop crying and when I come home from work I see she been out the yard to go get some flowers from the market that she arrange in the vase in the bedroom where it look real pretty.

11

Weather

Then Finley tell me that the police get themselves a new sergeant from Montego Bay. They put him in the North Street police station to help fight corruption, which I think is rich because half my money going to the police to make sure them look the other way. So anyway I say to him, 'Maybe we should go meet this sergeant,' but Finley not sure if that is such a good idea.

'What you going say to him anyway?'

'Maybe we just say hello, and wish him well with him duties, which most likely him going have to start right there in the police station,' and we laugh. 'Well, after all them sending him after us so the least we can do is shake the man's hand.' So Finley say he will think on it. Sun Tzu say, *'By weather I mean the interaction of natural forces; the effects of winter's cold and summer's heat, and the conduct of military operations in accordance with the seasons.'*

A week later Finley's big idea is to get Round One Chin to invite Sergeant Brown to address the Wholesale Provision Merchants' Association. Chin not sure if he too happy 'bout it because even though he think maybe it a good idea to hear what Sergeant Brown got to say, he nervous 'bout getting involved with the police. He say everybody happy paying the protection and keeping Chinatown business in Chinatown. He say we don't need to be inviting no outsiders to start interfering with us. We can handle everything ourselves just like we been doing since Zhang get here all them years back. So I have to say to him it alright, we not going do nothing but listen to the man for a few minutes.

So a couple month later Sergeant Brown come to the meeting, and at the appointed moment Chin stand up on the platform and announce how pleased he is to have with us this evening 'Sergeant Clifton Brown of the North Street police station who is going to talk to us about how his work controlling corruption in the downtown area is going to help the Chinese merchants' community'. And we all clap our hands. I take Finley and Hampton with me as well because I reckon we all interested in seeing what this man look like and finding out what he got to say.

When Sergeant Brown stand up, me and Hampton just look at each other. Later on when I get introduced to him I put out my hand to shake and then I clasp both my hands 'round his. And I hold his hand a long time while I look him in the eye. And the longer I am holding his hand, and the longer I am looking him in the eye, the more he is realising that we have a bond now and I will be relying on him to fix any little problems we have. Because just the way we recognise him, is just the same way him recognise me.

When we walking home afterwards I say to Hampton, 'How did Sergeant Brown seem to you that night we catch him in the alley with that bwoy?'

'That not nuh bwoy, man.'

'Sure it a bwoy.'

'No, man. You make it sound like it a child. It a man alright and him young, but it nuh bwoy. You going give Judge Finley the wrong idea.'

'Alright, how did Sergeant Brown seem to you the night we catch him in the alley with that *young man?*' I say it like that for Hampton sake.

'Calm.'

'Calm, like him do it before.'

'Yah man, like him do it plenty time before.'

'I reckon a man in his position got to be desperate to go take a chance like that, eh? And if him so desperate, and him so calm, then I reckon it not the first time. And it not going be the last.'

I look at Finley. 'What we need is someone to keep an eye on him. Someone he not going suspect. Someone maybe like a *young man.*'

And Finley say, 'My wife got a nephew, Milton, his papa just get run down by a drunk Englishman driving reckless down Constant Spring Road, now Milton the head of the family with a mama and four children to keep.'

'He know how to look after himself?'

'Yah, man.'

'Tell him to come see me.'

When Milton turn up the next day I see that he is nothing but a boy. And I think well I was only a boy myself when I start up in this business so maybe the situation not too bad. I reckon that he too young to be going picking up the money from Gloria. Them girls would make mincemeat outta him and relish every minute they spend making him blush all over his body. So that was definitely out. But you can't pay a man to be doing nothing but follow Sergeant Brown day and night so I settle to let Milton do some driving – chicken and eggs and maybe drop off a few cigarettes, even though any half-conscious policeman would notice that this boy ain't nearly old enough to be driving no van.

Still, and this is exactly the sort of thing Sergeant Brown need to be looking out for, those boys of his always happy to see that US dollar bill. They can make anything happen or not happen, disappear, come back, turn upside down when you flash them a few bills of old George Washington, or even better Mr Abraham Lincoln. And if things get really serious then you just pull out Mr Andrew Jackson for them. Because with the police, these is the faces you know you can always rely on.

So that was it even though I had a little worry in the back of my mind 'bout what Milton was letting himself in for with Clifton Brown. Especially because them little pouty lips and smooth skin make him look so young.

12

The Employment of Secret Agents

A couple months after we set Milton on Sergeant Brown's tail Judge Finley come to Matthews Lane with Milton bringing a message that Sergeant Brown want to talk to me, so I say for him to come meet me over the Blue Lagoon but Finley say it more complicated than that because Milton got something to tell me.

So then this is when Milton step up and I look at him standing there almost like he hiding behind Finley and I say, 'Come on then.'

Finley step aside and sorta push Milton forward with a little helping hand at his back.

'I didn't mean for it to happen. It just happen. Just like that.'

I just look at Finley because I can't imagine how much time this nephew of his is going to take to tell me nothing.

'Him jump me. Him just catch me by surprise.'

'Who jump you, Milton?'

'I was following him like you say: Sergeant Brown. And then I come 'round the corner and him jump me. And the next thing I know him grab my pants and rip it open and all the buttons just pop off and him drag them down and bend me over a barrel.'

By now Milton sweating and shaking and I getting ready to hear the worst.

'Him bend me over the barrel and when I feel the full weight of him leaning down on top of me I thought Jesus Christ. It all happen so fast I just lay there waiting for it. And then him put his mouth right next to my ear and say, tell yu boss I want to see him.'

'That is it? That is what you have to tell me? So when all this happen?'

'Just two week after you tell me to go follow him.'

'And all this long time go by and you no tell me?' Then I say to Finley, 'How long you know 'bout this?'

'Just this morning him tell me. Milton too 'fraid to tell you. Him take fright 'bout what you going do to him for being so careless.'

'He should take fright. What kind of stupid thing is that and then him no tell nobody 'bout it? Maybe Clifton Brown should have finish the job the bwoy such a jackass.'

But then I think about it and I think maybe it my fault anyway for sending a little bwoy to go trail a man like Clifton Brown. Maybe I should just count my blessings that nothing bad actually happen to him.

'Go on,' I say to him like to tell him to get outta the yard, and then just as he get to the gate I shout, 'Go get yourself a belt to hold up your pants.'

When I finally go meet Clifton Brown he catch up in a dark corner in the Blue Lagoon playing with a Red Stripe like he don't really mean to be drinking it. When him look up at me him seem sorta sour so I just sit down and tell the barman to bring me a beer.

'How come you no pay me no mind with the message I send you?'

'I here nuh?'

'And it take you all this long time to come see me after I done talk to that bwoy of yours weeks ago?'

I think to myself you rough up my bwoy and frighten him half to death. So maybe that your idea of a joke but it don't mean I owe you no explanation so I just say, 'I here now so tell me what you want.'

'That bwoy of yours busy following me all night and all day he is driving chickens and cigarettes all over town. And apart from it all being stolen goods you and me both know that bwoy not got no driving licence.'

'Driving licence! Is that what you worried 'bout?' And I just throw my head back and laugh. 'I can't believe you drive all the way over here to talk to me 'bout Milton driving licence. You really telling me yu not got nothing better to do than that?'

'I can throw his arse in jail, yu know. And yours as well with all this navy liquor and gambling and whore houses yu running.'

'My arse in jail? And what going happen to your arse when I get through telling everything I know 'bout you and them bwoys you taking down the alley? Whose arse you think they going be interested in then?'

Clifton start play with the beer bottle turning it round in his hand like he studying every inch of the label. Then he say, 'It don't have to be like this, yu know. We have a opportunity here to help each other.'

I look at him and I think to myself OK he got a point because us helping each other was what this was all about in the first place anyway. That was why I set Milton on his tail to get some leverage. So what it matter if it him making me a offer instead of the other way round? Sun Tzu say, '*When the envoys speak in apologetic terms the enemy wishes a respite.*'

So I say to him, 'If it was anybody else but me catch you with that bwoy in that alley that night they would have cut off your cock and beat you so bad they would have leave you for dead.'

But he don't say nothing.

I sit back and look at him because it suddenly dawn on me what a hard life Clifton making for himself and what a dangerous place Jamaica is for a man like him.

'So what you want to do, Clifton?'

And he lay out his terms, what protection he providing, how much cut he want, and I say yes because it all seem reasonable enough. But what I realise is that all Clifton really want is to be with some people who know what he is and not looking to knife him over it. Clifton lonely and him buying himself some friends.

So I say to him to forget 'bout the beer and I tell the barman to bring us a bottle of Appleton.

By the time I leave the Blue Lagoon I was feeling good. Good enough to want to go to Chinatown and see if I could pick up something to make Fay feel better. Because although she stop crying well over six months now all I hear from Ma is how Fay moody and lazy. And how she just sit still and silent and won't do nothing to help out. Not that she is there in Matthews Lane that much because in truth Fay spend half her time up in New Kingston running back to her papa's house any time she fancy. But Ma don't care 'bout all that. All Ma tell me is how Fay idle, she won't fry a few fritters or pick the duck feathers for the pillows. She won't even do a bit of cooking. Nothing. According to Ma, Fay still waiting for some house-maid to make her bed and tidy up the place, and put the food on the table in front of her, and clear up when she finish eat because her whole life Fay never even do so much as pick up a chopstick, not even to feed herself, because Miss Cicely always have them use a knife and fork, English style. Fay don't even know how to pick up the rice bowl. And I know this bit is true because I see her every day outta the corner of my eye staring at me like she would rather starve to death than put the bowl to her mouth. It get so bad I had to go buy a fork, just the one, so now she can sit there dainty taking all night to eat a bowl of rice.

Ma say Fay try to get Miss Tilly run 'round after her but she, Ma, put a stop to that: 'Tilly here to help me make a living not play maid to you.' That is what she tell Fay. So now Fay don't even bother to say good morning or good evening to Tilly because, to her, Tilly don't exist.

I say to Ma that maybe she could try talk to Fay, in English because she don't seem to understand that Fay Chinese not too good.

'Me talk English? She no Chinese girl? She talk Chinese.'

And I say, 'No, Ma. You talk English plenty good enough when you talking to Tilly. Just try do the same thing with Fay.'

But Ma not doing it. She clicking and clucking with her tongue and she crashing 'round the kitchen complaining 'bout Fay all the time but never a word will she say to Fay unless it outta some sort of spite.

I say to Fay maybe she can try do something with Ma.

'Do you have a suggestion?'

'I dunno, Fay. What do women do together? There must be something you can do? Maybe you go shopping or you show her how to arrange the flowers in the vase so nice like you do?'

Fay just sit there and look at me and I know exactly what she thinking because I can't see Ma going shopping with her neither, and as far as flower arranging I think my mother would sooner chop up the flowers and cook them.

'Well maybe you can try wash a few pots or something.'

So I am standing in the shop and it is a jade ring that catch my eye. Dark green jade sitting on a 22-carat-gold band, and I buy it. I have them wrap the box in some soft green tissue paper and put a bow on it. And even though this is not the first time I try sweeten Fay with something like this I feel uplifted. That maybe this time I might manage to get something she find some favour with because I think she really been trying her best to get along in the house with Ma and I know it not easy.

All the way back to Matthews Lane there is a spring in my step, with this jade ring in my pocket rubbing against my thigh feeling like a nice shiny big red apple for the teacher. Not that I know anything 'bout apples and teachers but I seen enough American movies to know how good it feel when you got a thing like that you going give to somebody.

But when I get back to Matthews Lane Fay not there, Ma say she gone back to her father's. And I don't know why, but this time I just see red. Maybe it was because the ring was sitting there in my pocket. And I just run out the house and jump in the car.

All the time I am driving with my hand down on the horn I can see in my mind's eye the signs on the highway that say 'Undertakers Love Overtakers'. Even when I hit Cross Roads I just ignore the sign that say 'Careful Drivers Stop at Red Lights' and just press my foot on the gas and keep going. When I get to Lady Musgrave Road I turn into the driveway so fast I can smell the rubber the tyres is leaving on the road.

But it is just the same thing. The housemaid Ethyl come out to tell me that Fay not there. She gone out with her sister Daphne. I think Ethyl feel sorry for me just standing there like that because she tell me to sit down on the veranda and offer to bring me a glass of lemonade. But it is not lemonade I want, so she bring me a glass of Appleton.

She put the glass down on the table next to me and say, 'Miss Fay and Miss Daphne most likely gone out to celebrate about the baby.' Well it was a good job I was already sitting down because otherwise I would have fall down. I look at Ethyl and I can see she think that maybe she say something outta turn, so she run inside without saying another word.

When I come round it was dark and I could smell the evening scent off the angel trumpet. But I know I not been sleeping all this while because there is three empty glasses on the table next to me. Then I hear a car door slam and the next thing Henry Wong is coming up the veranda steps. His tall, square frame look tired and weary. When he see me sitting there he take a hand and brush the greying hair back off his forehead and then he come and sit down next to me. Him take my hand in his. Gentle like.

'Is my fault,' him say to me. 'You think you good father. Give children everything they want. But maybe it not so good. Maybe they just grow up good for nothing. Fay not bad girl. She just spoil.'

I was looking at him and wondering how come he manage to live in a house full of women like this.

'Fay tell me 'bout Matthews Lane, how the house small and how you got no help. And I tell her you are a young man, just making your way. When business get better you will move her to a better house, get some help, make things good. She just need to have some patience. When I married her mother I was just a young man like you. Just got the one shop, but when business get better, everything get better. Patience, Pao, that is what it takes. That is what I tell Fay, that she has to stay with you and have patience. Anyway, I tell her, it better to be downtown with your own people. Better than living up here in this desert like me.'

'Did Miss Cicely keep running back to her father every other week as well?'

'No, that was a different situation.' And then him look sorta sad and pause for a minute. 'Women are not like men, Pao, they change with the wind. That is why we men have to steady ourselves. Make a firm anchor with a good business and work hard.' Then he stop and think a minute. And then he say, 'You go home now. You don't want to be having no talk with Fay at this time of night and with everything else,' him sort of motioning towards the empty glasses. 'Tomorrow is plenty time to sort things out.'

The next morning when I go up to the house, Fay already come and gone again. Ethyl look sheepish when she have to tell me but she still look sorry for me. So I say to her, 'Ethyl, you know where my shop is down West Street?'

'Yes, Mr Philip.'

'Next time you get a day off come see me will you?' And she agree to do it the next week Wednesday.

Then just as I start to leave Fay and Daphne turn up. Daphne fussing 'round Fay because Fay her older sister and she know she got to show respect. But it also because Daphne plain and every-body get taken with Fay like they don't even know Daphne is there. Daphne used to being invisible.

So I get outta the car and stand up in front of Fay in the drive-way. She look truculent like she going just kiss her teeth and walk inside. But she don't, she just stand up there with her hand on her hip while Daphne go inside the house.

'What you doing here, Pao?'

'What you doing here, Fay?'

'This is my home.'

'No, this is your papa's home. Your home is with me, downtown in Matthews Lane.' And then she do exactly what I think, she kiss her teeth and walk off. I follow her up the steps on to the veranda.

'You got no business here, you know.'

'You is my business. A wife supposed to stay with her husband, not making a fool outta him every week running back to her papa.'

'Is that what you are worried about, me making a fool out of you? Well don't fuss yourself about that. You are making a fine job of it yourself.'

And she start to walk inside so I grab her hand to pull her back, but she just jerk it away from me and start yelling like she want to wise up the whole neighbourhood to what she have to say to me.

'Take your hand off me. Who do you think you are, grabbing after me like that? You are not downtown now with your little whores and hoodlums. You are in a respectable place and you need to act like it.'

'You think this is respectable, you and me bawling at each other right out here on the veranda?'

'You should be the last person on this earth to talk about what is respectable. If you weren't so pathetic you would make me laugh.'

Well that make me mad. I just fix her with a stare cold as ice and she stop because I think she remember who she was talking to. So she calm down and I say to her, 'Is it true you pregnant?' But she don't want to answer me, so I have to ask her again.

'Is it true you pregnant?'

But she still don't say nothing so I take a deep breath and I fix her with my eyes and I say to her, 'Remember you are a Catholic.'

And just then I put my hand in my pocket and I feel the box still sitting there. So I pull it out and I hold it out to her. She look at it there in my hand, and then she look at me in the face.

'Take it.'

'What is it?'

'Take it and see.' So she reach out and take it from me.

'Go on, open it.'

She unwrap the bow and tear off the paper. When she open the box she just stare at the ring. And then she reach inside the box with her right hand and pick it up. And she raise up her arm, and swing, and throw the ring into the yard.

'That would be the companion piece to the jade necklace you bought for your whore in East Kingston.' She look at me. 'You think I didn't know?' And then she just walk inside and close the door, which was the first time I even seen that door shut.

Three days later she come back to Matthews Lane, most likely after her papa tell her to. But she don't say nothing to me 'bout the baby or the ring or anything else. And I don't say nothing to her.

When Ethyl come see me the next week she bring me back the ring she fetch outta the flower bed.

'I think you might want this back.'

And she hand it to me in the box she must have pick up off the veranda. I take it from her and say thank you and put it in my pocket.

Ethyl is young. She want something more than being down on her knees scrubbing the Wongs' mahogany floor, and picking up after Fay and Daphne, and their little brother Kenneth who Miss Cicely produce long after everybody think she past her time.

Ethyl is looking to better herself. So I tell her I will pay for her to learn shorthand and typing on her day off, and buy a little typewriter and all the books she need so she can practise. And pay for the examination when the time come. And she is happy with that. So that is our secret, because if Miss Cicely catch wind of all of this she will fire Ethyl just like that. Maids are twenty a penny for a person like Miss Cicely in a place like Jamaica.

Ethyl come to see me every week after that and she bring me the news from Lady Musgrave Road. This is a good arrangement because just like Sun Tzu say, the thirteenth principle of the art of war is the employment of secret agents.

'What is called "foreknowledge" cannot be elicited from spirits, nor from gods, nor by analogy with past events, nor from calculations. It must be obtained from men who know the enemy situation.'

13

Offensive Strategy

The next time I see Gloria I take the ring with me because Fay is right, it will look good next to the necklace that Gloria keep lock up in a box at the back of her wardrobe and only get out on special occasions. But the ring she want put on straight away. It fit her like it was bought for her. So she straighten it on her finger and stretch out her arm to admire how gracious it look pon her hand. It suit her. Really and truly. The thing make her skin look rich and succulent. And she so pleased with it I think maybe it mean something more to her than it do to me. So I don't bother say nothing 'bout Fay and all her antics and carrying on. Not that Gloria want to hear anything 'bout Fay because that was the one condition Gloria had after I get married. She didn't want to hear nothing 'bout Fay. We was just going to carry on act like Fay didn't even exist because being married to Fay didn't change nothing between me and Gloria. I still pick up the money from her. I still giving her protection. I still drinking Lipton's Yellow Label tea with her. I still seeing her three times a week. I still talking to her 'bout things because Gloria is the only person who ever care to listen to me talk 'bout myself and what this life mean to me.

Then she say to me, 'I have something to tell you.'

And I say, 'What?'

And she say, 'I going to have a baby.' Well I just reach out and find the arm of a chair to steady myself, and I sit down because it feel like me knees going buckle under me.

'So how long you know this?'

'Last week. Well I think two months gone already. I just wanted to be sure.' I can tell Gloria don't know what kinda face to put on. She don't know whether to look happy or worried or vexed because she don't know how I am going take the news. And truth is I don't know either.

So I say, 'What you going do?'

And she say, 'How you mean?'

'What you going do . . . with it?'

'You mean get rid of it?'

'No. I mean what you want to do? You want to keep it or what?'

'What you want to do?' And she look at me now like she scared what the answer going be.

'It not got nothing to do with me, Gloria. Is not my baby, is yours.'

'You no know it take two people to make a baby?'

'You saying it mine? How you so sure?'

She just stand there and look at me. Then she say, 'OK, if you want say the baby not yours then fine. I will go about my business and sort this out myself.'

'I'm not saying that, Gloria. I just surprised that's all. If you say the baby mine then it mine. But it not for me to decide 'bout it. It not going change my life like it going change yours.' And that is when her face soften, because she could see that I was really giving her a choice. And it was almost like she never thought I would take it that way. Actually just give her the choice like that.

So I say to her, 'I am good with whatever you want to do. But if you decide to have it you going have to let me look after you better than this place.' And I just look 'round the room the way it decorate for entertaining men and she knew exactly what I mean. 'Long time now I been wanting you to stop all this anyway, but sure as eggs is eggs this ain't no business for a pregnant woman.'

And she laugh and say, 'Some men come on strong with a pregnant woman.'

'Not on top of my son.'

'Who say it going be a boy? Maybe it be a girl. Maybe she become the first woman prime minister of Jamaica.'

'Maybe.'

After that Gloria start look for a different place to live. She and her sister Marcia going all over Kingston, but truth is I have my heart set on some place in Barbican. It new, it clean, it good neighbourhood. But I don't say nothing to Gloria because if I say Barbican she going move to Mona Heights. She don't like me telling her nothing. She say I not got no right, especially after I decide to go marry somebody else. But in the end there was no need to worry. Gloria and Marcia find a nice three-bedroom place, two bathroom, nice tidy yard right up there in Barbican.

The thing I couldn't figure out was how come after all these years Gloria get pregnant at exactly the same time as Fay. So I decide that maybe it was something to do with me. Or maybe it was something Gloria decide for herself.

When Ethyl come see me at the shop she tell me that Fay start going down to Bishop's Lodge visiting with some priest, and him visiting her up at Lady Musgrave Road as well. Him called Father Michael Kealey and him young and good looking, so Ethyl say anyway. She say he look like the movie star Jeff Chandler, 'but a little bit browner than when he was the Indian chief Cochise in Broken Arrow'. Ethyl say he even got the wavy grey hair and the dimple in his chin. So now this is something else for me to go sort out.

I set Finley to go see what he can find out and sure enough Father Kealey is some young sprat straight outta the seminary in Washington USA although he a Kingston boy that they school up in St George's College with all them Jesuits. Ethyl tell me that him and Fay spend all hours of the day sitting on the veranda and on the swing way out yonder under the big mango tree, and all the time them talking and talking.

Seem like it been going on for months but is only just now Ethyl decide to tell me. She say she didn't know what to make of it but she say last week when Father Kealey come knocking up the house in the middle of the night it make Mr Henry so vex he go out there and tell the Father to go home.

'Mr Henry not a man quick to his temper, so that is when I reckon that maybe something not so right with Miss Fay and Father. And Miss Cicely don't care for it neither. When they out there on the veranda she play the piano loud. Loud. And sing all them tunes Mr John Wesley make up that she learn when she was a Methodist, all 'bout how sinners going burn in hell and things like that.

'Then yesterday Miss Cicely and Miss Fay have one almighty knockdown drag-out 'bout how Miss Fay running 'round with a priest and what she doing with Father Kealey. And Miss Cicely saying how Miss Fay been spoil her whole life. And how she make them send her to Immaculate Conception to be a boarder when the school only down the road from the house because all she want do is mix with her rich friends and pretend she white like them. And Miss Cicely say 'bout how Miss Fay spend all her time going to parties and playing tennis when she should have been doing her lessons which, according to Miss Cicely, tennis not no proper pastime for a Jamaican girl anyway. And Miss Cicely say they only let Miss Fay in the tennis club because she half Chinese and her papa rich.

'And then that is when it really get bad because Miss Cicely say Miss Fay think she better than everybody else because her skin so light and she can get away with forgetting where she come from. Well, Mr Philip, that is when Miss Fay start up telling her mother 'bout how is not she that is ashamed of her colour but is Miss Cicely shamed. Is Miss Cicely got all the airs and graces and acting like she white Englishwoman with her Earl Grey tea and Victoria sponge.

'Well the whole house can hear this a going on and when it go quiet we all think Miss Cicely done mash up Miss Fay in the mouth shut her up. But it didn't seem so because next thing somebody slam down the lid on the piano so hard it make the whole house rock. And Miss Fay is yelling how Miss Cicely never care for her, and how she been vengeful to her all her life because she jealous, and how all the fighting with Miss Cicely –' And then Ethyl stop, suddenly, like she 'fraid her mouth run away with her and she don't know if she should carry on with what she is telling me.

So I say, 'Go on, is alright.' But Ethyl still too 'fraid to tell me so I have to say to her again, 'Go on.' Only this time I say to her, 'Is fine. You want a glass of water or some lemonade or something?'

And she say, 'Yes, a glass of water, thank you, Mr Philip.' And she wriggle herself on the chair like she easing her back, and I tell Hampton to go fetch her a glass of ice water. She just sit there quiet, and when Hampton come back she drink down the whole glass of water like she was dying of thirst.

Then she say, 'Miss Fay say that it was all the fighting with her mother that make her done marry you just to get away from Miss Cicely. But is only now she discover that . . .' And she stop again.

'Go on, Ethyl. It OK, really.'

'Discover that living with you is just as bad as living with her mother. Worse, because you is a thief, and you pimping women and carrying on all sort of nastiness all over town.'

'So what Miss Cicely say to that?'

'Miss Cicely say she grow up in a plantation hut they used to use for the slaves. She say the floor was just hard mud and the place was pure misery. "You could smell the misery in the walls, and every day I used to pray, Lord have mercy on my soul." That is what she say to Miss Fay. And then she say, "If that was good enough for me, then Matthews Lane is plenty good enough for you." And that is how it end, because after that all we hear is the car start up in the driveway and Miss Fay was gone.

'When I go in the music room afterwards I half expect to find that Miss Fay drop the baby right there on the floor, the argument so bad.'

So I decide the only thing for it is for me to go see this man. I ring up and make an appointment and when the time come I take a shower and put on a good suit.

When I get down to Bishop's Lodge I find this calm, gentle man who talk in a whisper like he 'fraid God going overhear him. And when I shake his hand his skin so soft I think my hand just going sink and disappear into his palm. Everything 'bout him just sort of suck you in, but it not unpleasant. In truth, it feel sort of reassuring.

I tell him I know my wife coming to see him. I don't want to know what she talking to him about. I know that is between him and her, him being a priest and all. But I just want him to meet me, to know I am a person in flesh and blood. I don't want to be just something he imagine based on what Fay have to say about me. That maybe me and him can just get to know each other. Not talk 'bout Fay or anything like that. Maybe I could even help with some of the good work him doing in his ministry. I just want him to come to know me as a person, and a human being.

Him look at me some long time with his hand covering him mouth like he don't want to say nothing before he was good and ready. And then him say to me, 'The good Lord already knows you are a person in flesh and blood and the door of His house is open to you. All that He asks in return is that your heart is open to Him.'

Afterwards when I go visit Miss Cicely I make sure to take plenty grapenut ice cream and I sit on the veranda with her drinking lemonade and watching Edmond working in the garden just like old times.

I start going up there regular but I never mention nothing 'bout Fay even though sometimes she right there in the house. I just carry on with Miss Cicely like Fay not there. Every now and again Daphne come out and sit with us. Daphne nuh say much. She just sit there and look at me and smile. And she like to pour the tea and fuss 'round me over every drop of milk and triangle of sandwich.

I enjoying myself. The only thing bugging me is Fay little brother Kenneth who keep sneaking up to me asking me if there is anything I got for him to do. And every time I just ease him back because the boy too eager to take to the street when by right he should be in school getting himself a education.

When Fay near her time they take her into the hospital up Old Hope Road. She lay up there over a week and then they get fed up and decide to do whatever they do to make the baby come. I think Fay ready too because she not protesting so it must be what she want.

The baby is a boy. I tell Fay I going call him Xiuquan after Zhang and my brother that went to America. She don't say nothing but when I leaving the hospital I hear her cooing up the baby in her arms and calling him Karl.

Gloria have a girl in the public hospital. That is where she choose to have it. She name the baby Esther. Is Gloria's mother name and all of them come from country to see the baby. Them pleased and proud. Marcia just keep saying 'Auntie Marcia' to the baby all the time she rocking her up and down in her arms. Gloria look settled and happy with the baby in the new house, and even though I keep trying to get her to get some help she just say no.

When Fay come home from the hospital with the baby she surprise me. I thought she would just put him down and leave Ma and Tilly to tend to him. But it wasn't so. Fay get real motherly so I get to think that maybe it was what she was needing all along because it seem like she finally find something she actually want to do. And for the first time since I know her Fay actually look happy.

Even Ma seem like she happy to have Fay and the baby in the house. She talking to Fay 'bout the baby clothes and she cooing the baby and loving him anytime Fay put him down and it seem like she can get away with a few minutes of picking him up and holding him to her.

Ma say, 'He just like Pao when he baby.'

Fay say, 'What was Pao like?'

'Pao strong boy, and smart. Very smart. He learn everything quicker than any baby. And he happy. His papa throw him up in air and Pao laugh. Just like throw baby . . .' And I think Jesus Christ and I stand up so I can see outta the window at what is going on and sure enough Ma got the baby under him armpit and she tossing him into the air and him chuckling and Fay standing there next to the table hanging on to it like she need to take hold of something to stop herself from grabbing the baby from Ma. I impressed by her self-control.

After three or four toss Ma wear herself out and she give the baby back to Fay and Fay put him down. So I sit back in the chair and carry on read the paper. Then Ma say, 'You miss your mama?'

'Not really.'

'So why you keep go back?' Well I think to myself this I got to hear so I draw up my chair closer and catch up under the window where they can't see me.

'It's complicated.'

'What mean complicated?'

'Mama and I argue but . . .'

I can hear Ma stop beating the batter for the fritters and I can picture her just standing there looking at Fay waiting for her to finish.

'I miss the house and being at home with my sister and brother.'

'Ah yes. And your papa? You miss your papa?'

'Yes.'

'Yes, when you leave a place there is a lot to miss. Like when you leave a country. A country like China and you come on a ship to another place. There is a lot to miss. But not go back, eh? Too far. Too far and too long ago for anything.'

'Do you still miss China?'

'Every day. The rice fields and the open sky. The village, the family and their father. He was a good man. Honourable man. Good farmer. Like Xiuquan. He make good farmer like his papa.'

'You miss Xiuquan?'

'Ah miss, miss, miss. Too much talk 'bout miss. What good it do you? This happen, that happen. War, death, a new country, a son leave, a baby born. Who tell the world to make these things happen? That is why the Buddha say to be happy is to suffer less, and to suffer less is to be free from wanting. You accept what you have. Now I am here with Pao and Zhang.'

It good to hear Ma and Fay actually talk to each other. It a relief more than anything to think maybe the war between them not going go on for ever. That maybe Xiuquan going help that. But two things still true.

First, even though Zhang proud like he got a grandson name after him, Fay won't never call the baby Xiuquan. She call him Karl all the time and everybody in the house notice it but they don't say nothing 'bout it. Second, Fay still going to Bishop's Lodge so the Father Kealey thing not done with yet.

Sun Tzu say, 'What is of supreme importance in war is to attack the enemy's strategy and disrupt his alliances.' So when I find out that the young Queen Elizabeth is coming to Jamaica on a two-day visit on her way to Australia I tell Clifton Brown that I need a invitation for Cicely Wong to this here big party they going hold up at Kings House.

'How the hell you think I going do that?'

'You policeman, you fix it. How you do it your business. If you need money I give it to you. But you have to make the contacts, man. You have to set up the situation. I want two invitation. One for Miss Cicely and another one in case she want take somebody with her.'

Miss Cicely take Daphne with her, and she can't thank me enough. After all these years of Earl Grey tea and Victoria sponge she finally get to meet the Queen of England. She actually get introduced to her. That is how good Clifton Brown is.

Three week later I make Hampton go with Miss Cicely and Daphne to Miami on a little shopping trip. They over the moon. They have such a good time they bring me a tie and some after-shave and a bath robe, although god knows what they think I going do with that. But it not enough for Daphne to just give me the things. She want to invite me to dinner so we can sit down and eat and open up the parcels like it something special.

So I go up to Lady Musgrave Road and sit down there eating this chicken with Miss Cicely and Daphne and the little brother, Kenneth, who keep looking at me like he can't wait for the dinner to be over so he can corner me and beg me again to take him on. I tired of telling this boy no so I chewing my food good and slow and I chatting with Miss Cicely in between every mouthful hoping that the boy get fed up of waiting and go find himself something else to do.

Sure enough when him finish eat him get restless because I am chewing and chatting, and chatting and chewing, and no look like I going get done this side of New Year. So Kenneth get up and take off and I think thank god.

Then after dinner Miss Cicely say we should go sit on the veranda and we do it. Daphne sit down there hanging on every single word that passing between me and Miss Cicely 'bout her meeting with the Queen and the shopping trip to Miami. And that is when Daphne rush inside and bring out these parcels for me to unwrap. It feel nice that somebody want to give me something. That they want to say thank you. It not something that happen that much. In fact I can't remember the last time I get a present from anybody.

And then just as I try look pleased and grateful for the gifts they bring me and start to say thank you, Daphne get up and come over to me and kiss me. Just like that. On the cheek. And then she sit herself down again and straighten her skirt. I so surprised I just look at her, but she glancing past me like maybe somebody coming up behind but there not nobody there. So I look again at Miss Cicely but it don't seem like she notice anything at all.

By this time I am making regular donations to Father Kealey's orphan fund and his projects for poor relief and education in the rural areas. And him already done tell me to call him Michael and I tell him to call me Pao.

Sometimes we just sit and chat at Bishop's Lodge, him telling me 'bout how his projects doing and me just making conversation.

Other times we go somewhere grab some lunch. Michael is a man of discretion. He never mention Fay to me. And just the same way, I know he never mention me to Fay because she not say nothing to me 'bout him and I know if she knew I was seeing him she would have something to say 'bout it.

So I reckon I manage to do what Sun Tzu say. I disrupt Fay's alliances. Not that Fay see Miss Cicely that way, but she treat the house at Lady Musgrave Road like a sanctuary and now that was mine because Miss Cicely and Daphne and Ethyl belong to me. Just like Father Kealey was coming to me with his God and his hope to find some goodness in me. And the same way Henry Wong would take me in as a full son-in-law, because that was my next move.

14

Deception

By the mid 1950s Jamaica was on the up, especially because they discover the bauxite. But the big profit was going to the overseas aluminium companies who invested in the mining, because up to 1954 Busta's government let the bauxite ore be shipped out for 10 cents a ton. When the government change in 1955, Norman Manley negotiate a new royalty and tax at $1.40 a ton. It was a pittance when you compare it to the profit the aluminium companies was making but still Jamaica was earning and people had jobs and training. It was good but it didn't stop me from noticing that the whole thing was just like the same way the plantation profits gone to England back in the old days. It was just like a new version of that, including them passing some laws to secure the special rights and status of the foreigners *to make them feel more confident*, that is how they put it anyway.

But when all was said and done there was still money to be made, so there was improvements in industry and agriculture, and especially tourism. Suddenly hotels was jumping up all over the place. Jamaica was happy and dancing and getting fat. So whereas in the 1940s Kingston was busting with US sailors, in the 1950s Ocho Rios was ripe with the rich and famous – Rock Hudson, Katharine Hepburn, Noël Coward, Clark Gable, John F. Kennedy – a whole load of them, sunning and swimming and having themselves a ball. Jamaica was like a party-time paradise for white people. Some of them staying in that same hotel me and Fay go for the honeymoon.

So that was when I say to Henry Wong that we should go into business together. He had the wholesalers and wine merchants and I had a van and the men, so next thing Hampton and Milton was busy running food and liquor to every major hotel on the north coast and me and Henry Wong was partners, which vex Fay but there wasn't a damn thing she could do about it. Henry was a businessman. Making money was all he was interested in.

I understand how she feel though because she had nowhere to turn. There wasn't a single soul that she could complain to about me. And then to make matters worse she get pregnant again. She was as mad as hell. So I make sure to tell Father Kealey good and quick so that way there was nothing she could do apart from have the baby when it come due and give it a home, because she wasn't going shame herself in front of Him by doing anything else.

In truth I did feel bad about it though because I know that the time when she must have got pregnant is when I force myself on her. Not that Fay was ever willing as such but that time it was bad. There was all sort of twisting and turning, and shoving and scratching. She even try to hit me with the bedside lamp but the electric cord stop her short.

I don't know what come over me. I just thought I would teach her a lesson for looking down her nose at me and acting like she better than the rest of us; better than everybody that was important to me like Ma and Zhang, and Finley and the boys; like she was above us all. And having that look on her face, like she smell something rotten. It remind me of the way a white man would look at you when you accidentally run into him coming outta Gloria's house, like you are the scum that is going in to collect the protection money, not him is the scum that is coming outta there after doing god knows what and paying for it – and the only reason I got to be there is to protect these women against him and his nastiness. Somehow they never see it that way. They just have that look. Whatever service you providing for them you get the same look, like they think you a cockroach and you lucky they don't just lift up their foot and pulp you.

So I just grab her arms and I pin her down on the bed and do it to her, even though she was crying and throwing her legs about all the time.

It soon done anyway and afterwards I didn't feel no better, but it turn out she get pregnant. So I couldn't say nothing 'bout how she angry and didn't want nothing to do with the baby. It was inside her and she was glad when it come out.

I went up to the hospital to fetch them back and I swear she would have left the baby there if I didn't pick it up and put it in the car. I just rest the little basket thing on the back seat because Fay wouldn't even hold it for the drive back to Matthews Lane. And even three week later the doctor is ringing me up asking what the baby name is because we supposed to register the birth. But I can't get no sense outta Fay so I just look at the little thing laying there and I say into the phone, 'Mui.'

'Mui?'

'Mui. Little sister.' And I spell it for him. 'M-U-I.' And then I just hear the click when Dr Morrison hang up the telephone. Maybe I even hear him sigh before he put down the receiver. I dunno. I could just tell he was none too pleased with having to ring me up like that, a busy man like him, come all the way from Scotland to help us out here in the islands.

Although what these people still doing here I dunno. But we seem to be grateful for something because even while Mr Manley is busy campaigning for self-government we still busy organising all sorta things to celebrate three hundred years since the landing of Penn and Venables. Why we want to do that I don't know. It was like we think the English give us something to be proud of, something more than slavery and a government that still running the place from four thousand miles away. It didn't make me feel proud to be Jamaican. More like it remind me that we was still colonised, and what was there to celebrate about a thing like that?

But it no matter, all this eating and drinking was good for business and that at least was alright with me.

Then one day I come 'cross Dr Morrison stand up in the hot noonday sun in the middle of King Street. Right out there with the cars and carts, and sweat and noise like him willing someone to come run him down. So now I am in two minds 'bout whether to go drag him back or just let fate take its course. Maybe Dr Morrison tired of being a doctor, maybe the hospital wearing him down, maybe he just think this is a quick and sure way back to Edinburgh. That is his business, but then I start think 'bout the poor man that is going to go to jail for running down this white man in broad daylight and I decide that I better go fetch him. So I run out 'cross the street and I grab him.

After I drag him off the street I take him and sit him down in a bar and order some Appleton. The barman look at me like 'What the hell you doing with a white man in here?' like maybe I am about to fleece him and he don't want no trouble in his bar. But whatever he think he bring the rum anyway and pour out two glasses.

Morrison gulp down the whole lot in one swallow and put the empty glass on the table and say to me, 'I am a Presbyterian, I don't drink alcohol.' So I just stare at him and reckon that I must be looking at a desperate man. I don't say nothing, I just motion to the barman to bring the bottle and I pour Morrison another drink. When he pick up the glass him say to me, 'It would have been better for you to have left me there.'

'Is that bad, eh?'

'Yes.' And he take a sip from the glass and then catch a little drip with his finger and lick it off like a real professional drinker. I just wait because sooner or later this man is going to tell me the whole sorry story 'bout how he come to be in the middle of King Street dancing with death. That is how people are. They want to tell anybody who have the time and patience to listen.

So it turn out Morrison got a wife, good Presbyterian woman who volunteer at some church place for young mothers and I think so what so special about that in a place like this and he say, 'No,

I mean young. Children. Some of these girls are nine or ten years old.' So I shake my head like I think OK. Mrs Morrison come all the way to Jamaica to bring the word of God to these poor unfortunate girls. Back in Scotland she see an advertisement in her church magazine and decide that she have to come help. Morrison just follow after her because he think she such a Christian woman, and he want to be as good a Christian as she. But he not. He weak because he can't give her the one thing she really want. The one grace that God has bestowed on every woman – that she should hear the patter of tiny feet. That is how he say it. And I have to think to myself what the hell is this man talking about before I realise that he mean she want a baby. That is it? That is what all of this is about? Some damn fool woman want a baby? No, I think it can't be, but I don't say nothing, I just pour him another drink and wonder why she don't just adopt one. She certainly in the right place for it. But then I think maybe this good Christian woman didn't reckon on raising no dark-skin baby so maybe that is why she still unfulfilled like Morrison say.

And as I am sitting there looking at Morrison with his ginger hair and flabby white hands I start thinking 'bout how having a baby just don't mean the same thing to a Jamaican woman. Maybe never been the same, and sure as hell not since slavery. Because to a Jamaican woman having a child is just the continuation of life, maybe even the continuation of misery. She don't see it as her personal achievement. She just see it as something she got to do. Well that is how it seem to me anyway.

When my eyes focus I see Morrison is almost crying into the glass what with all the rum he been swallowing. And I realise that all I am waiting for is him getting to the part 'bout King Street and the traffic. But instead he go all quiet and start get himself together like he about to leave. So I stand up with him and I say, 'Is OK, you know, whatever you want to talk about.'

But he look at me like he don't quite believe and he say, 'Thank you for your kindness today but I really must be going. Margaret will be wondering what has happened to me.' And so I let him go even though he almost fall down when he open the door and the sunlight hit him in the eye.

A few days later I find out from Judge Finley that Morrison got tabs all over town that he can't pay. The man is a gambler. The horses especially. Seem like the totes at Caymanas Park rub their hands together when they see him coming, he is such a big-time loser. Then he also got bookies downtown and the worst thing, he now got Louis DeFreitas on his tail trying to collect.

'You mean that slimy piece of half-white boy from over Tivoli Gardens?'

'Yah, man.'

'How Morrison get mix up with him?'

'Just accident. Morrison just looking for anybody that will take a bet from him. He don't know nothing 'bout who connected to who and who is running what. He just looking out for the next race. So now DeFreitas send some boys to talk to him the other afternoon and things get sorta rough. That is what I hear anyway. And afterwards he go to cross King Street and then halfway he just stop and stand up there just like you find him. Me think maybe he didn't mean nothing serious by it, he just sorta stop in the street.'

When I get back to Matthews Lane the place is crowded. This is the same routine Mondays, Wednesdays and Fridays. Zhang is up the top of the yard playing dominoes with Tartan Socks McKenzie and Round Chin and Mr Lee from the Chinatown Committee. Ma and the old women packing up the mah-jongg tiles and the little Formica table they sit at down the bottom of the yard. The baby is laying in her cot wearing a old T-shirt of mine and sucking on a mango stone. There is no Fay and no Xiuquan, because just like always wherever she go she take him with her.

I pick up the baby and coo her a bit while I say goodbye to Madame Chin and Madame Fong and I watch Tilly running fresh water over the ham choi and rinsing it for dinner. After dinner when the house empty and Ma gone to temple I tell Zhang 'bout Morrison and DeFreitas and he say to me, 'So what you want with this doctor anyway?'

'I paying out a lot of money to doctors, what with Fay and the children and Gloria and the baby, and then there is the normal things to do with the girls.'

'You mean your whores?'

'Why you always got to call them that?'

'Because that is what they is.' And I just look at him because even after all these years he just can't stop drawing attention to it and reminding me how he feel about it even though it is the money from these girls that is helping to put food on the table. Somehow the two things don't match up in his head. Maybe because he still getting everything he want for free – the herbalist, the barber, the pharmacy, clothes, shoes – hell he still even eating in Chinatown when he want to for free.

'Well it cost me a lot of money and I just reckon that if I can get me a doctor then I can make some saving.'

'You no pay him?'

'No, he work for a favour to me.'

'What favour you do him?'

'I write off his gambling tabs.'

'You buy them up?'

'I reckon it worth it because he pay it back over and over year after year and he still owe me. And I can save him face as well because I don't mention none of it to his wife so he can carry on being a good Christian as far as she is concerned.'

'DeFreitas not honest businessman. He find out you want doctor he raise price of tabs. Then maybe it not such good bargain.' Zhang look away from me, off somewhere like he thinking. Then he say, 'You have to make DeFreitas give you the tab, like you taking it to do him a favour.' Sun Tzu say, '*To subdue the enemy without fighting is the acme of skill.*'

Next morning I call Clifton Brown and tell him to meet me over the Blue Lagoon.

'You want me to go threaten DeFreitas over this doctor?'

'I want you to go take some boys in uniform and a big police van and drive over to West Kingston and tell him that you can't have him roughing up this white man in broad daylight in a public place like that. Tell him Morrison complain to you and he is a white man and a respected doctor and you just can't have it. DeFreitas got to leave the doctor alone.'

'What about the money?'

'Tell him you don't give a shit about his money. The way he acting making you look bad, after all you supposed to be fighting corruption and you can't have him acting like he don't respect your authority. Tell him to forget about the doctor otherwise you going shut him down, his whole operation, and you going make it mean and nasty so whatever Morrison owe him be a small price to pay.'

And that work out just fine because a week later news was all over town 'bout how DeFreitas was looking to shift Morrison's tabs. So I offer him half of what he was asking and he take it. And the next day I tell Finley to go buy up the rest of Morrison's tabs.

15

Force

Sun Tzu say, '*He who understands how to use both large and small forces will be victorious.*'

But Morrison running up more and more money he owe to bookies all over town and I am having trouble explaining to these men that I have no intention of picking up any more of his tabs, that whatever they doing with Morrison they have to think of as extending a personal courtesy to me. So finally I decide is time I go have a little talk with him.

I take a drive up to the hospital one rainy afternoon and they show me into a upstairs office that got his name on the door in shiny brass letters, 'Dr George Morrison', and where a skinny little nurse with a white uniform and buck teeth tell me to wait. Outta the window I look down into a little garden with bird of paradise and a frangipani growing in the middle of it. It look pretty, what with the little wooden seat round the tree, and it sound peaceful with the raindrops dripping off the banana leaves. When Morrison come into the room he walk over to the window and stand next to me looking into the garden.

'You like?'

'Yeah, it look like a pretty space. Calm and peaceful like.'

'It has given me many hours of pleasure.'

'I surprised a man like you got time for a thing like that.'

'I am a very keen gardener.' Then he jut out his chin towards the window and say, 'This is one of the few pleasures I still allow myself.' He have a little think to himself and then he say, 'How can I help you? Is the baby fine? And your good wife, is she well?'

I look at him and I smile to myself because I can't understand how come he manage to sound so proper and formal for a man with his secrets, and what he think he doing acting like that with me after we been drinking Appleton together and him telling me all 'bout his personal business with his wife and how she can't get a baby and such. Or maybe he just got a bad memory. I notice that 'bout white people. They got bad memories.

So I say to him, 'They both good, doctor. Thank you for asking but they not what bring me here today.'

He raise one eyebrow and look at me like he can't imagine what I have come there for. So I reach in my pocket and I pull out a couple of his tabs and I hold them up in front of him. He look at them like he got no idea what they are, and then I see the panic creep 'cross his face, and that is the first time he look at me. Really focus on me.

So I say, 'You know what these are?' But he don't say nothing, he just stand there shaking his head like he think that maybe he in a dream and he soon going wake up. So I wave the tabs around, like rock them from side to side in my hand and I say to him, 'These belong to me now. Actually, all your tabs belong to me now. I done buy up all of them. Even the ones from your friend Louis DeFreitas.'

Morrison look worried but him still can't say nothing to me. Is like his whole body gone into shock and all he can do is sweat because now his doughy white face is wet and red and clammy.

So I tell him, 'I not going hurt you, yu know. I didn't spend good money on these so I can do you damage.'

But he still don't say nothing, so I say, 'What you think happen after all that business in King Street? Yu no notice how everything gone quiet on that front?'

He start to open his mouth, then almost like he was squeezing the air outta his lungs he say, 'I thought perhaps he had gone away.'

'Gone away! DeFreitas? You think DeFreitas go away and just forget that you owe him money?'

'I thought he had perhaps been detained by the authorities. He seemed that sort.'

Well that is when I really laugh, right out loud. I nearly bust my gut. When I finally calm myself down and him standing there like he still don't understand what is going on I say to him, 'No, DeFreitas not gone nowhere. And none of them others neither. They all still right here in town, but now you owe me instead of them. And what I come to tell you is that it time for you to settle up.'

Morrison sit down in his big old leather chair and listen to me. And he agree to everything. Funny thing was, afterwards he take my hand and shake it. It seem like him so frighten of DeFreitas he actually grateful to me for stepping in.

So now I had me my very own personal physician, and the children had a doctor and the girls could rest easy 'bout all their little trials and tribulations. And in exchange Dr George Morrison had the full protection of the Yang family and a clean slate with everybody, except me. Just before I leave I say to him, 'You have to curb your gambling.'

When I turn outta the hospital I drive up Old Hope Road, down Tom Redcam Avenue pass Up Park Camp and head out along Windward Road where the sea breeze whip through the car going 'cross the Palisadoes to Port Royal. Father Kealey got a special liking for the fried fish and bammy they sell out there. When I get there he already park up and sitting at a table admiring the view.

'I love to see the sunlight shimmering on the sea and catching the peaks in the water like that. It just sort of glistens, doesn't it?' I smile at him because he always remind me about the simple things in life that I should take more time to appreciate. So I just stand there for a time looking at him and the sea and thinking yes, him right.

And just then I can't imagine ever being any place other than Jamaica. I can't imagine any other view that could be better for the spirit than this. And I think to myself I don't know what Father

Kealey doing to me but every time I meet up with him it seem like I start thinking about this life and the hereafter, and right and wrong, and all that sort of thing even before he open his mouth. Is like he just sorta carry all of that God and goodness 'round with him. Like there is always a little ray of light shining down on exactly the spot he is standing on, or where he is sitting waiting for his fried fish.

When the waitress gone inside with the order he start telling me 'bout the new school he setting up for the children in Cockpit Country. He excited. I can tell because I know how much it please him every time he take his God to some place new. And how he rejoice when folks start to understand that the Bible got more to it than learning how one word follow another.

The waitress come and put down the food and then right as he start picking at the red snapper he suddenly ask me, 'How is the baby?' I so surprised I just repeat the question in my head. 'How is the baby?' Well he never ever ask me anything like that before. Never. And even before I get round to answering him he say, 'I see Karl often and he is growing into a fine boy but Mui I have not yet met.' All the time he is saying this to me he is staring into his plate, almost like he concentrating on his food and just making chat with me that he not too concerned about. And I look at the side of his head and I think yes, Ethyl right. He is a good-looking man. Younger than me. And yes, Ethyl right again. With the face and the hair and the dimple him look just like Jeff Chandler in *Broken Arrow*, and *East of Sumatra* and *Away All Boats*. And I think to myself what is this good-looking, younger-than-me man doing asking me 'bout the baby? What is his business with her?

I dunno how much time go by, but now I see him stop searching his plate and just sitting there looking at me expecting something. So I say, 'The baby fine but she not such a baby no more.'

So he satisfied with that and turn back to his fish. And I start to think 'bout what we been talking 'bout all this time. I really search my memory, and all I can come up with is all the things him say to me 'bout the orphan fund and poor relief and education in the rural areas. And how early on he ask me why everybody call me Uncle because he catch wind of it and want me to tell him what it mean. So I tell him the same thing Hampton tell me when I just come to Jamaica about how people call Zhang Uncle because he not your father but he look after you. You can count on him to help you.

Then one time he try talk to me 'bout greed. And another time it was all 'bout pride. And the best one was when he start talk to me 'bout lust and I wonder what he know about a thing like that. After all they take him straight outta St George's College and put him in the seminary for seven years and now he come back and want talk to me 'bout lust? But then I think well he a man and they have him married to God all this time so maybe he is exactly the person to know 'bout lust. Anyway, I reckon he was really trying to say something to me 'bout Gloria so I decide to give him a wide berth and pretend I didn't know what he was talking about.

In truth I think he just happy to talk and he not all that concerned about what I am listening to. But the day he tell me I could think about going to confession that was when I put my foot down and he not mention it since.

'Anyway,' I say to him, 'I would have to be a Catholic.'

And he say, 'Yes, we can work on that.'

So I didn't go see him for three months after that to give him some time to cool off.

But now he is sitting there calm as you like asking me about the baby. He even know her name! He call her by her name. The name I give her. Not even Fay call her by her name. She just keep saying 'the child' when she force to mention her, which not that often because most of the time Fay just act like Mui don't exist.

So I say to him, 'One day I bring her and you can get introduced if you like.'

And he say, 'Yes, I would like that.' And then he just change the subject and start talking 'bout his new school. And I know it time for me to put my hand in my pocket because either he is running low or there is some big project he got in his mind. So I just listen and I don't say nothing to him about no money. That is not the way we do things. But he know and I know that come next Sunday he is going to open up his collection box and find a fat roll of US dollar bills that will bring a smile to his lips.

I eating the fish and bammy and thinking to myself what is it about this man that make me feel so calm? The baby thing aside, I just like to sit with him and listen to the deep, rich peacefulness in his voice. It don't even matter what he talking about, I just feel like when I am with him it is safe. I don't have to be looking over my shoulder or finding some dark corner in the Blue Lagoon. I can sit right out here in the sunshine, right here in broad daylight and it don't matter who see me there. I can say to him what I want and it not going come back to haunt me. And the things I don't tell him is because I protecting him, not because I protecting myself.

And even though I start up with all of this just to cut 'cross Fay, it seem like it worth something to me. It worth something to have somebody who always look at you like they think you OK. Who never got a look in their eye like they 'fraid of you. And who treat you like they believe you mean well. They believe you have good intention and a true heart.

When I get back to the shop in West Street Finley is waiting for me. He hand me a cold beer and he say, 'All this driving food all over the north coast putting a strain on business in town.'

'Yeah?'

'So I think we need to go get some more help.'

I say to him, 'What you think 'bout Kenneth Wong?'

'Yu mean Miss Fay little brother?'

'Yah, man.'

'The bwoy too young and foolish.'

So Finley fix on that. I say to him, 'You got someone in mind?'

'You remember that round-face boy hang with DeFreitas when we kids? Married that no-arse girl from Spanish Town.'

'You mean Samuels.'

'Same one. He come round yesterday asking if we got something for him.'

'He not running with DeFreitas no more?'

'He say not. Say he not been with DeFreitas for years. He been driving a Checker Cab but he can't make ends meet no more. Not now he got four children to feed and clothe and school and everything.'

'So you want take him on?'

Finley stop and he think. And then he just walk out the back. Five minutes later he come back with two jugs of oysters, a bottle of hot red pepper sauce and a couple of cold Red Stripe. So I turn up two empty orange crates and lean them up outside against the wall in the shade. And we sit down.

'His eyes too pale and shifty and I don't trust him. I only mentioning him to you because he come 'round yesterday and I think I should tell you.'

'You ever actually hear anything 'bout him make you think him risky? Anything like he lazy or he cheat you?'

'No.'

'So what you got against the man?'

Finley screw up his nose and look at me outta the corner of his eye and say, 'Something I don't like 'bout the way he smell.'

'He smell?'

'No.'

'Then you got to give the man a chance to prove himself. If he don't work out we let him go. He need the money and fair is fair.'

Finley wait a good long time and he swallow a good few oysters before he say to me, 'You spending too much time with the Father.'

16

The Modifying of Tactics

In 1961 they have a referendum to see if we should come outta the West Indies Federation because although Norman Manley think it good for Jamaica to be part of a united voice for the thirteen English-speaking Caribbean islands, Busta say Jamaica got a big-island mentality and we should go it alone. He say that the smaller islands going drag us down. So Manley call the referendum and lose, and we pull outta the Federation.

After that it was full steam ahead for Independence. And in February 1962 Manley and Busta go up to England to ask Her Majesty the Queen to let us go and she say yes. So that was it, Independent Jamaica.

There was so much excitement I couldn't hardly believe it. Lord Creator even make up a calypso 'bout how good Independence was going to be for all of us.

Then one hot afternoon Round Chin granddaughter come to see me. She called Merleen and she come to the shop still wearing her school uniform. As soon as I see her standing in the doorway like that I knew it was trouble. The girl look like she was shivering even though it must have been a hundred degrees outside. So I tell her to come in and send Hampton to fetch her something cool to drink.

She settle herself and drink down the lemonade and that is when she start to cry. Just some little drops outta the corner of her eye and she take out a pretty little kerchief with a flower embroider on the edge and she mop her face. She just dab it, ladylike. And I wait because it obvious that there ain't no point rushing this child. Then she say, 'Uncle, I hope you don't mind me coming to see you like this but I hear tell that you help people and I got my fingers crossed that maybe you can help me.'

I look at her and I see she not shivering because she cold, she shivering because she 'fraid. So I say, 'Is alright. You can tell me what you want.'

'I came here to the shop because my grandfather is always at your house playing dominoes with Uncle Zhang and I can't have anybody know that I came to see you.'

I just look at her and nod my head. And then I give Hampton a look that let him know it time to make himself scarce. After Hampton gone, she carry on.

'I hope you don't think me rude but whether you decide to help me or not I have to ask you to promise you will keep the secret I am going to tell you.'

'Well it depend on what that secret is, because it might work out that I got to go tell somebody so that I can help you.'

'I think that if my grandfather finds out he will kill me.'

'Maybe you better just tell me what it is you have on your mind and we can figure it out from there.'

So she tell me. And I listen. And I think yes she right. She in a bad situation, and if all of this get out Mr Chin most likely coming to me to fix it and that prospect I didn't fancy none.

So I ask her, 'How old you now?' And she say twelve and I say, 'Who else yu tell 'bout this?'

'No one, I just came to you.'

'Good. So we keep it that way then. You come here this time tomorrow and I have somebody come see you. You don't worry no more. You just leave this with me.' And that is when she really start to bawl. She grab my hand like she going kiss it but all she do is hold it to her cheek and keep saying, 'Thank you, thank you,' till I tell her is time she better be getting home. But even when she leaving the shop she still crying like she never going to stop. I think it was relief more than anything had that girl sobbing like that.

Next day Morrison ask Merleen a lot of questions and then him take her 'round back and examine her. And when she leave him tell me, 'Yes, it seems most likely that she is pregnant.' But him done take some urine and blood sample so he can go check for sure.

So I say to him, 'So what you going to do?'

'What do you mean, what am I going to do?'

'What you going do to get rid of it?'

'I'm not going to get rid of it! That is against the law.'

'What you talking 'bout against the law? She twelve years old and pregnant! Who you think been breaking the law?'

'I am a doctor. I have taken an oath. It is against the law.'

'So how come you no worried 'bout the law when you working over East Kingston?'

'That is an entirely different situation. Those women are . . . well, they are what they are, and this girl here is an innocent child.'

'That is right, she is an innocent child and when her grandfather find out he going kill her for sure. So then she going be a dead innocent child. Is that the blood you want on yu hands?'

Morrison look at me and then him say, 'Maybe Margaret can do something.'

'No, man! Nobody got to know 'bout this. You have to come up with something better than that.'

'When did it become my responsibility?'

'When you refuse to get rid of it. I already promise this girl that we going fix it. So now you have to do something, yu hear me?'

So the next day Morrison come to me and say he and his wife going adopt the baby and I say no. But then he plead with me 'bout how Margaret want a baby and I know how important it is to her and how she make a good mother and how she will love the baby and look after it and treat it good and how he already tell her that he sure I going let her have the baby.

'Yu mad? Yu completely lose your mind? I can't let you adopt that baby. What you going use for papers? We not registering that baby in Merleen Chin name, yu understand me?'

'No, I can fix that. I'll register the baby at the hospital and say that the mother died in childbirth. Father unknown.'

'No, man.'

'No, I have it all worked out. I have a house up in the hills in Cedar Valley. Margaret and Merleen will live up there and I will go up at weekends to check on them and look after Merleen, and deliver the baby when it comes due. And afterwards everybody will come back to Kingston.'

I just look at him in complete disbelief even though he standing there looking so hopeful.

'I thought yesterday yu tell me yu not going break no law, now today yu going falsify documents up at the hospital?'

'Margaret wants the baby.'

'She want this half-Chinese baby so bad?'

'This is her chance. It is not going to happen any other way.'

So I say OK but we can't settle nothing till I talk to Merleen 'bout it. She have to agree as well because right now she think we going get rid of it.

And he say OK. And then I say to him, 'So what you expect me to tell Mr Chin 'bout what Merleen doing up in Cedar Valley?'

'Surely you don't expect me to think of everything?'

I see he got a point so I say OK and leave it at that.

So now I have to go do something 'bout Merleen's baby father, a English army captain from up the camp. And as it turn out, Morrison know him. Meet him at some cocktail party at Kings House and I think yes that about right because these white people always like to stick together.

'What else you know 'bout him?'

'I've heard about two other young girls with whom he was associated.'

'Associated! You mean this man do it before?'

'I don't know that it involved any pregnancy, but I do under-stand that he has been involved in at least two such liaisons.'

107

Amazing. You got one doing what he doing with children, and another one talking 'bout liaisons. So I tell Morrison to tell this army captain to come meet me over the Blue Lagoon and to bring the money with him.

'How much it cost for an abortion anyway?'

'How do you expect me to know a thing like that?'

'Well go find out, man, and tell the captain to bring the money in US dollars. I don't want no pounds, shillings and pence.'

When I meet up with Captain Charles Meacham him look just like I expect him to. Not so much because he tall and broad but because he so straight. He is upright, and stiff like a piece of board. And even though he not wearing his uniform you can tell that he think he rule the whole British Empire. Him alone. And him alone command everything and everybody in it.

He walk up to the table and hold out the money to me. Just like that. He not even got the decency to put it in a envelope. So I just sit there with my elbow on the arm of the chair and my hand on my chin and I tell him to sit down. And even though he look surprise, he do it anyway.

I say to him, 'It look like you trying to make a bad habit outta this?'

And he look at me and lift up his head and say, 'I know who you are.'

'And who is that?'

'Just some local thug who thinks he has the upper hand and can use it to intimidate an officer of the British army.'

'So you reckon it working or not? The intimidation thing, I mean.' Meacham just look at me and put the money on the table and get up and walk out.

When I get back to the shop I tell Finley to go open a bank account for Merleen and put the money in it.

So now we all set with the Cedar Valley thing because when I talk to Merleen she say she happier to think the baby going have a home rather than it not even get a chance to live at all. I tell her she really need to think careful 'bout it because this mean she going have to carry the baby for the whole nine months and she only twelve years old. And she tell me that she think about it and it OK. She done meet with Mrs Morrison and she think she a nice lady. And the doctor seem a nice man too. And they done take her to Cedar Valley and she think the house nice. It in a quiet little valley with a river run through it, and a little river-water swimming pool, and beautiful hills, and sugar cane and orange trees. She think it all going to be just fine. And Mr Morrison being a doctor and all, she know everything going to work out good. So I say OK and then she ask me what she going tell her grandfather and I say to her, 'Is OK, you don't need to say nothing to him. I going sort all that out. You just get yourself ready because we going do this soon before you start show.'

But there is no way I can talk to Mr Chin 'bout any of this. Mr Chin is a whole generation older than me. It not seemly for me to go talk to him 'bout anything so personal as his granddaughter's condition. The only way 'round it is I have to go explain the whole thing to Zhang, because he is the only one old enough and honourable enough to go talk to Mr Chin.

When I tell Zhang he mad as hell. He mad at Meacham, and he mad at Merleen.

'He beat her? He force her?'

'No. Meacham tell her she a woman and he treat her like she grown and it make her feel important.'

'She bad girl?'

'No, she just young, that is all. She just young and she make a mistake.'

'And you not know better? Now you mix up in it?'

'What you want me to do? Just leave the child crying on my doorstep?'

'You tell her grandfather.'

'And what you think going happen then?' And that is when Zhang stop because he know the answer to the question just the same as I know, and Merleen know as well.

'What captain say?'

'When she tell him he laugh. But he done pay me the money already so at least he accepting the baby is his.'

Zhang shake his head from side to side and start mutter to himself 'money, money' and then he turn and walk off up the yard to his room. And all I hear is his wooden slippers slapping on the concrete path.

When I tell Gloria 'bout it, it turn out that she know about Meacham as well. He ask some girlfriend of hers if she had any girls and when she say yes he say, 'I mean young, young girls,' and she say, 'Go 'way, man, what you think this is?' and that was the end of it. But she know he was asking 'round the place.

Then she say to me, 'Is Zhang going help you?'

'I dunno.'

'So what you going do?'

And that is when I realise that this time I really done get myself in a jam because there is no way that this can turn out OK unless we can save face for Mr Chin. And Zhang is the only person that can do that.

So the next few days I worry myself sick. I can't eat, I can't sleep, all I can do is fret 'bout how Merleen belly going start swelling up soon and how everybody going lose face and it being a damn mess. I so worried I even tell Father Kealey 'bout it, which afterwards I think most probably a mistake, but all he say to me is that he will pray for me. And I think well maybe I need all the help I can get.

Then finally Zhang say to me, 'Chin come dim sum tomorrow. Eleven o'clock. Make sure you here.'

Early morning Zhang get up and prepare everything himself. Chicken soup, glutinous rice and sausage, pork and peanut dumpling, prawn dumpling, roast pork buns, chicken feet, beef and ginger dumplings, choi sum. A feast for Mr Chin.

I don't know what he say to everyone, but by the time I get up the house is empty. And Tilly and Ma even take Mui with them wherever they gone. I shower and get ready. And eleven o'clock on the dot Mr Chin is at the gate.

Zhang welcome him and we all sit down to eat. Zhang happy

and gracious. He waiting on Mr Chin hand and foot. Nothing is too much trouble.

'More rice, Chin, more pork, more soup?' Zhang cook enough food for ten people. Then he chat 'bout the news from China and how business is doing in Mr Chin's bakery now that his son running it for him. Finally, when Mr Chin cannot swallow another morsel, Zhang invite him to walk up to the top of the yard where he has put out a straight-back chair and his own rocking chair under a bit of shade next to the duck pond.

I look at the two of them a walk up the path with their heads bow and I can't imagine what Zhang going say to him. Then they sit down and Zhang invite Mr Chin to sit in his rocking chair, and the two of them start talk.

They stay up there over three hours, with Zhang motioning to me to bring more tea every time the pot go cold. And when they finish, they walk down the path together to where I am still sitting and waiting.

I stand up when they get to me. Zhang say, 'Mr Chin's grand-daughter is going away on an educational trip and he would like you to see to the arrangements.' And that was it. Mr Chin just stand there and nod his head in agreement. And then they bow to each other, slow and low, and Mr Chin walk outta the gate.

Then Zhang look round at the mess of pots and bowls and wave his arm at them and say to me, 'This need clean up.' And him turn and walk back up the yard and step into his room taking the rocking chair with him.

17

Favourable and Unfavourable Factors

Everybody and everything was getting ready. Even the British army decide to leave us in peace. We so happy to wave goodbye to the Royal Hampshire Regiment because it was three hundred years since they been lording it over man and beast and it was well time for them to be gone. That was when Charles Meacham take off as well. So by the time Merleen come back from Cedar Valley Meacham wasn't there to say no goodbye.

After the British gone everybody just focus on one thing: 6 August 1962. Independence Day. Man, woman and child was cleaning up and painting up, and decorating the whole town with flags and bunting in readiness for this eight days of celebration. They line the street waving and cheering when Princess Margaret get here and thousands of them crowd into the National Stadium the night before.

I didn't bother go up the stadium because I didn't feel like watching no marching bands in their little uniform with the one out the front twiddling the stick, or no boy scouts, or girl guides, or police parade, or dancers in *traditional costumes*. I didn't feel like listening to no speeches from Her Royal Highness, or Manley or Busta for that matter. Instead I go over the Blue Lagoon for a quiet drink with the boys. And just at midnight when I know they was going pull down the Union Jack and haul up the Jamaican flag I raise my glass for a toast, 'Jamaica, land we love', and me and the boys clink our glasses. And right after that we step outside to see the fireworks in the night sky high above the National Stadium.

And if I think I already hear enough of Lord Creator then that was a big mistake because the next day was Independence Day and I was listening to him ten times over with every verse repeating itself booming outta every car, house, store, bar and street-corner jook joint all at the same time. They play that record till the groove must have been going flat, and every time he sing the chorus there was a whole heap a hooting and hollering, and clapping and cheering, and just downright merriment. There was people singing and dancing and waving the new national flag, and wrapping it 'round themselves like to show how much they in love with it. Yellow for our natural riches, black for the struggle and green for hope.

There was men in shirts and women in frocks that they make outta them same three colours, because we was Independent and everybody was believing Lord Creator when he tell us that we was going to live in unity, and have progress and prosperity. It was happiness. You couldn't paint a picture of happier happiness if you had your whole life to do it.

Me and Zhang and Ma go take a look at some of the celebrations and processions that going on all 'round town. And I take Mui with me because I have no idea where Fay gone, and like always, she got the boy with her. One thing I notice these days though is that sometimes when she go out she taking Mui as well. She taking the two of them with her. I got no idea where all of this come from. Maybe Father Kealey tell her it time she pay the child some mind. Anyway, I not saying nothing to her 'bout it.

Hampton and Judge Finley somewhere downtown, I dunno where, but it wasn't the sort of day you want to go try find anybody. You just choose your space on the sidewalk and you stand your ground.

All over town there was steel bands, and calypso and reggae and ska. So the sound of 'Yellow Bird' was blending into Lord Creator, and Byron Lee and Prince Buster and the Skatalites, and it didn't matter a damn because it was Independence Day. Independent Jamaica. That day was our future, and it was full of hope that out of the many, that the British bring from all corners the world to serve them, we could be one people.

I never see nothing of Fay all day. In truth I don't think she that bothered 'bout Independence. But she not the only one. Seem like maybe different people have their own reasons for thinking that Independence was a good thing or not. For some of them Independence was the sign that we finally free. We finally drive out the old slave masters. The British gone and slavery is over. For others, like Norman Manley, we was finally taking charge of our own destiny. Jamaica was growing up, taking responsibility for ourselves. Jamaica had come of age. Then some thought that when we cut our ties with England then maybe we make some better ones with America. And on top of that, there was those who wasn't in favour. They felt safer under the British or more like they thought Her Majesty would carry on look after us better than we could look after ourselves. And then of course, there was those who just didn't care one way or another. I think that maybe that was where Fay at, indifferent about the whole thing because she didn't think that Independence was going improve her life any. And especially because the newly elected prime minister was Bustamante which didn't please her none because Busta so strong with the union. Maybe Fay worried 'bout what going happen to her little rich girl friends from Immaculate who all married to their American- or English-educated doctor, dentist, lawyer, accountant and all them little light-skin boys that running the bank and the insurance company. Or maybe she just think that if Busta get higher wages for workers it going mean her papa business don't do so good and she going have to take a cut in her allowance, which is what been on her mind all along because even years back when I ask her if things so bad with Miss Cicely why she nuh just leave Lady Musgrave Road and go find somewhere else to live she say to me, 'Who would do that?'

'Well, you didn't have to go marry me, or anybody for that matter. You are a grown woman. You could have just leave.'

'And live on what?'

'You could have get a job.' She just look at me. That is all she do, like the words I am saying don't make no sense to her.

But actually, I get it all wrong because afterwards when I ask her 'bout it she say to me, 'My whole life has been spent being white for Cicely to stop her feeling ashamed, and being black for Cicely to stop her feeling alone. I had to be Catholic for Cicely because Methodist was too black, and I had to hold back at school for Cicely because being smart was too white. I had to spend with style for Cicely so she could show off her new wealth and class, and I had to be prim and chaste for Cicely so she could protect the reputation of black womanhood. And where me being Chinese came into all of this for her I don't know. But whatever I did she picked and poked and prodded, and found fault with me because in Jamaica the colour of your skin still counts for everything.' And then she stop. And then she say, 'You think Independence is going to change that?'

Gloria more enthusiastic 'bout Independence, but then she black so maybe it more straightforward for her, like the white man not ruling over the black man no more. So that is something to celebrate, even if you a woman. But maybe it not so simple for those of us that too white to be black, or too black to be white, or too Chinese to be either. And what I realise from Fay is that it not just to do with the colour of your skin. It to do with how you feel about yourself and what you think about your life.

But none of this matter to Zhang. He very happy 'bout Independence, but when I catch him with that glint in his eye I know he not thinking 'bout Jamaica. He thinking 'bout China and wondering what it would have been like to have been there with Mao Zedong on 1 October 1949.

Well I know for sure that it would have been nothing like this because the Chinese have got no idea about making music or how to jig and jive. Not like Jamaicans. Jamaicans can dance. The only part the Chinese would have keep up with was the food, and that day there was a mountain of it. Rice and curry goat, chicken and rice and peas, fried fish, fried chicken, fritters and dumpling, ackee and saltfish, festival, breadfruit, fried plantain, patties, coconut cake, plantain tart – well just about everything you could think of that you could wash down with a Red Stripe, or a Heineken, depending on your persuasion. And everybody that wasn't beating a steel drum, or strumming a guitar, or blowing a trombone, or just flinging their arms in the air, was carrying a plate of food.

Me, I wasn't sure what we was so busy celebrating because all that happen so far was Her Majesty say OK. But it seem like everybody think we already do what we need to, whereas for me Independence was just the beginning of something we might do. At least when Mao Zedong was marching he just done win a war after twenty-five years of fighting. Busta on the other hand still had to show us that he could do something to improve the country, especially in agriculture and industry, and education and employment. And to make it even more of a challenge for him, he got more people to look after because less and less of them feel like they want to go set sail for England.

I feel sorry for Manley though. He was the premier under the colonial government and he put so much effort into us getting our freedom, what with the vote in 1944 and the whole thing with the Federation, and working so hard for Independence. And then after all of that he had to go sit down and watch Busta become the first prime minister of an Independent Jamaica. That musta hurt.

Then no more than a week after all that done one day I go see Gloria and find she in a mood 'bout where Esther going go to school to finish her education.

I say to her, 'The child only ten years old. What you fret yourself about?'

And she say to me, 'Ten years old, that is exactly when you have to be fretting. Next year she not a baby any more. She got to go

116

to high school and where you think she going go? Where Karl going go? Him being the same age and all.'

'I guess he go to St George's. I should imagine that is what Fay have in mind.'

'And where little Mui going go, Immaculate Conception?'

'She seven years old, Gloria! Rest yourself nuh.'

'No, man. You have to take some interest in this.'

'We can't be sending Esther to Immaculate, Gloria. You know that. Them nuns will be asking all sorta questions 'bout who her papa is. What you want to do, bring down a whole heap of scandal on my head?'

'What scandal? Who you think dunno that Esther your child?'

'Fay. Fay dunno nothing 'bout it. It one thing me being here with you like this but it a whole different thing if she know you got a child.'

'You think Fay dunno? What daydream you living in if you think Fay don't know?'

And just when I look 'round I see the door closing. Slow and gentle and quiet. And I realise that just how me and Gloria standing up in the kitchen, Esther is behind the dining-room door listening to every word that she don't want to hear.

The whole thing vex me. All this commotion over what? As if it matter which school the child go to. I didn't go to no school at all and I still learn to read and write and count good enough to carry on my business.

But Gloria won't let this thing go. She on and on about Immaculate till it get so bad I can hardly stand to go over there to see her no more. It not about the money. She know that I happy to pay. Is just that Esther skin really dark. The child didn't even ease up a couple of shades. And a child that dark in a school like Immaculate, everybody going want to know who her papa is. And I just didn't think I could bring that much shame on Fay. Having it so public like that whether or not she know. Even though Fay don't seem to think that much of me, I didn't think I could do that to her.

So next time I go collect Mui from Father Michael, because she spend regular time with him now, I ask him what he think 'bout the whole school thing. And he say to me that Gloria only want the best for Esther. And that even though things changing in Jamaica we still not yet at a point where it don't matter which school you go to, because right now in Jamaica it is still the darker-skinned Jamaican that is digging the road, and the lighter-skinned Jamaican that is running the office, and the Chinese that is selling the groceries, and the Lebanese running the dry-goods stores, and the Indians growing the vegetables. And even though, over time, all of this is going to change, we are not there yet. But since he understand my situation with Fay and Immaculate maybe I should consider some other schools. And that Alpha Academy is a fine school and St Andrew is a very good school even though it not Catholic.

So that same evening I go see Gloria and I say to her that maybe she could consider St Andrew or Alpha Academy because I hear tell that they both very good schools.

I say to her, 'Our girl will do fine at either one of them.'

But whereas I expect Gloria to be glad with the news, she not. She vex.

'You think Immaculate too good for Esther because she so dark?'

'No, Gloria. You know it not like that at all.'

'I know you think you enlightened because you got me all these years and your little gang of black boys you run with. And I know you think Independence done change everything, but honest to god, Pao, sometimes I think you just live in your own little world and you can't see what is going on right in front of you no matter how much you think you open your eyes. Is like you don't know you in Jamaica and it 1962. More like you think you in China and the workers just done winning the revolution.

'But there wasn't no revolution, and the workers didn't win it. The same thing that was going on before is the same thing that is going on now. The British take all the profit from the plantations, and they still taking it. And now the Americans and the rest of them going take the big profit from the bauxite and all the hotels and factories they busy throwing up all over the place, and Jamaica going to be left exactly where we always been.

'Jamaica look good on the surface, but unless you make sure you daughter get a good education she going end up with the same choices I had, the same two choices that is waiting for her because she is a woman and because of the colour of her skin. And I don't see her wanting to be no domestic, not any more than I did.'

Well, that whole speech really take me by surprise. It knock me back because I never hear Gloria talk so much in one continuous stream before, so it tell me that she feel real strong 'bout all of this. So that is when I say to myself if she really want the child to go to Immaculate then I just going have to figure out how I going tell Fay 'bout the whole thing.

But as it turn out, Gloria not that way inclined. She was just trying to make a point with me. She agree that St Andrew is a good school and she go get Esther's name put down. Esther got to take a entrance exam and she pass it. So they ask Gloria for the school fees and I pay it. The day they go get the school uniform Gloria make Esther dress up and come show me the white blouse and little red and grey check skirt thing. The child look genuinely happy but after she finish twirl 'round in front of me she just walk off, so I reckon there wasn't nothing she wanted to say to me 'bout it.

So what with all Gloria's talk 'bout money and everything she make me feel nervous and make me think that maybe I should be putting something aside for a rainy day, or for when things turn really bad.

I dunno what to expect any more with the way she carrying on, but it seem to me that the island doing good with tourism and the bauxite and all the foreign investment bringing jobs and training. We getting all the latest new-fangled equipment from America and they say our gross national product is growing. We doing good. The place even look good.

But anyway she frighten me enough to make me think I go build myself a safe because I sure as hell not putting any of my money

119

in any bank. Next thing you know they asking all sort of questions 'bout where it come from and I definitely not getting into any kind of conversation over a thing like that.

So I decide the best place is under the shower. Ain't nobody going to think of looking there. I tell Hampton to dig the hole and fix it up, and make sure it watertight. But it cause so much commotion I couldn't stop everybody in the house from taking an interest, especially Mui who seem happy to spend all day just sitting on the little bench in there watching Hampton sweat and strain.

18

Opportunity

Well now, the Jamaican woman feeling on top of the world because they convinced Carol Joan Crawford going win the Miss World competition, which will be the first time a Jamaican do it. So every one of them start fetch up like they think they the most beautiful thing that grace every man day even if him minding him own business just walking down the street. And you can't do nothing with them they all get so feisty. Not that they need much encouragement in that direction.

And if that not enough to make the nation feel proud they decide to hold a anniversary celebration for Independence Day just in case we didn't get enough chance to sing and dance and eat the first time 'round.

This time they planning a military and police parade from George VI Memorial Park all the way up to Cross Roads. And they hoping we not tired of cheering because they think we going line the route and wave the flag for the whole thing again. And the jewel in the crown? The prime minister going take a salute at the march past.

I can't make up my mind whether to go or not. I think that maybe I must have something better to do than go stand up in the street in the hot sun and watch them congratulate themselves, because I start think to myself that maybe Gloria right. They keep telling us 'bout all the progress they making and sure enough I can see they building the Esso oil refinery downtown, and the big hotels in New Kingston and suchlike. They got cement pouring outta the Carib works like there is no tomorrow. But I also hear some heavy rumblings from West Kingston 'bout unemployment and how the people over there poor and vex. So what I figure now is, Independence is good for the young and the old but only for some of them, the ones that already got something to invest in the progress because they are the ones that going reap the prosperity. And what happen to unity in all of that I not quite sure.

So the Friday night before the anniversary celebrations the telephone ring. It is Morrison. And in truth it is more like one o'clock in the morning.

'What you doing ringing the house at this time of night, man? You not got no bed to go to?'

'I have just received a telephone call from Captain Meacham.'

'I thought he left when the British army make their retreat last year.'

'He is back for the celebrations. He brought his daughter with him to show her Jamaica.'

'So what this got to do with me?'

When I finish talk to Morrison, I get dressed and get in the car and take a ride 'cross Windward Road to Club Havana. The parking lot got cars park up every which way and the Cuban salsa is pumping out so loud I bet they can hear it halfway 'cross the Palisadoes. But since there nobody out there it no matter.

I circle the car park a couple of time to see what I can see and then I park up on a verge and get out. I got a flashlight in the trunk. The car park not that big which explain why it so pack. So it not long before I see it up in a corner sorta nearly under a bush. But it not actually hid as such. I just take my foot and ease it over and when the body slump on it back that is when I see him face, and then my eye catch sight of the knife. It look like some kinda butcher knife just laying there on the ground. I get out a kerchief and pick it up by the point and I throw it in a old crocus bag I got in the back of the car.

I drive over to the Blue Lagoon and telephone the police, and tell Clifton Brown to come meet me there.

When Clifton turn up a good hour later he already been to Club Havana and he already got the name and address of a waitress that run off this evening before she finish work. Him tell me he got to go back to *the scene*, that the way he say it, because he have to catch up with what his men doing. So I say for him to meet me at the waitress house in an hour. Then just before him leave he say to me, 'Is two bodies down there, yu know, not just one.'

I get back in the car and I drive up to New Kingston where Meacham holed up in the house he rent for his vacation. When I reach the house he open the door before I even knock it. Morrison is sitting in the living room with a glass of Appleton in his hand so I reckon he just forget again that he a Presbyterian.

When I see him it remind me that I not paid no visit to Mrs Morrison and the baby since they come back from Cedar Valley. I know they call the baby John, and Morrison already tell me that Margaret *delighted* that you can't tell from looking at him that the baby half Chinese. I don't say nothing 'bout it though because Meacham think we get rid of the baby, and he already look embarrass that he have to call me out like this. So I just make a mental note to myself 'bout making a visit.

Captain Meacham tense. He don't like what going on. He don't like being in this position with me, not a second time. It already stuck in his craw over the thing with Merleen and the baby. So I just say to him, 'Where your daughter at?'

And he say, 'In her bedroom.'

'Well she better come out here and tell me what happen so we can all go get some sleep tonight.'

When Meacham gone to get the girl I say to Morrison, 'He know this going cost him?'

And Morrison say, 'Yes. I told him. He said I am the only person he knows still on the island. That is why he called me.'

'Yu must mean the only white person, because it seem like he still know me, and he still know Merleen and any number of other girls that he love and leave just the same way he leave her, although I don't suppose that love come into it that much.'

Meacham daughter white and skinny. She look like she could do with a good meal inside her. And she got dark brown hair, cut short. Her name Helena, and she only eighteen year old.

According to her, she take the big kitchen knife from the house in case she need to protect herself when she go down to Club Havana. This is how she tell it anyway. She say she lucky to have the knife with her because the boys just follow her out to the car park and jump her for no reason at all.

I listen to all of this and then I say to them, 'She can say self-defence if you want, but you know yourself questions going be ask 'bout what she doing at Club Havana in the first place, a young white girl on her own, drinking liquor and carrying on. And then she go kill two boys with a big knife that she herself take down there.'

I look at Meacham and I say to him, 'It don't look good, Charles, I have to tell you that. Not with the Jamaican police. Not with the fact that these boys had no weapon of their own. Not at the moment with the Independence celebrations and everything people have on their minds 'bout the British and colonialism and slavery and all of that. Because they will think to themselves well now we have freedom but we still have some little white English girl who think she can come down here and murder two Jamaican boys for no good reason and get away with it. And that not good. Really, is very bad timing. That is what it is. Bad timing. And in truth I don't think a Jamaican jail is going suit your daughter. No, Fort Augusta not going suit her at all.'

So I tell him the only thing to do is get the girl off the island as soon as possible.

'Just you take her back to England.'

Then afterwards I say to him, 'Where the clothes she wearing at the time?'

'They are on the back veranda.'

So I tell Morrison to take them home with him and burn them because I don't trust Meacham to take much care with anything he do.

Then I say to him, 'What about the car she driving?'

'Parked out the back.'

When I go look at the car it one of them old English Rover. A nasty-looking grey thing that sit up stiff and straight just like Meacham.

I look at him and I say, 'Where you get a thing like that?'

'I borrowed it from an ex-army friend.'

So I turn to Morrison and I say, 'So he still have at least one ex-army friend here on the island then.'

But Morrison just want to shush me because he don't want me getting on the subject 'bout how the English only want to know you when it suit them. Or more like, when they got some little job need doing that they don't want to soil they little white hands over. Is 1963, we independent, but we still servicing them.

When I open the car door I see the seat got blood all over it, and the steering wheel and the gear-stick as well. Blood all over the interior where she open the car door from the inside to get out. I close the door and I walk back inside, and the two of them follow me. I pick up the telephone and I ring Hampton.

'Yu need to go get Milton and the two of yu come over here with what yu need to clean up a car.'

'What! Yu mean right now?'

'What yu think I ringing yu for this hour of night if I don't want yu come do this thing right now?'

Then just before I leave the house Meacham say to me, 'She dropped the knife. Do you think there is much chance that the police will find it?'

'None at all,' I say to him. 'Not that the Jamaican police incompetent or lazy, you understand. But I already got the knife. I pick it up in the car park earlier this evening and I keeping it nice and safe for you.'

By the time I cut 'cross town to the waitress house Clifton Brown already there waiting outside for me in a parked car. When we knock the door a man face appear at a side window and then him come and open up.

125

'Is you, Uncle. We 'fraid maybe it be the police.' And he let us in.

The waitress turn out to be him little sister, a girl of just sixteen. She lock herself in the bathroom she so 'fraid, but when her brother tell her to come out she do it. And just as she pass him by, him reach out and box her, like a slap in the back of her head. But the slap seem to get weaker from when it leave him hand to when it reach her head. Then him sit her down and tell her to tell me what happen. So it seem like him vex with her, but him still care for her and worried for her as well.

'The white girl been coming down the club all week. And every night she talk to me a little. And I talk back. Then tonight she ask me if I want go sit out in her car with her, where it a bit more quiet and we can talk. And I say alright.' She stop and she look at me like she wondering if she want to go on. And I look at Clifton because he the one that need encourage her now she on his territory. He the one that need set her mind at ease.

So he say to her, 'I think we know where you going with this and it alright. Believe me, you in fine company with this.' Both she and me look at him sorta quizzical, but then she carry on.

'When my break come, I go out there and one thing and another, and then she say to me if I want get in the back seat of the car with her. She say we can get more comfortable. I don't know what come over me, I just say yes. We was in there for a while and then the next thing I know there was this banging on the car window and a lot of laughing and hooting. And when I look 'round there was two boys. Just children really. But they acting like they gone mad, screaming and running 'round and banging on the car. I just panic in case all their carry-on attract someone attention. Anyway, before I know what was happening she jump outta the car with this carving knife and was slashing at one of these boys. She was in a frenzy. I never seen nothing like it in my life. It was like she just become a completely different person. And while all this was going on the other boy just stand there staring at her. So I was shouting, 'Run, run,' but he didn't move. It was as if he was glued to the spot and then she swing 'round with the

126

knife and catch him throat. And that was when I run, and come home because I didn't know where else to go.'

So now me and Clifton both know we got a situation. After all, the perversions of white people is one thing, but Jamaicans doing that sort of nastiness, no. And definitely not a young girl like this. Not in Jamaica. Once she set foot inside that car she become guilty. And judge and jury wouldn't be too fussy 'bout what them punishing her for.

I say to Clifton, 'We have to get this girl off the island tonight. Yu going have to take her to Cuba.'

'Cuba! How me going do that?'

'Yu have to take a launch, man.'

'I can't take out a police launch at four o'clock in the morning for no good reason and take it to Cuba. Yu mad?'

'Well you of all people, Clifton Brown, I would have thought would understand a situation like this. If this girl stay here tonight she going end up in jail for sure, while her little white girlfriend flying free back to England on the morning breeze. Is that what yu want to happen to her? Look at her, she nothing but a child.'

When I look at him I can see that I got him convinced, so I say, 'Alright then, but yu going have to keep her somewhere safe tonight and then yu can put her on the morning flight to Miami. All yu need for that is some US identification and a ticket.'

'What identification? What the hell you talking 'bout?'

'Passport, man. Driving licence.'

'And where yu think I going get that?'

'Is independence weekend! Yu know how many Americans out there right now drinking liquor and living it up. Go arrest somebody and let them cool off in jail while yu take them papers. How come yu can't ever think nothing for yourself, Clifton?'

Just before him go I tell him to try keep the thing outta the newspapers at least till after the holiday weekend done.

When I go back to Matthews Lane I put the knife in the safe and try get a couple hours sleep before daybreak.

The next morning Meacham come see me on him way to the airport. He park the nasty grey Rover car outside the shop across the street, and I see the girl sitting there like butter wouldn't melt in her mouth.

Him come in the shop and I say to him, 'The car clean enough for you?'

And him say, 'Yes.' Then him just hand me a envelope and when I look inside it I see it full of US dollars. I half begin to wonder where him get so much money from so fast overnight, especially on a holiday weekend, but then I realise I don't care. At least he have the good manners this time to put it in a envelope, not like how he just hand me the naked bills when he pay me to get rid of Merleen's baby.

I think him see himself as paying for a service. And I think him expect me to go give him the knife. But then I start think 'bout how this man going fly outta here and leave me with all his responsibility. I got Merleen Chin and baby John Morrison, and I got Marguerite Lopez, which is what the waitress call after Clifton done sort out the business with the driving licence.

I got all these people to look out for and put through school and everything. So I look at Meacham and I say to him, 'I was thinking of something regular.'

Clifton do the business with the newspaper thing as well because the story didn't reach the *Gleaner* till the Wednesday morning, 7 August. It make page four, squeeze between the Coral Gardens murder case and a hit and run in Savanna-la-Mar. There it was. 'No clues in stabbing of youths.'

On Friday 2nd August two youths were found stabbed to death in the car park of Club Havana on the Windward Road in Kingston. The youths, Winston Morgan and Aubrey Williams, both aged 13 years old, were from Kingston in the parish of St Andrew. Police have no clues and have yet to arrest anyone in connection with these fatal woundings.

19

Reputation

A week or so after that I go visit Margaret Morrison and the baby. I take some peanut brittle for her and a little shirt and pants thing for the baby that far too big for him but Margaret say is OK he will grow into it.

Well, Mrs Morrison right. You can't tell from looking at him that his mother Chinese. Baby John look just like a regular big-frame baby white boy. Funny thing is he even got a full head of ginger hair just like George. If you didn't know no better you would even think that George Morrison him papa.

Margaret entertain me royal with tea and shortbread biscuits. She so happy with the baby she can't thank me enough. She say it change her whole life. She say it give her life meaning. She say every day she thank the Lord that He bring baby John to her. She say she and George happier than they ever been their whole lives. I never hear anybody carry on so much over a pickney. I feel like I want to say to her, 'Is just a baby, you know, Margaret,' but I don't say nothing because it would hurt her feelings, and I don't mean to do that.

Then she turn to face me, and she turn her whole body right 'round so she looking at me square and direct.

And she say to me, 'I would like to ask something of you. You don't have to give me your answer straight away, but I would like it if you would at least consider it. I beg you, just think about it before you respond.'

I can't imagine what she going say to me.

But then she say, 'George and I would like to ask you to be John's godfather.'

Well, you could have knock me down with a feather. 'Margaret, I honoured that you ask me, but . . .'

She put her finger to her lip like to say shhh, and then she say, 'Take some time to think about it. Please. It would mean such a lot to us and I don't want the decision to be hasty. Please just think about it.'

Next time I see George I tell him he got to talk Margaret out of it.

'I can't be no baby godfather. All the things you and me do together and then I going stand up in church and say what?'

'I have spoken to her about it repeatedly, but Margaret has her heart set on this. I don't know what else to say to you, Pao.'

'Is not me you need talk to. Is her.'

But Morrison not paying me no mind. It seem like he actually want me to be the baby godfather as well. He just prefer to lay the whole thing on Margaret like it her idea alone. This is what I guess anyway after him say to me, 'You talk about the things we have done together and what of it? Wasn't it kindness that you showed to Merleen Chin, and the waitress from Club Havana, and even Meacham's daughter? You care for your children and Zhang and your mother. Even the girls in East Kingston tell me how lucky they feel with you looking out for them. Anyway, we don't know anyone who would make a better godfather for John, because in a way you are the person who gave him life. So who better to help him understand how to live it?'

I reckon all this talking with Margaret make Morrison done lose his mind, so I just shrug my shoulders and walk off. I can understand Margaret maybe thinking she doing something good by the child because she dunno nothing. But Morrison should know better. Maybe he just forget what we been doing. Like every now and again he forget he not supposed to be drinking liquor.

Father Michael think maybe the godfather thing OK if I ask

God for forgiveness and go to confession and Holy Communion and I say, 'No, man. We already been through all of this.'

'Then why don't you just say no?' That stop me dead in my tracks.

'I think you need to face it, Pao, there is something that the Lord is trying to make out of you. Some lesson He wants you to learn. Some corner He wants you to turn. Maybe you just need to let Him do His work with you as He is doing with Karl and Mui.'

So right then I see in his face for the first time ever that maybe he think he make a mistake.

'What you mean, Karl and Mui?'

He take a deep breath. 'Both Karl and Mui have been baptised and received their First Holy communion. Karl attends Mass regularly with Fay, and Mui also attends during the time that she spends with me.'

I just look at him in complete disbelief. 'And this is what you been doing with her all this time she coming here and I think you taking an interest in the child?'

'I am taking an interest in her. Mui belongs to a group of young people who are studying the Catechism in preparation for their Confirmation.'

Well right then I feel like just swinging my arm and boxing him. I can't believe how he betray my trust like this.

'And you never think, in all the time that you and me spend together, you never think that maybe you mention any of this to me?'

'Mui asked me not to.'

'Mui asked you not to? Mui is a child. You and me are grown men. Is you and me should be talking to one another not just you go talking to some child.'

I can hear myself now and I can hear how much I shouting. Michael just stand there, calm in him little space that always surround him. He just stand there with him hands clasp in front of him.

Then after some long time him say to me in that still voice he got, 'I know you think that you are a bad person. But in this life good and evil are not always as clearly delineated as you think. Good people sometimes commit bad deeds. And bad consequences are sometimes unintended or unforeseen. Virtue does not reside in particular actions. It resides in the settled moral state of the individual.' Then he stop and draw breath and say, 'One thing I do know is that you can never come too late to redemption.'

I just walk out his room and slam his little door.

When I ask Mui 'bout it she say it true. She ask Father Michael not to tell me because she know it only make me vex and she really want carry on with it. She really like Father Michael, and then she say to me, 'And Papa, there is really a lot to learn, you know.'

20

Manoeuvre

So right in the middle of all of us sitting there in the shop counting the money from the weekly pick-up, I got Samuels giving me some long political speech 'bout how bad everything getting in West Kingston. All 'bout unemployment and poverty; and how the people losing hope; and how they running outta patience; and how it all going lead to open warfare in the streets. And him telling me all of this as if I can't see for myself how West Kingston busy dividing itself up. Like everybody don't know that Trench Town belong to the People's National Party and the Labour Party got Tivoli Gardens, and how all the rest of them fall. Every little township lining up to face off with next door, and this is Samuels's explanation for why, even after I already tell him to stop it, he still busy selling guns in Chinatown.

So I say to him, 'I tell you this before, and I going tell you again. West Kingston is West Kingston, and this is Chinatown.'

'Yu nuh see what happen with the Chinese riots already?'

Well now this just make everybody stop. And them all turn 'round and look at me because they know how vex it make me the way people like to talk 'bout the *Chinese riots*. So I say to him, 'Don't say nothing to me 'bout no Chinese riot. There was no Chinese rioting. It was the Chinese that was catching hell, and Chinese shops burned and homes vandalise, and people harassed in the street.'

'That is what I mean. The Chinaman got to protect himself.'

So right then I just jump outta my seat and grab Samuels in the collar with my left hand and make like a two-finger gun with my right hand and stick it in his temple and shout, 'POW, POW.' Real loud.

And then I sit down and I say to him, 'How you like that for this Chinaman protecting himself? I expect one of your .365 Magnum sound a bit louder than that.' But Samuels not paying me no mind, so I just say to him, 'I don't want you selling no more of Louis DeFreitas's guns in Chinatown, you hear me?'

And he look at me and say, 'What make you think they come from Louis DeFreitas?'

'Don't mess with me, man. I know where they come from. And I know DeFreitas getting them on special delivery straight from the CIA.'

'Nobody know that. That is pure rumour.'

'How you think all them guns getting on the island? You think the rude boys flying up to Miami and bringing them back shove in their hip pocket?' Samuels just sit there and look at me so I say to him, 'This here is a family. It not no posse with anybody looking to make themselves a reputation so that they can go sing a song and make a record 'bout it.'

I ask Zhang what him think because I know for sure Samuels not going do as I tell him to. Him making too much money with DeFreitas. And I don't want no guns in Chinatown because the next thing is everybody going have to be going heavy every time they step out the yard. But the thing that really worrying me is that maybe this thing with Samuels is the way DeFreitas going find to creep into my territory.

Zhang say to me, 'Sun Tzu say, "*What is difficult about manoeuvre is to make the devious route the most direct and to turn misfortune to advantage. Thus, march by an indirect route and divert the enemy by enticing him with a bait.*" '

Zhang say Sun Tzu also say, '*Those who excel in war first cultivate their own humanity and justice.*' So the first thing I do is start reclaim the neighbourhood. I have to make them so loyal to me they would never think of doing any kind of business with DeFreitas. I start visiting with people not just for the weekend pick-up, but in the middle of the week as well. Calling in sometimes just to share a bowl of tea with them; taking the time to ask 'How is business?' or 'How is the family?' On occasion I take a small gift for the baby or a present for the son or daughter's wedding; I exchanging recipes and news of this week's best buys. I taking part in the neighbourhood gossip 'bout Madame Huang's daughter who make terrible pickle: 'Never going to get a husband with pickle like that.'

I listening and I talking; I listening and I listening. I just taking the time and making a effort.

Then I get the boys go give a hand 'round the place, so they doing something useful, unloading a delivery truck, reorganising a warehouse, repainting a shop. Something practical so people can see the benefit. Pretty soon I am giving advice, people asking me to sort out them little disputes, I putting injustice to right. I not just fixing things behind closed doors no more. My authority is out in the open. I step out from under Zhang shadow.

Then I start ask people if they buy gun from Samuels. And it turn out that they do it because Samuels work for me and they think is what I want. So I tell them no. And I say to them, 'We going put the gunrunners outta business.'

I tell them I will buy back any gun they buy from Samuels for twice the price they pay him for it. All I ask of them is that they broadcast the price they get from me and say it the same as what they pay Samuels in the first place. So pretty soon news going reach DeFreitas that Samuels holding out on him, and him not going like that.

I tell Judge Finley to arrange a meeting with DeFreitas and I pack up all the guns in a old crocus bag. A couple days later we take a slow drive to West Kingston, me, Judge Finley and Hampton. All the way there I thinking 'bout what Zhang tell me 'bout Sun Tzu and the devious route and enticing the enemy with a bait.

DeFreitas operate outta a three-storey wooden house on the

135

edge of Tivoli Gardens. It got one of them plastic multicoloured beaded curtain thing hanging in the doorway that lead from the street into this dark, dingy little bar where them playing 'My Boy Lollipop' on the jukebox. Then a couple of his men take us up some rickety stairs to his office that on the first floor. All the way up there we squeezing past the traffic of women who live up the top floor and service the customers from the bar downstairs.

When we get in the room it empty apart from one straight-back chair and a large mahogany desk that DeFreitas sitting behind. He look like him been sitting there all morning trying to strike the right pose. Him look pale and sick, and he got this thin line above him lip I guess him must think is a moustache. Him men stand up behind him with them feet apart and them arms folded, like they think they going scare somebody.

DeFreitas nod him head and tell me to sit. So I do it. The place stink of stale sweat and beer and tobacco. It almost like it oozing outta the wall. Hampton put the sack of guns on the desk.

I look straight at DeFreitas and I say to him in the meekest voice I can muster, 'I am offering these guns back to you because I don't want any trouble. You have them. Sell them again anywhere you like, just not in Chinatown.'

DeFreitas just smirk at me. 'And who you think you are that you can come here and tell me where to do my business?'

Sun Tzu say, '*Pretend inferiority and encourage his arrogance.*' So I say, 'I am just a small businessman and you is a big man with the whole of West Kingston at your feet. I hoping you accept these guns as a gift. A sign of my respect. After all West Kingston is big and Chinatown is small. Your power is great and mine modest. So all I want to ask yu is if you could leave the Chinese to me.'

DeFreitas scrutinise me, then him eyes pass over the sack of guns. I can tell him thinking 'bout how much money he going make again the second time 'round. He stand up and start pace the room. He got a walking stick with a handle like a silver fox head. He go over to the window and start look out. Him rubbing him neck. Him staring at the floor. Him taking so long over this, I start wonder if I read this thing all wrong.

When him come back, him rest the walking stick on the side of the desk and put both hands palm down on the surface. Him body rigid. And when him lean forward, the long nail on the little finger of him left hand scrape against the wood.

'I want Samuels.'

'Samuels? What you want with Samuels?'

DeFreitas don't like that and him snap at me, 'That between me and him.'

I wait. I know timing is everything. So I just sit there.

'We got a very small family. Well, we all here, apart from Milton who is just a boy. How I going manage without Samuels?'

'Him give you some trouble nuh? Over these guns.'

'True, but we have come to an understanding now.'

'Give me Samuels and I stay outta Chinatown.' I sit for a minute and I just look at him. Then him say, 'Take it or leave it. I not haggling with you.'

Sun Tzu say, *'One anxious to defend his reputation pays no regard to anything else.'*

Driving back to Chinatown Hampton say to me, 'What we going do 'bout Samuels's chores?'

'Kenneth Wong been pestering me this long time to give him something to do. Divvy up Samuels's jobs and let Kenneth run some errands with Milton.'

'You mean Miss Fay little brother?'

'How many Kenneth Wong you know?'

'She not going like that. Her little brother involve with you and your business.'

'You worry 'bout your own business, and I will worry 'bout Fay. Anyway, is just for now, till we find someone else.'

I wind down the car window and stick my elbow on the sill. And then a funny feeling come over me so I tell Hampton to pull into a gas station and I go inside and buy a cigar, a big, fat Montecristo.

137

I get back in the car and I light it. And I take a satisfying puff. And I think to myself well that is the first big thing I manage to do without thinking in the back of my mind that Zhang was there to fix it if it all go wrong. The first big thing that I fully responsible for. It seem like I change today. I grow up. I am forty years old and I finally become a man.

It feel good to watch the smoke curl outta the window and drift away on the gentle afternoon breeze.

21

Death Ground

'*Ground in which the army survives only if it fights with the courage of desperation is called "death".*' Therefore, Sun Tzu say: '*In death ground, fight.*'

Three month later Mrs Samuels come see me. Samuels dead. Shot in the back of the head. He been missing three weeks but the police just come tell her last week that they find his body shot and burned and left in a alley. She know who do it. But there no point going to the police over a thing like that. They not going move against a man like Louis DeFreitas. She even go see DeFreitas herself to plead with him, and beg him for some support. But all he say to her is for her to come see me. He tell her I will take care of everything.

She wait before she come because she didn't want bother me. She know Samuels not work for me no more, that he working for DeFreitas at the time he die, so really is DeFreitas's responsibility. But she dunno what to do because she got four children to feed, and she got to keep a roof over their head, and she got school fees, and she only earning a little money work part-time in Mr Chung shop. She fret so much she can't think, she can't eat, she can't sleep. She dunno which way to turn. She dunno what she going to do. And she start cry.

So I tell her she right. Samuels really DeFreitas's responsibility but, I say, in truth I feel partly responsible because if Samuels was still working for me there is no way DeFreitas would have lay a finger on him. DeFreitas know the rules, you can't go rough up somebody else's man. So in view of this, then I happy to help her.

I tell her to hush herself and blow her nose. I take care of everything. Rent, school fees, Blue Cross medical insurance, clothes for the children, a little extra every month, whatever she need to make ends meet and make a good home for her and the children. She don't have to worry about a thing. And I just touch her light on the arm.

That is when she really start to bawl. It get so bad I have to call Hampton to come drive her home. And even as she going outta the gate she still thanking me, and waving at me, and telling me what a good man I am.

When I tell Judge Finley what happen he say to me, 'So what, you surprise DeFreitas kill him?'

'Yes. I never think he go do a thing like that.'

'I thought that was exactly what you had in mind the day you jump up and *pow* two shots in his head.'

'No, man. I was just making a point.'

'So what you think DeFreitas was going do with him?'

'I think maybe he give Samuels a good hiding and teach him a lesson. Maybe bust him down the ladder. I never imagine he would go kill a man over a thing like that.'

'Well then you must be the only man in Kingston who think that way, because right now a man can get shot just for wearing the wrong colour shirt in the wrong part of town. So maybe this be a warning to you to throw out every green or orange shirt you got in case anybody think you supporting the Labour Party or the PNP.'

Next day Fay come tearing into Matthews Lane and straight into the bedroom where she start flinging open drawers and emptying everything into a suitcase she got open up on the bed. I go stand up in the doorway and I say to her, 'What you think you doing?'

'What does it look like I am doing?'

'Well, it look like you going somewhere. But it seem to me like you already gone from here so I dunno why you think you need to take anything else.'

Right then she stop what she doing and she turn and look at me.

'I heard about Samuels.'

But I don't say nothing to her. The two of us just stand there. She looking at me, and me looking straight back at her.

'Cat got your tongue?'

When I look at her I see that she really hate me. Her face look hard and her mouth got a real cruel twist. If she was a man she would have thump me. She would have try to mash me up just so she can let off some steam and work out how she feel. But she not a man and she can't do that. She can only stand there and think that maybe she can wear me down with her stare.

But just then she grab the vase and throw it at me. It hit the doorframe and smash, and it shower all the water and glass over me because the flowers was still standing in it. I feel like I going just jump on her and beat her till I wipe that look off her face. But I don't move a muscle. I just stand there. And I brush myself down a little, try wipe off some of the excess water. And then I turn 'round and go back down the couple of step, and sit down at the table and pour myself a bowl of tea.

I expect she going carry on packing but she don't. She follow me. And then she start talking while I sitting there with my back to her.

'He was shot in the back of the head and his body burned. That is execution style. You think I don't know that?'

I don't say nothing to her.

'One minute Samuels is working for you, the next minute he is being executed in West Kingston. And I suppose you are going to tell me that this has nothing to do with you.'

'I not telling you anything, Fay.'

'I married you because I couldn't stand to live with my mother any more. She thinks that I went to board at Immaculate so I could pretend to be white, but that wasn't it. I went up there to get away from her. I couldn't stand her pretensions, and I couldn't stand looking at how ashamed she is of herself and of the life she thinks she would have had if she had not married my father; if she had not elevated herself from being the descendant of an ex-slave.

'But believe me, I had no idea of the squalor you would expect me to live in. I didn't even know that places like this existed. And then to bring children up in it? No self-respecting person would even call this place a house never mind a home.

'And as for you, I have no idea what it is you think you are doing. But you are nothing but a dirty little crook. You are not smart. You are not powerful. You are just a sleazy little hoodlum who thinks he is a big shot because his pocket is stuffed full of money. Yang Pao, the big man of Chinatown. You and Louis DeFreitas make a good match. You belong together with your drugs, and guns and murder.'

'I am not a drug dealer, and I don't run no guns, and I didn't murder nobody.'

'Well with your little whores then. I think you are still running her, aren't you? Your whore in East Kingston?'

I just get up and turn 'round and launch myself at her. I knock her down and we start fight. We rolling on the ground grabbing and pushing and trying to ease away so we can get some space to land a good punch. We twisting and kicking and scratching and biting and we got elbows and knees going in every direction.

Then suddenly I realise how long it is since I touch her. How long it been since I feel her warm body next to me. And then I can't tell if I am pushing her away or pulling her towards me. She putting up a good fight either way. She surprise me how strong and agile she get. I even forget I fighting with a woman. I just trying to defend myself. I just trying to get outta this tangle in one piece.

Then outta the corner of my eye I see Xiuquan stand up by the gate and I realise she must have leave him in the car outside. Then I see Mui in her pyjamas stand on the step. And Hampton is shouting something and Ma is running down the yard with her arms waving in the air. In the middle of all of this commotion I manage to make some distance between me and Fay so now we standing up and I got her by the shoulder at arm's length.

And that is when she spit in my face. And I let her go. And everything stop.

Xiuquan run up to her and grab her hand. And then she walk over to Mui and take her hand as well. So now she got both children one on each side. So I say to her, 'What you think you doing?'

And she say to me, 'You don't think I am going to leave them here with you, do you?'

'You not going anywhere with them children.'

'What, so I can leave them here to grow up with pimps and whores, and thieves and thugs and murderers? So that one day maybe they become just like you? Is that what they should aspire to? To become just like Papa? Papa's little boy and girl?'

That is when I slap her nasty face. But I regret it straight away because I didn't want the children to be seeing me do a thing like that. And anyway, it come 'cross a bit too heavy because it leave my handprint like a big red mark on her left cheek just so.

And she start cry. So I reach in my pocket and pull out a handkerchief and offer it to her and she take it. And just for that small little moment when she take the kerchief from me and start mop her face she look soft and gentle at me like maybe she remember another time long ago at the Jamaica Inn when she take my handkerchief just like that.

And just as she let go of the children hand, Mui step 'cross and stand up next to me. And Xiuquan look at me like him dunno what to do. Or maybe him do, but he too 'fraid to do it, because him got a sorta longing look in his eye.

So I just say to her, 'You a grown woman, Fay. You can do what you want, but the children staying here with me.'

She look at Zhang and Ma and Hampton standing there. And then she look at the children, and then at me, and she say, 'This isn't over.' And she turn and walk outta the gate. I half expect Xiuquan to run after her, but he don't. Him just stand there watching her back as she close the gate behind her.

22
Truce

One good thing come outta it anyway. Xiuquan and Mui finally start act like they brother and sister. Every day now they gone out the street somewhere together. They gone up the US navy base, or they fishing off the wharf, or they gone swimming with Hampton at Hellshire Beach or over Lime Cay. It a pleasure for me to see the two of them go down the street hand in hand even if they just go roam 'round town and come back.

It seem like we got a family. Tilly still come every day, Zhang got Round Chin and Tartan Socks, and sometime Judge Finley play dominoes. Ma got her mah-jongg friends three times a week. Every now and again she take the children to temple with her, and Zhang busy telling them the same stories him tell us when we young, 'bout the revolution and Sun Yat-sen and Mao Zedong, and the counter-revolutionary Chiang Kai-shek.

We settled now. We not got nobody disrupting the place coming in and out like she can't make up her mind if she staying. I read the newspaper and I smoke a cigar which is a regular thing for me now when I feel relax and happy and content with life. Although I don't do it over Gloria's because she don't like the smell.

I say to her, 'This here is a real good Havana cigar. I would have thought you would like the smell of that,' because more and more Gloria looking to Cuba and praising all the changes going on over there with education and health and employment.

I start take the children with me when I make the weekly pick-up 'round town on a Saturday. I introduce them to the shopkeepers and market traders; to people in grocery stores and laundries and pharmacies; hardware stores, barber's; people who just stand on the street with me and talk and smile and bow their heads; and who happy to see me. People who want to make a fuss of Mui and Xiuquan, to give them gifts and pamper them, and tell Mui how beautiful she is like her mama and Xiuquan strong like his papa. I start teach them tai chi and I tell them that Yang Lu-Ch'an who founded and develop Yang-style tai chi during the Manchu dynasty was my great-grandfather. But Ma tell them it not true. We just share our name with the great master.

But Zhang don't like it. He think that maybe them coming with me not such a good idea. So I remind him that he done the same thing when me and Xiuquan young and him say, 'That long time back. Now maybe it set bad example.'

I not paying him no mind because I want the children to know Chinatown and Chinatown to know them. I want them to have run of the place just the same way it was for us when we young. Zhang say times changing, that it not the same as when he first come to Jamaica. Back then it was because Chin ask him, and he was doing a service.

'Things different now. Everybody worried 'bout what legal and how they show taxman what they doing. People think different 'bout you protecting them. They think different 'bout favour they ask you. You not Uncle no more. You Mr Fixit. In old days they happy you call in to share a bowl of tea. Now you need appointment so they can clear all their fancy guests out the way before you turn up. Now they worried maybe one day you ask them do something for you. In old days they looking what to do for you before you ask.'

Maybe Zhang got a point. Anyway I think it time the children meet Gloria. Fay gone and who knows what going happen next. But Gloria no think it such a good idea because she dunno how I going explain to them who she is, and I say it no matter, we can just meet by accident. So that is what we plan to do. Me and the children going to be walking down King Street and stop outside Times Store just at the moment when Gloria step outta the shop like she been doing some shopping in there. And then everybody get introduce and we go get a ice cream together. And this place is good because it got a soda fountain right upstairs in there. Gloria not so keen on the plan but she go along with it anyway.

So Saturday come and I take the children with me on the weekly collection 'round Chinatown and afterwards I say to them 'bout how they fancy going down to Times Store for a ice cream and they say yes. We walk down King Street and just as we reach Times Store Gloria see us coming and step outta the shop right there in front of us. It work perfect.

I act surprise and I say to her, 'Hello, Gloria. It such a surprise to see you.'

And she say, 'Yes, quite a surprise.' And then she look down at the children standing either side of me and she say, 'And these must be your children? I have heard so much about you.'

And right then Mui just put out her hand and take Gloria's and shake it and say, 'I'm Mui.'

Gloria stand there shaking Mui's hand and then afterwards she turn to Xiuquan and say, 'You must be Xiuquan?'

But Xiuquan just stare at her. Him no offer no hand for no shaking and him face look vex. Then him say to her, 'My name is not Xiuquan. It is Karl.'

I grab him by the hand and drag him into Times Store while I saying to him, 'Yu twelve years old and yu so rude already?'

The four of us sit down with the ice cream. Mui got this big mountain of banana and ice cream and nuts and syrup and god knows what while Xiuquan got to make me force him to have two scoop of vanilla. Gloria order a cup of coffee and I just take some ice water.

So we sitting there squeeze into this little corner table and Mui say, 'You are a friend of Papa's?'

'Yes, a very old friend.'

'How do you know him?'

'Your papa helped me when my sister had some trouble. He helped us to sort things out.'

Mui sitting next to Gloria and she look 'cross the table at me. Then she take a spoon of ice cream and say, 'Yes, my papa is good at helping people.' And then she pause, and then she say, 'Do you have any children, Miss Gloria?'

'I have a daughter. She is called Esther. She is about the same age as Karl.' Gloria look at Xiuquan, but he got his back half turn to her with the ice-cream dish in his hand.

'Yu nuh look at somebody when they talking to yu? And put the dish on the table. Yu not just going sit there eating the thing out yu hand.'

But Gloria try hush me down. Maybe she think it not so good me chastising the child like that first time she meet him. So she say, 'How is school, Karl?'

But before Xiuquan answer Mui start talk. She talk 'bout everything that she do at school like all the singing and the spelling, and she paint picture and read storybook, and write her composition, and how the nuns strict, and how she go to church every morning and say the rosary on her knees, and how she go to Mass at the cathedral on Sunday, and how at the catechism class she learn why God made her, and how she love Father Michael.

And then she start ask Gloria 'bout what her daughter do at school, and if she go to church, and if she know Father Michael. So Gloria have to explain to her that Esther not a Catholic.

'Not a Catholic?'

'No.'

'And you are not a Catholic, Miss Gloria?'

'No, Mui, I am not. I was brought up Baptist by my mama.'

Then Mui turn to me and say, 'Papa, do you know that Esther is not a Catholic?'

Well I think the child gone too far now. I just can't decide what to say to her in case Gloria think I overreacting. But right then before I fix anything in my mind Xiuquan turn 'round and say, 'Yes he does.' And then he get up from the table and walk off.

When we get back to Matthews Lane I say to him, 'How come yu so rude to a woman yu just meet? Yu think she do something to yu?'

But him not answering me. Him just standing there willing me to go do something or say something else to him. Then him say, 'I may be twelve years old but I am not deaf and blind. I hear and I see, and I have heard that woman's name before. Many, many times. And I have seen the upset it causes my mother.'

'This is the way yu talk to me?'

'I am not afraid of you.' And he just walk off.

Mui stand there. And then after Xiuquan gone she say, 'What I don't know, Papa, is anything about Esther.' She stand there staring up at me for a good long while, and then she turn 'round and walk off. I look at her strong little legs going up the yard and her hair in them two plaits hanging down her back and I think to myself well I don't know nothing 'bout Esther neither. I know she older than Mui and taller and darker, and she got the African hair like her mother, even though she got a little Chinese round the eyes. And I know she quieter than Mui and less like she think she can say anything to me she want to. And that is it. But then I think, she a child. What you supposed to know?

Another thing that happen about two weeks after the fight with Fay was Michael telephone me and say he want talk to me. That never happen before. Michael never summon me like that before and I didn't take to it. I go see him anyway because we still not get over the business 'bout Mui and the catechism classes.

When I get to Bishop's Lodge he tell me to come walk with him in the garden. He walk 'round a long time without saying nothing, and I just follow on next to him. The garden full of poinsettia and bird of paradise and them little wild banana plant. It beautiful and peaceful. It remind me of the botanical garden up Old Hope Road except Michael garden not got no bandstand.

After some long time he say to me, 'We have known each other for many years, Pao, and in all of that time I have made it a rule not to discuss Fay with you. Or you with her for that matter. But she came to see me two days ago and, well, her face is very badly bruised and her left eye is black and turning yellow. She told me her version of what happened and I wanted for us to talk to see how we can find a peaceful resolution to the situation.'

I didn't say nothing at first because I not sure that he come to a stop. And then I didn't say nothing because I didn't know what to say to him. I just walking along and asking myself which side he on. And then I look at him walking so slow with his hands clasp in front like he praying, and wearing this long black cassock and I think well maybe he not on any side. Maybe he just genuinely trying to sort this thing out.

'There nothing to resolve, Michael. Fay decide to leave and that is what she done. I feel bad 'bout her face though. I really do. I regret it the moment I do it. But you have to understand it was some brawl that went on there that night.'

'I understand that. It is not my intention to reproach you about it. Fay admits she was equally responsible for what happened. The problem is that as long as you have the children the situation is not resolved.'

Right then I just stop, because I suddenly realise that is she put him up to this. And him only get me come over here so he can plead for her and get me give her the children. Well, Xiuquan for sure anyway.

'I not going give her the children, Michael. So if that all you got to say to me I think I will be going about me business.' And I turn and walk off.

I get halfway down the path when him shout after me, 'Pao, I know there is something you want to resolve otherwise you would not have come here today.'

I turn 'round, and I walk back to where he still standing.

'I still angry with you, Michael, over all this thing with Mui.'

'I am a priest. I want everyone to find God and share in His glory, including you, Pao.'

'You got no right doing it behind my back like that. If Fay bring Xiuquan to you so as you can turn him into a Catholic then that is one thing. But I didn't bring Mui to you for that.'

Michael just look at me like he got no idea what I am talking about.

'When you ask me that day at Port Royal about her, you get me wondering 'bout all the time you spend with Fay, and all the hours of day and night at Lady Musgrave Road, and how Miss Cicely not happy 'bout whatever she think going on between the two of you. So I think maybe, when it come to Mui, you have your own personal reason for being interested in her.'

And then something happen that I never seen before. Michael blush. I didn't know before that a black man could colour up like that. Even though he a bit on the light side. Right then the back door of the lodge open and when me and Michael turn 'round we see the housekeeper come out and start walk towards us.

Then Michael say to me, 'A long time ago, before Mui was born, Fay asked me to write to Rome to request special dispensation for her to divorce you. They declined and without a divorce she cannot file for legal custody of the children.'

I dunno why him telling me all this right now. I dunno if Fay know him telling me or if he just decide himself to go for broke trying to get me to give up the children.

When the housekeeper get up to us she say the archbishop on the telephone. I tell Michael is OK, go get the phone. We finish this another time.

And another thing since the fight with Fay is that Henry Wong start spending all him time down Chinatown. Him sitting in Barry Street from dawn till dusk and playing mah-jongg till all hours. When I ask him what going on him say him can't stand it at Lady Musgrave Road no longer. Since Fay come back she and Miss Cicely do nothing but argue morning, noon and night. Argue, argue, argue. Anything they find they can argue over. They can even argue over the fact that a couple hours pass and them no cuss. Henry say it bad.

'All I do is leave the house before Fay get up and stay out till after Cicely gone to bed. And even then it not always work out, because sometime when Fay come in early morning Cicely get up out her bed and they get started. If the neighbours closer I sure they call the police by now.'

So I wait for Ethyl to come tell me what going on up there. Because even though I been paying for shorthand and typing lessons all this long while Ethyl can't pass the test yet so she still the Wongs' housemaid. I tell her is OK, we can just keep carry on till she get there. And she happy with that because she like the idea that one day she going work in a nice cool air-condition office.

'Mr Philip, it like a war zone in that house up there. Every day Miss Cicely playing the piano and singing at the top of her voice. Her favourite one at the moment is "Sinners, Turn: Why Will You Die?" I know it by heart myself now because Miss Cicely play it a hundred times a day, especially when Father Michael visiting. She thump down on them keys, because she play it loud but she no play it too good, and she sing, *Dead, already dead within, Spiritually dead in sin, Dead to God while here you breathe, Pant ye after second death?* She play it over and over. *Will you still in sin remain, Greedy of eternal pain? O you dying sinners, why, Why will you forever die?* She sing all fourteen verses of Mr Wesley's song just like she learn it when she was a Methodist before she turn Roman Catholic, so I dunno what Father Michael make of that.

'Then all the time Miss Cicely quoting the Bible like she say, *He that soweth to his flesh shall of flesh reap corruption, but he that soweth to the Spirit shall of the Spirit reap life everlasting.* She love say things like that when she know Miss Fay can hear her. So they argue 'bout that and how Miss Fay running to Bishop's Lodge all the time and how Father following her from one end of town to the other. And when Miss Fay tell her Father Michael her counsel Miss Cicely say, *You should let the word of the Lord be a lamp unto your feet, and a light unto your path.*

'But truth is I never see nothing going on with the Father. I never even see him stand close to Miss Fay or touch her or anything like that. He just always got his hands clasp in front of him or resting in his lap. And he always keep so still. You never see him like make no sudden movement. None of the help say they notice anything so I dunno what go on but for sure Miss Cicely not happy 'bout it.

'Then when they not arguing 'bout the Father Miss Cicely say it not seemly for a married woman to be constantly running between her husband and father and dragging the children with her, and going out with her friends every night, going to every nightclub and party in town.'

And then Ethyl sorta lower her voice and look down and say, 'Because Miss Fay go out at night a lot.'

And then she carry on, 'And Miss Fay say it not her fault she have a lot of friends and it better than if she running 'round town with some jock. Well that word now, "jock", really get Miss Cicely started on some long speech that she finish off by saying, *You too busy fretting about your social standing when you should be saying to yourself the Lord is my rock, and my fortress, and my deliverer.*

'And even in the middle of them arguing Miss Cicely will just stop and say something like, *We pay all that money for your schooling and you can't even stand up straight. Why you need to lean on the doorpost?* And then she tell Miss Fay to act like she a respectable woman. Another time she say to her, *Take your hands off your hips! What you think this is? You think you big enough now to be standing there akimbo scowling at me?* And if Miss Fay interrupt her, Miss Cicely say, *I am talking. I am talking to you here if you don't mind.*

'But the worst time was when Miss Fay say that Mr Stanley run off to England just to get away from her, Miss Cicely that is.'

Ethyl talking so fast I have to put my hand up like a policeman say stop so as I can ask her who Stanley is because I got no idea who she talking 'bout.

'Mr Stanley Miss Cicely's firstborn.'

'Miss Cicely got another child?'

'Yes, sah. But Mr Henry not him father. I dunno who him papa except I hear Miss Fay say something 'bout Mr Johnson marrying

Miss Cicely off to Mr Henry. And that make Miss Cicely vex 'cause she say, *Mr Johnson was your grandfather, God rest his soul, and you will talk about him with a civil tongue in your head. He didn't do nothing to you.* So I dunno what all that about, except it seem like Mr Johnson Miss Cicely's papa.'

'So what 'bout Stanley going to England?'

'Miss Fay say Mr Stanley run off to England to get away from Miss Cicely hounding him every day 'bout how he stupid and lazy and irresponsible, and how he never going 'mount to anything. And Miss Cicely say it not true, Mr Stanley go to join the Royal Air Force, to serve his Queen and country in a time of need. And Miss Fay say no, Mr Stanley sick and tired of Miss Cicely because no matter what he do Miss Cicely never forgive him for being as black as her.

'The latest thing is a letter come from England for Miss Fay. It come from Mr Stanley and it say he can make arrangements for her to go there. She write a reply to him and she say she need a divorce so she can get the children from you, but the Church not going give it to her. I know it bad of me but I been taking the liberty to steam open the envelope when they come and when she give me the letter to take to the post office.'

Then she stop and she just sit there and look at me. And then she say, 'I think that all I got to tell you right now, Mr Philip.'

So I say, 'Thank you, Ethyl. You must be hungry you come here straight from work. Maybe you go get . . .' but before I finish talk Hampton jump up and start mumble something and shake out him legs and brush down him shirt and pants, look like him trying to make an impression.

And then finally him say, 'I can take Miss Ethyl for some dinner and drive her home after if that alright with you?'

I just look at him. And then I say, 'Yah, man.'

After the two of them leave I lock up the shop and walk 'round to Matthews Lane. When I get there, there is a big commotion going on. Mui talking so fast I can't make no sense outta what she saying. Ma trying to get her calm down when the telephone ring. It Clifton Brown.

'I got Karl down here at the police station.'

'What you got him doing down there?'

'He get arrested by accident. I just trying to sort things out now and I bring him over the house in a hour or so.'

When Clifton turn up he got Xiuquan and two police constables with him that I never seen before. He say they young, they new to the neighbourhood, they didn't know no better. They make a mistake. I reckon everything they do must be a mistake the two of them look so dimwitted. And with one of them so tall and the other one so short they just like Mutt and Jeff out on another one of them get-rich-quick scheme. I almost expect one of them to say 'Oowah!'

But these two constables not no comic strip, because when they see Xiuquan lifting the bow and arrow outta the store they shout at him to stop, and when he start running, they chase him till they finally catch up with him halfway down Barry Street and they take him back to the station.

When I ask Xiuquan what him think he doing he say they frighten him when they start shout, and him just in a hurry to run back home.

So I say to him, 'But you no pay for the things you take outta the shop?'

'Pay? We never pay for anything. It was a gift. It is always a gift.'

'So if it a gift how come yu start running when yu see the police coming?'

But before he get to answer Mui say, 'Because you cannot always trust the police to understand your situation.'

I think to myself yes, she right. But I also know another Xiuquan that take off just like that when the police turn up.

Just then I look 'round and catch Zhang walking off up the yard to his room.

Clifton push the constables forward to come apologise to me, and they both tell me them sorry. They nuh know who Xiuquan is. They nuh know him my boy. Arresting him a mistake they regret and they promise it never happen again.

I tell them is OK, these things happen. No harm done. And I open some Red Stripes and pass them 'round. The constables sit down and drink the beer, and they smile at me, but I can tell they none too happy 'bout the whole situation.

Sun Tzu say, '*When without a previous understanding the enemy asks for a truce, he is plotting.*'

23

Waging War

West Kingston was like a powder keg just waiting for something to come put a match to it. So that day when Edward Seaga stand up at the hundredth anniversary of the Paul Bogle Uprising, and when the crowd start heckle him, an' him say to them, 'If they think they are bad I can bring the crowds of West Kingston. We can deal with them, in any way, at any time. It will be fire for fire. Blood for blood.' Well that is when the mayhem really start up in earnest, and I wonder if it was a wise move for him to stop being a music promoter and become a politician. Not that all the shooting was Mr Seaga's fault because it was going on long before that. I think the blood-for-blood thing just ease it up a notch.

Anyway, it was just like Gloria say to me. It was open warfare in the street. And this was 1965, just three years after Independence when we was out on them same streets parading and dancing and singing 'bout unity. Now everybody was just out there gunning down one another. It get so bad that one day they report that in a two-hour period on one West Kingston street they fire two thousand rounds of ammunition. How they work out a thing like that I dunno. I don't even know how people can afford to buy so much gun and bullet. And how come they so happy to spend so much time and money just trying to gun down their neighbour.

I say to Judge Finley that it was exactly the sort of thing I worried we was headed for when Samuels take up with Louis DeFreitas, and how good it was that we stamp it out straight away. How good it was that we keep them guns outta Chinatown because I didn't want nothing to do with what was going on.

And him say to me, 'What about unity and being brothers in arms?'

'This is not unity. Unity is when you gather together to face a common enemy. Who is the enemy in West Kingston?'

'They think it is the man next door with the gun that is trying to kill them.'

'Killing your neighbour not going solve unemployment and all the misery that go with that. Their enemy not their neighbour. Their enemy is the masa that is making himself rich while all them boys bleeding to death in the street. If you want talk 'bout brothers in arms then maybe we need to get together and go get back the land that still owned by British landlords. And maybe we need to go see 'bout how we going stop these foreign investors from just taking out all the profit as fast as we can make it for them, so Jamaica can get to keep something for herself. And then maybe we wouldn't need so much foreign aid. But the ordinary man can't do nothing 'bout these people. He don't even know where to find them. All he can do is take up a gun and fire it at the people he see every day. And the worst thing about it is he doing it with a gun he get from the CIA. The masa don't even have to beat the slave himself no more. We doing it for him.'

But there is not a soul listening to me, except Mui.

So then the next thing we realise is, we got to go do something 'bout Kenneth Wong, because it seem like somehow Kenneth get himself all mix up in the middle of everything. Like he use the excuse of running a few errands for me to go turn himself into his idea of public enemy number one. So I think I go solve that by hiring Desmond Drummond and telling Kenneth he don't work for me no more. Not now I got Desmond. I think this going fix it because Desmond a long-time friend of Milton who turn out to be one seriously big, bad bwoy so I think that will send Kenneth running back to his mama. But it not so. Kenneth still going 'round the place acting like him working for me. So people start get confuse over whether it Desmond they dealing with or Kenneth, and I have to talk to the boy over and over and explain to him that he should go back to school and try get some qualification. But him not interested. Him say he don't need it. His papa nuh got no qualification, I nuh got no qualification, but we still rich, so what he need qualification for? And I tell him things changing. He can't spend his life just run 'round town like me. Maybe he should go ask his papa to work in the supermarket business. But him just shrug and walk off and I know him not going do it.

When I go talk to him 'bout what him doing he say he not interested in politics.

'But you running with one of the biggest political gang of rude boys in West Kingston!'

'Louis is my friend.'

'Louis DeFreitas is not your friend. Him not nobody friend. DeFreitas only DeFreitas's friend. You get thick with a man like that and yu heading for trouble. DeFreitas busy talking politics now but him only a punk. Him don't care 'bout unemployment and education, him only interested in what advantage or money he can get outta a situation. And right now everybody say is the CIA backing him to be causing all this violence so they can destabilise the country.'

'I tell you I not interested in politics. Louis been good to me. He let me work and him pay me.'

'Yu can't trust him. Louis DeFreitas will just as soon put you out front to take a bullet in your chest as shoot you in the back himself if that work out better for him.'

But Kenneth not listening to me. I start thinking it all my fault anyway, because there is no way a boy like Kenneth Wong was going meet a man like DeFreitas unless he was on the street running errands for me.

Finley say to me, 'Maybe you shouldn't take it so hard. After all, Kenneth was bugging you anyway. That was the way he was heading. He would have got himself involved somehow whether or not it had anything to do with you.'

A part of me know Finley right, but another part of me still feel responsible. I got no idea what to do with Kenneth. Sun Tzu say, '*Too frequent rewards indicate that the general is at the end of his resources; too frequent punishments that he is in acute distress.*'

So I decide to go talk to Henry Wong 'bout it. But it turn out Henry don't know nothing 'bout what Kenneth doing. Him say the boy just come in and outta the house and eat his meals and leave his dirty laundry behind. Kenneth don't talk to nobody, and when he in the house he lock himself in his bedroom, which he put a big padlock on the door so nobody can go in there when him out.

All Henry know is Kenneth got a lot a money. He buy a lot of fancy clothes and a record player and a whole heap of records him busy playing in there. And he buy a car and driving it 'round even though he got no driving licence.

Henry say the boy been off the rails a long time. Even before he legal to leave school him stop going while Henry still paying the school fees. And Henry say him think the boy smoking ganja in the house because the maids say they can smell it. Henry dunno what to do with him and all Miss Cicely say is she praying for him, but Henry not counting on that doing much good.

'I not know what to say to you, Pao. If you got a idea I happy to listen. But is Cicely that really deal with children.'

Three days after that, on a hot Thursday afternoon, Henry Wong collapse in the street. They take him to the public hospital because they dunno who he is and that he rich. And down there they decide it was a stroke that cut him down. When I hear 'bout it I ring George Morrison and tell him to take a ambulance downtown and bring Henry back up to Old Hope Road. Later when I go see him he paralysed down one side and he in a bad way.

After a few days Morrison say Henry not going get any better and he may be more comfortable at the Chinese Sanatorium, so that where we move him to. This is a nice place. It clean and calm and the nurses really seem like they care for him. Like they mean it, they not just doing their job. But when I go see him all him say to me is how he want me to bring him some rice and peas and chicken and saltfish fritters and bammy.

I want make sure that somebody go up there with food every day so I make out a rota for Finley and Hampton and Milton. And then Zhang surprise me when him say he going go as well, because I can't remember the last time Zhang leave the house to go any further than Barry Street for the Chinese newspaper. How him going make it up to North Street I dunno. But then it turn out that Tartan Socks McKenzie say he going drive him so that work out fine.

The last time I go visit Henry him reach out him shaky good hand and grab my sleeve and pull me to him, and whisper to me, 'I done tell Cicely already, I want you to have the business.'

When Henry die, Cicely decide to have the funeral in Holy Trinity Cathedral, which was the second time I go there that year. The first time was when I go watch Michael get consecrated Roman Catholic Bishop of Kingston, which was what the archbishop telephone him 'bout the day we was in the garden at Bishop's Lodge. Michael look proud and serene that day the same way he look now, because Fay insist that is him conduct the funeral and although Ethyl tell me Cicely muttering 'bout it, somehow Fay and her come to some agreement because is Michael standing up there saying, '*In nomine Patris, et Filii, et Spiritus Sancti.*'

I surprise myself when they start recite because I never think I had any emotion 'bout all this church thing. After all, I already go to church and become John Morrison godfather and I didn't feel nothing at all. But just now I can feel a little something in my chest when all the voices start ring out: 'I confess to Almighty God, to blessed Mary ever Virgin, to blessed Michael the Archangel, to blessed John the Baptist, to the holy Apostles Peter and Paul, to all the saints and to you, Father, that I have sinned exceedingly in thought, word and deed.' And then for no reason at all I just start pound my chest, three times like the rest of them: 'Mea culpa, mea culpa, mea maxima culpa.'

I look down and I see Mui just stand there gawking at me and suddenly I come over like I suffocating, and I realise it the smell of burning frankincense, and I think I going start cry. But this not got nothing to do with Henry Wong, it just the smell of incense, and the jangle of the little bells, and the purple and white and gold of Michael's get-up, and the candle burning by the coffin, and the sprinkling of holy water.

When Michael begin sing the Preface, I gather myself together, and Mui turn 'round and start look forward like she should have been doing all this time instead a staring at me.

Michael do the commemoration: 'Remember also, O Lord, Thy servant Henry who has gone before us with the sign of faith, and rests in the sleep of peace.' And after a while it over. And the soprano start sing Ave Maria in Latin.

When I see Fay outside in the cathedral garden I realise it the first time I come face to face with her since the fight we have that night at Matthews Lane. She look good. She look better than how I picture her when I was sitting in the cathedral staring at the back of her head with the black mantilla hanging down. She look like how she used to look before we get married, fresh and alive. She don't seem like she that bothered Henry dead. Is like she take it in her stride, which surprise me because I thought the two of them was close. When she come over to me I make sure I hang on tight to the children, one on each side. She bend down and she try talk to the two of them but they not got nothing to say to her so she straighten up again. I say to her, 'The children quiet right now but it don't mean they don't miss you. Anytime you want to come home is alright with us.' And she just look at me and walk off.

It turn out that Henry die without making a will and so Cicely get everything. The next week after the funeral she call me and ask me to come up Lady Musgrave Road because she got something she want talk to me about. When I get up there she have Ethyl lay out afternoon tea on the veranda just like we used to take it together in the early days. Tin salmon and cucumber sandwiches, cut into little triangles, Earl Grey tea, and Victoria sponge cake.

She spread a little white napkin 'cross her knees and she pour the tea, steadying the teapot lid with her left hand. She even got little cubes of processed white sugar and a pair of tweezer things to lift them up, which make me smile to myself when I think of how much good raw cane sugar we got on this island.

After she stir the tea, she put a piece of quarter sandwich on her little plate and she say to me, 'I have always liked you, Philip, you know that. I sincerely hope so anyway. It is my belief that a man would have to have the patience of Job to make a lasting marriage with Fay, because even though she is my own flesh and blood, I know what a trial she can be. So even though things have not worked out between you, I do not see that as a slight on you in any way. And I hope that you will extend to me the same courtesy in understanding that a mother does what she can even if the children do not turn out as she hopes.'

I sit there balancing this cup and saucer trying to make sure I don't rattle it too much when I reaching over to take the plate and sandwich she passing to me. And I want rest something down, but the little table just a bit too far away for me to do it without standing up and I don't want interrupt Miss Cicely's flow. So I just sit there holding on to everything, which mean I not got nuh hand free to drink the tea or eat the sandwich.

'Which brings me to the reason I asked you here today. As you know, Henry had it in mind that you should have his businesses.'

This is when my ears start prick up.

'I understand that. After all, you are his only son-in-law, and mine, and the two of you are partners in supplying groceries and suchlike to the hotels. And I know you have been doing that together for some good time. But this is my problem: Kenneth. What will Kenneth inherit if I grant this wish of Henry's?'

And she stop. I don't know if she expect me to give a answer. So I just look at her hoping she going carry on.

'Kenneth is not an easy boy. I am sure you have noticed. And even though I have prayed for many long hours, it seems that my prayers are in vain. This is the thing.'

So now I waiting for it.

'If you could see your way to helping Kenneth to learn about the supermarket business then perhaps in a few years' time, when he has mastered his trade so to speak, we could divide the business so that you could have, for instance, the wine merchants and wholesalers, and Kenneth could have the supermarkets. How does that sound to you?'

'Well, Miss Cicely, I think it is very fine of you to be thinking about Kenneth's future. It is what a good mother would do. But I am not sure if Kenneth is that interested in the supermarket business.'

'Let's just give it a try, shall we? And in the meantime let us say that you have control of Henry's business concerns. You are the general manager if you like. Carte blanche. And Kenneth is your apprentice. And as for income, let us just split that fifty-fifty between the two of us, and you can pay Kenneth a salary out of your share. How is that? More tea, Philip?'

When I drive outta Lady Musgrave Road I reckon I feel like how Bill musta feel the first time I meet him. Miss Cicely some shrewd businesswoman. And all this time I think all she doing is making embroidery and shouting at the help and answering all them letters Ethyl tell me she get every week. But she fix me alright, because sorting out Kenneth was the only way I was going to get my hands on Henry Wong's business.

24

Employing Troops

Kenneth not too impressed when I tell him 'bout Miss Cicely's plan. Seem she already explain it all to him and he already done tell her he not doing it, but she not listening to him.

'I ain't no shopkeeper! What you people trying to do to me?'

'Is not me, Kenneth, believe me. I only doing it because it what Miss Cicely ask me to do to try put you on some decent path. She worried 'bout you, that's all.'

'She not worried 'bout me. Since when she worried 'bout anything apart from the good Lord? I dunno what she doing with you, man, but I don't need nobody come put me on any path. I got my own path already.'

Well, I think to myself, Kenneth on the path to hell that is for sure. Not that I got any room to talk.

After a couple of week him show up down the shop and say him going give the supermarket thing a go. Turn out Miss Cicely threaten to throw him outta the house, so Ethyl tell me anyway. And even though Louis DeFreitas him big buddy, Kenneth not so keen to go live in West Kingston without him tennis court and swimming pool and maids. So him make a deal with his mother and he turn up to me.

But even though I try and try, I can't do nothing with Kenneth. Him show up at eight o'clock in the morning but then him gone by ten. Sometime him no come till four o'clock in the afternoon, and when I ask him where he been he just tell me it none of my business. Every job I give him to do he leave half done, or later I find out that he get Milton or Desmond to finish it for him. Then it start happen regular that I get a telephone call from this hotel or another say they nuh get no delivery, and it turn out that Kenneth just leave the van somewhere when him take off to go do something for DeFreitas. Even if I give him a job in the office he can't do it properly. He make mistakes, and he do things untidy, and he talk bad to the customers, but he don't care. I talk to him and talk to him but it nuh make no difference.

All this time I am putting my back into this because I can see it a way for us to get outta the other business, which we need to because just like Zhang say, people feel different these days 'bout the protection. They still paying it, but they got some feeling 'bout it. Plus with all the violence and trouble, the pai-ke-p'iao is slowing because people nuh feel like gambling away their money when the future so uncertain. Then the chicken thing just stop because the Chinaman go get himself arrested. And the business with the girls never pay so good anyway because I always feel bad 'bout taking away them hard-earned living.

We still got the navy surplus even though Bill long gone and we been through I can't remember how many sergeants since then. And we making money from surplus off the hotel construction sites and damaged goods off the docks. In truth, though, it was the hotel business that was really keeping things together. And now Miss Cicely give us a chance to clean up and do things legal and we had to make it work.

But then everything sorta overtake me because the shooting was still going on. It get so bad that on Sunday 2 October 1966 the government declare a State of Emergency in Western Kingston. And in the middle of all this Kenneth get shot. Him never even make it to the hospital. Him just lay there in the street and bleed to death because it took five hours before the police get the situation under control enough to go pick up the wounded.

The first thing I hear about it is when Fay yelling and screaming at me down the telephone 'bout how it all my fault her little brother get killed. That she dunno how I involved in it but she sure it must be me. Kenneth a good boy from a good family just starting to make his way, and now, thanks to me, him dead. She just screaming at me and crying and blubbering so half the time I can't understand a word she saying, except I get something 'bout how she not going let me kill Karl as well. The way she talking to me is like she think I take the gun and shoot Kenneth myself.

I jump in the car and drive up to Lady Musgrave Road. Miss Cicely sitting on the veranda, so I go up to her and I kneel down on the tile floor in front of her, on both knees, and I say to her, 'Miss Cicely, I am so sorry. I just hear about what happen to Kenneth.'

She look down at me and I see how her eyes red from crying, and then she take my two hands and hold them in hers. Her hands fat and warm and comforting.

'It is not your fault, Philip. I know you did your best. Kenneth was not a good boy. We tried. What more can we do? This is just the Lord's way of punishing me for all the things that I should have done and didn't do, and all the things I did that I should have thought better of. This is for me to ponder, not for you to blame yourself.'

After that, everybody start worry 'bout what Fay going to do, because even though Ethyl come tell us a long time since 'bout the letter Fay send to her brother in England nobody really pay it no mind. But now with this Kenneth thing we think maybe we should be taking things a bit more serious.

Judge Finley say to me, 'You think she going try take the children with her when she go to England?'

'She can't do that! How she going do that? Xiuquan fourteen and Mui eleven, and there is not a man alive going help her do a thing like that. Not any man that want to keep on breathing that is. And sure as hell is hell Fay can't pull off a thing like that on her own.'

'Well maybe we should just take some precaution anyway.'

So we decide that Milton and Desmond going take it in turn to watch the children all the time them outta the house. The children don't like it but I tell them it for their own good.

Mui say, 'But we still got to go to school and go see Father Michael.'

And I say OK, but the men going wait for them right outside and when they come outta school or Bishop's Lodge they got to come straight home with Milton or Desmond. And they agree.

A couple of month later Clifton go up to Miami to see Margy Lopez. This is what she start call herself within weeks of being in Florida. The first time she write it in a letter to me I have to ask her on the telephone, 'What this Margy thing? How you pronouncing that? Is it Margy like in Marge?'

'No, Uncle, the "g" not soft like that. It hard like in Marguerite. Margy.'

Anyway, all this time she been living up there she been staying with some of Clifton family. They make a good home for her and now she nineteen she want go to college. I got all the money Charles Meacham been paying every month and I give it to Clifton to take up there with him. Because even though they got all sort of currency restriction they not going search a policeman boarding the plane.

I say to him, 'Is you that keep her outta jail that night and put her on the plane to Miami.'

And him smile and say to me, 'We lucky we didn't all end up in jail that night.'

As soon as Clifton get up there Margy telephone me to say thank you.

'So what you going study at college then?'

'Cosmetics.'

'Cosmetics?'

'You know, lipstick and powder and face cream and such.'

'They got college course for that?'

'They got college courses for everything, Uncle.'

Two days after Clifton gone Milton screech the car up outside the shop and come running in like him tail on fire.

'She take them. She done take them right out from under me.'

'What you talking 'bout?'

'She take them. Miss Fay. She take them.'

I start grab Milton and shake him and slap him a bit to try get some sense outta him till Judge Finley step between us and ease me back. Then I just start spin 'round on the spot because I can't think and I dunno what to do. Hampton put him hand on my shoulder and rest me into a chair.

Finley go over to the telephone and dial the Wong house. Ethyl answer the phone and tell him that Fay not there but she get Miss Daphne for him if he want and him say yes. When Daphne come to the phone she don't want talk to Finley, she want talk to me.

'Fay isn't here, Pao. She went to England this afternoon and she took the children with her.' I don't say nothing because I can't understand what I think I hear her saying to me.

Then I hear her say, 'Are you there? Pao. Are you still there?' I just sitting there holding the receiver.

Finley take it from me and say into it, 'Miss Daphne, it is me, Finley. I wonder if you could kindly tell me what is happening because we not making any sense of it at this end.'

'Fay has gone to England and she has taken the children with her.'

I get up straight away right then and jump in the car and drive to Bishop's Lodge. But Michael not there. So I run 'round to the cathedral and when I open the door I see him laying there in the dark church, flat out on the floor, prostrate in front of the altar. So right then I know him guilty. I run up the aisle and grab him up but he just hang there limp on my arm, and when I look into his face I see that the punishment he getting from his God worse than whatever I was going to do to him. So I just let him go and he fall back on the ground.

It turn out that Fay get the two young police constables that arrest Xiuquan to grab Milton outside Xiuquan's school. And while Mutt was arresting him, Jeff was busy dragging Mui outta the car and forcing her into a taxi cab that Fay got waiting there with her already inside it. And after Xiuquan get into the taxi as well it go to the airport while Milton get haul down the police station and they keep him there till after the plane leave. And they get away with all of this down the station because Clifton in Miami.

'But how many people it take to pull off a thing like that? Where she get the money? Where she get passports? How she organise a thing like that and nobody know nothing 'bout it?'

I tell Judge Finley that we going to England to go get the children back. But he say we can't do that. England not like here. They not going let some Jamaicans just waltz in there and take two children outta they white country. That is kidnapping and the English authorities not going take kindly to that sorta thing.

When Clifton come back from Miami I tell him I want the two constables to pay for it. I want them throat cut and them bodies throw in the sea. I want them beat till they eyes pop outta the socket. I want him cut off their cocks and shove it down their throat. I want him chop off them hands and feet, and arms and legs.

And then I want him to go find the taxi driver and do the same thing to him. And the clerk she get the passport from, and the one who sell her the ticket, and the red cap that carry her bag into the terminal, and the woman who pass her through to them BOAC flight to London Heathrow.

But Clifton and Finley say we can't do none of that. The only people we know for sure involved, that knew what they was doing, was the two constables, and we can't go murder them. They policemen and you can't just go kill two Kingston policemen and it not bring down a heap of trouble on your head.

'So then what you saying is that there is nothing we can do.'

Clifton and Finley do a deep sigh. The two of them at the same time. And then they look at each other. And then they look at me, but they no say nothing.

Then Finley say, 'It would be very bad for business. Plus we could all end up in jail. And it wouldn't bring Mui and Xiuquan back to us.'

Zhang say to me, Sun Tzu say, '*There are some roads not to follow; some troops not to strike; some cities not to assault; and some ground which should not be contested.*'

I open a bottle of Appleton. And when it finish, I open another one.

25

Human Relations

I drink so much I couldn't do nothing. I couldn't even see straight most of the time. All I could do was walk up to Barry Street to fetch the next bottle. Then one day Hampton come in the yard and him got Ethyl follow behind. This is the first time Ethyl ever come to Matthews Lane. Every time she come see me before that she come to the shop. But since I nuh leave Matthews Lane since the children gone I guess this the only way she going see me.

I sitting in a little straight-back chair by the duck pond when the two of them come up the yard and Hampton step up and say to me, 'Ethyl got something to tell yu but she 'fraid in case yu vex with her and she worried what yu going do to her.'

'What I going do to her? You see me do anything to anybody?'

So Hampton step back and push Ethyl forward. She timid and when she start talk she whispering so much I can hardly hear a word she saying.

'You need to talk up, Ethyl.'

So she clear her throat and she say, 'Yes, Mr Philip.' And then after Hampton nod at her, she start, 'The Sunday before Miss Fay take the children I overhear her on the telephone. She was in the living room and I just go in there to put down a vase of fresh flowers like Miss Cicely ask me to and Miss Fay just turn 'round and wave her hand at me and tell me to get out. I didn't even get a chance to put down the vase. It was like she vex with me for going in there. So when I shut the door I just wait outside a little minute and listen. And that is when I hear her say "I will be in the taxi", which make me think that she just making some arrangement with one of her friends. But the way she say it seem a bit funny. And it funny that she didn't want me to hear her, because them not usually worried 'bout that sort of thing. Anyway, the next thing I hear is when she say, "Do you understand?" It nuh sound like . . . well I didn't know what it sound like, but now I realise what funny about it was maybe she was talking to a child. That she not talking to one of her friends after all.'

I just sit and stare at her standing there in front of me. Hampton tell her is OK, she done the right thing. He tell her to go wait down by the gate and he will come directly and drive her home. Then him sorta lean over me, and really look at me like him worried 'bout something.

And then him say to me, 'You alright?'

But I no answer.

So him say, 'I think it best she come tell yu. I reckon yu would want to know. And I think it better if it come from her.' Him wait a bit and then say, 'I going drive her home now if that alright with you.'

'Yes, is alright.' And just as him step away I reach out and grab his arm and say, 'Thank you, Hampton.' And then I shout out to Ethyl as she opening the gate to leave, 'Thank you, Ethyl.'

According to Sun Tzu, Mencius say, *'The appropriate season is not as important as the advantages of the ground; these are not as important as harmonious human relations.'*

The next day I take a shower and shave and get dressed and go 'round to see Michael. The housekeeper don't want to let me in but Michael hear my voice from the next room and shout to her that it OK, she can let me by. When I come into his study he ask the housekeeper, Miss Crawford he call her, to go put on some coffee, and he invite me to sit down in a armchair by the open window. This here is the first time I see him since I grab him up in the cathedral that day. Michael look like he lose some weight, and he look tired.

'I have been meaning to call you.' This is what him say as he sitting down in the armchair next to me.

The window reach down to the ground so when you sit down you can see the garden right there in front of you, and you can catch a nice breeze to take the edge off the afternoon heat.

'That day I grab you up in the cathedral I could see you was suffering. And now I come here and see you like this it seem like you still the same way. So maybe the confession thing switch 'round now and is you that need to tell me what you got on your mind.'

Michael look at me and I can see he got all sort of things going 'round in his head. Is like he can't even think where to begin there is so much he got to tell. But what strike me is it seem like he been waiting and wanting and wishing for me to come over here and ask him 'bout what happened and what he had to do with it.

Right then the door open and Miss Crawford come in with a tray with the coffee and cups and such. She put it on a side table and Michael thank her. When she gone Michael get up and pour the coffee. The rich, heavy smell of the Blue Mountain fill up the room.

When he hand me the cup him say, 'The week before it happened Fay asked me if she could visit with the children on the Sunday when they came to Mass, and I said no.'

Then he sit down next to me with the cup of coffee he pour for himself.

'I told her that if she wanted to visit with the children she would have to make arrangements with you. She became quite distraught over this. It took some time for her to calm down and compose herself. And then she asked me if I would at least allow her to talk to Karl on the telephone.'

Michael stop. I think he get startled at how I suddenly just right then put all my attention on him. It give out a kind of electric shock. So the two of us just sit there and wait for it to pass.

'I don't know why I agreed to it, but I said yes. So on the Sunday before that was what happened. She spoke with him on the phone. Right here in this room because I told Desmond that Karl had to come with me to collect some new missals.' Then him stop. And then him start again. 'I waited outside. I did not eavesdrop on their conversation, but when Karl came out he looked anxious and I asked him if he was OK. He said he was alright so we walked together back to the cathedral to meet up with Mui and Desmond and I thought nothing more of it. Not until after it happened. Because although I knew Fay was planning to go to England I never dreamed that she would take the children with her. I just never even conceived of it.'

'Yu knew she was going?'

'Yes, and I realise that I was an accomplice. Especially in relation to the children. I helped when I should have been trying to do something to stop it.'

'When I find you in the cathedral that day, and when I look at you, it don't seem to me now that you could have been crucifying yourself like that over a telephone call.' And then I thought maybe I shouldn't have said a word like *crucify*.

Michael look outta the window and right then it start to rain. That three-thirty Jamaican rain that flood the place in ten minutes and then ten minutes after that you can't tell it happen except for the fresh smell and the few drops of water still dripping off the banana leaf.

'She wanted me to go with her.'

'She wanted you to go with her? She wanted you to go with her to England?' When I see the flash of panic on Michael's face I suddenly remember where I was so I lower my voice to a whisper and I say, 'She wanted you to go with her to England?' And him nod. 'So what kinda thing is that? You take your priest with you when you kidnap your children and run four thousand miles away?'

Michael run his hand through him hair and then cover him mouth like there is something he don't want to say. He sit there like that with his hand over him mouth for a good while.

Then he say, 'Sin occurs in thought as well as in deed.'

It shock me. I dunno why because it what I been thinking all along anyway. Maybe I didn't expect him to admit it to me just like that.

'You mean in thought *and* deed?'

'No, Pao, just thought.'

And I think well that about right, because if Michael had anything to do with Mui I reckon Fay would have been more interested in the child. But then I think to myself, Michael torturing himself like this just for thinking 'bout it? So I reckon maybe it was more than thought. It was somewhere beyond thought, even if it was short of deed.

I say to him, 'Did you want to go with her?'

Michael think a long time and then him say, 'Some part of me did. Some part of me wanted to go. Some part of me wanted something with her. But the greater part of me knows that my calling is here.'

I look at him and right then I just get up and I raise Michael up outta the chair and I hug him. I hug him close because he was the only man on this earth who understand how I feel, the only man who understand what we lose. Not just because we lose Fay. But because we both lose the children as well.

When I get to Gloria's she open the door and she put her arms 'round me. I let myself lean into her, and right then it feel like the first time my body come to rest since the whole thing happen. So I just stand there and she carry on hold me while she say to me, 'I wonder how long it was going to be before you come.'

I want to tell Gloria everything 'bout what happen, and how Fay do it and 'bout the constables and the taxi driver and what it feel like with the children gone, but I not sure it fair on her. Not sure if it fair for her to have to listen to it when she got all her own feelings 'bout Fay and Mui and Xiuquan, and Esther. So I don't say nothing, I just follow her inside.

She go into the kitchen and start boil the kettle.

'You not got no Appleton?'

'From what Finley tell me you already had plenty enough of that. I fixing us some nice Lipton's.'

Esther come into the kitchen and look at me. And for the

first time it seem like maybe she feel something different from sour to see me standing there. And then she say, 'I'm sorry to hear about what happen,' and she go to the back door and step out into the yard.

Gloria put the tea bags in the pot and she pass the little strings through the handle, and then she pour in the boiling water. After she settle us down with the cup and saucer and everything she take my hand and say to me, 'It like old times, eh?'

And I say, 'Yes, except twenty years done pass us by.'

'I know you tell Clifton you want him to go murder everybody, but who you talk to, Pao? Who you talk to 'bout how you feel inside?'

'I don't talk to nobody. Who you think I going talk to?'

'Me. You can talk to me.'

'What, me talk to you 'bout Fay? I thought that was your one condition?'

'That a long time ago.'

I look at her and I realise she really mean it.

'Since the children gone it like somebody reach in my chest and pull out my heart, and I just walking 'round like a dead man. I don't want to do nothing. I don't even want to get outta bed in the morning. I don't want to shower or shave or dress myself. I don't want to go to work. I don't want to talk to nobody. All I want to do is see the bottom of a glass.

'And as for Fay, I know she never cared for me none, but what I realise today, just this afternoon, is that all the time I spend with Michael give me a feeling like I connected to her. Like being with him give me a way of being part of something that Fay care about, because I really wanted something between us to work. There was so many times I feel like maybe we could have had something good and then some calamity happen like when she go to Matthews Lane, or when she find out 'bout you or the thing with Samuels or when Kenneth get killed. So many times I think we was going step through a new door together but what happen instead was she go through the door on her own and slam it in my face. Just like what happen on the veranda that night up Lady Musgrave Road.

'I really wanted us to be a family, yu know. And now she gone and the children gone, what might have been is never going to be.'

And then I throw myself in Gloria's arms and I cry.

26

Sincerity

When I open my eyes I realise Matthews Lane completely silent. I still hear the dogs barking but that is way out there somewhere. Not here in the yard. The thing that I can't hear is life. I can't hear life going on. I can't hear Ma beating the batter or Tilly picking the saltfish and throwing the skin and bones in the pail, or Hampton sweeping the yard, or Zhang rustling the pages he turning on the Chinese newspaper.

So I get up and pull on some pants and step into the yard to see what going on. I stand on the step of my room and I look 'round. Ma got the bowl in the crook of her arm and the wooden spoon in her hand beating the batter for the saltfish fritters. And I see Tilly there at the sink washing off the saltfish she already soak and boil and drain off the salt water and now she picking off the fish and throwing the skin and bone into the pail. And I look up the yard and Hampton got a yard broom working his way down from the duck pond. And Zhang is sitting there with his rocking chair in the shade reading the paper. And there is not a sound from any one of them.

It so quiet I start wonder if I done lose my hearing. Is only the barking dogs telling me I not got no need to fret 'bout what all that Appleton do to me.

And then I look 'round again and I think it not so much that the place quiet. What wrong with Matthews Lane is that the place empty. The place done lose its energy. Maybe some would say it lose its chi because everybody was going about their business just the same as they always do except there was no substance to it. It was like they a bunch of duppies just waving their arms about but there was nothing there. No intention. Just their empty movement.

Then little by little as the days go by I start notice how Ma grumbling to herself that there is no little hands to help chop a few vegetables, or a little voice that showing interest in how you season the duck or pickle the cabbage. No one eager to wash the rice, or help set up the mah-jongg table, or greet your friends with a warm welcome and a hot bowl of tea, or light a extra incense stick at temple, or just sit with you and pick the bean sprouts, or help cut a few threads on your mending. Now you have to do everything on your own.

Zhang solemn as well. Like he dragging them wooden slippers up the concrete path rather than lift up his feet. All the news in the paper is bad news. Everybody he read about and everybody he know and everybody he talk to is dishonourable and cantankerous. There not one good thing in the whole of Zhang's world. Not like when you have somebody take some interest in history, and the revolution and what is honourable and noble, and wants to know what is the right thing to do in different circumstances, and is a good student of tai chi, who practise hard and ask sensible questions, and who is getting better every day at reading the Chinese newspaper, and who want to understand that there is a connection between the plight and destiny of poor men and women everywhere in the world.

Hampton huffing and puffing with every clunk of them weights on the bench press. Up and down. Up and down. Up and down. With the sweat pouring outta him in the midday sun. It almost like Hampton want to kill himself with exercise. Well what you going do when you not got nobody to play shove ha'penny, or go fishing off the wharf with a hook, line and sinker, or go swimming over Lime Cay, or to bring you two piece of wood that need nail together, or they got string and paper and they want to make a kite, or you need to go get some old truck tyre to take to the beach, or you got to make a cart with wheels that turn. What you going to do if there is no one to ask you 'bout what you and your friends used to get up to when you boys, and what you know 'bout Uncle Xiuquan, and what her papa like when he young? What you going to do apart from pile the next few pounds on the barbell?

The thing I can't understand is how come I no notice when all of this was going on. Mui so busy with everybody in the house, while I was driving from here to there with chickens and cigarettes and paying the child no mind. I try hard to think what it was I do with her because I wasn't making no cart or kite or singing the praises of Sun Yat-sen or Mao Zedong, or picking the root off the bean sprouts. Truth is all I was doing was reading the newspaper and smoking a cigar. I was sitting down in my room or in the little sun trap just outside, outta sight of all of this with the faint sound of it coming to me on a breeze drifting down the yard. And the only thing that I do that seem important to me was to haul the children 'round Chinatown thinking that this was going to be their inheritance like it was mine. And all that happen from that was Xiuquan go get himself arrested and bring me face to face with them two good-for-nothing constables.

I say to Zhang, 'What is it you think the children get from me? I mean it seem like everybody got something they do with them except me. They cooking and talking and playing and what not. What you think I do with them?'

'You teach them tai chi.'

'I start teach them. But every time they got a question is you they running to. Is you they want show off to how well they practise. Well, Mui anyway. Xiuquan don't seem like him that interested. What Xiuquan interested in, yu think?'

Zhang pour more tea and he look 'round the empty yard because Ma at temple and Hampton out doing his chores.

'Life not so easy for Xiuquan. Mui she spend much time Matthews Lane. Xiuquan he spend much time Lady Musgrave Road. Mui she learn ask question. Xiuquan he learn stay quiet.

Mui she ask question in own head and tell you what on her mind. Xiuquan he got question in head but he not telling you nothing. Or maybe he tell people up Lady Musgrave Road. I don't know.'

'What question she ask you?'

'Like she say, "In 1865 Paul Bogle and his comrades marched up to the courthouse in Morant Bay to protest about the injustice and abuses suffered by the people. He did not shoot his neighbour. He went to the authorities to air the many grievances of which the peasants of the parish complained. Why don't the people today go to the authorities with their grievances?" And I say to her, maybe because they do not believe that the authorities are going to listen to them. And she say, "The authorities didn't listen to Paul Bogle. They hanged him. That is why we struggled so hard for self-government and the right to government of the people, by the people, for the people. So how come a hundred years later the people still can't get their grievances heard?" '

'But where she get all of this from?'

'You. She get from listen to you. "Killing your neighbour not going solve unemployment and poverty. Foreign investors taking all the profit. The masa don't even have to beat the slave any more in Jamaica." This is you. Mui listen good and then she make up her own mind. The night you and Fay fight, Xiuquan confused but Mui know exactly where she want to be, and it with you.'

27
Courage

Sun Tzu say, *'If a general is not courageous he will be unable to conquer doubts or to create great plans.'*

I sit there on the veranda and I look at Miss Cicely and she just say to me, 'The children were silent when they were here. Maybe Mui played some game with the maids, but Karl sat silent and read his comic book under the mango tree, or comforted his mother who was often distraught.'

'And what about when Father Kealey come to visit?'

'That was strictly a private matter between him and Fay. The children did not seem to be a part of that although it was obvious that Mui thought a great deal of him, and he in turn was very fond of her.'

'But what about Xiuquan?'

'Like I said, Karl read his comic book and watched television.' And then she start look around like she already done finish with the conversation. She already done tell me everything and she can't think what else there may be to say. She even get up and walk over to the edge of the veranda to go check what Edmond busy doing 'round the side of the house. Then Ethyl bring some cool lemonade and pour it out, and Miss Cicely sit down and take a sip and say to me, 'The thing that interests me, Philip, is why you are so concerned about how the children spent their time here. And why now? It didn't seem to me that you were concerned previously.'

I dunno what to say to her. Miss Cicely don't think that children is a proper subject for men to be interested in. She tell me that a long time ago when I ask her 'bout marrying Fay. Or maybe it was more like Henry Wong didn't think it was a concern for men. So I decide to just tell her the truth.

'I miss them, Miss Cicely. Everybody miss them. Matthews Lane like a ghost town with everybody just going about their chores in silence. It like the life take outta the place.'

She look at me and then she have a little think to herself and she say, 'It is unusual for me to hear a man speak this way. I did not realise you had such feelings in you. I thought you just concentrated on business . . .' she pause a little '. . . and, well, the other things that men think about. You are quite a surprise, Philip. Really.'

'What was it like for you, Miss Cicely, having the children here, and now they gone?'

She take a sip of lemonade and pick up a fan off the table and start move the air. She fanning her face this side and that and I can see the relief it bringing her.

'The children brought a much-needed breath of fresh air into the house. Well Mui anyway. Karl was a different matter. He was always rather sullen. A very frightened boy. I suspect he spent too much time concerned about his mother. Not a healthy preoccupation for a boy, or any child I dare say. And although some children know how to balance their concerns with more carefree pastimes, Karl was not one of them. He was a sad boy in many ways. Devoted to Fay of course, and given the deficiencies of my relationship with her, Karl did not care for me a great deal.'

Miss Cicely examine her lemonade and then she carry on.

'Mui? Well, Mui is Mui. I'm sure you know what I mean, Philip. She is quite a free spirit, isn't she? A live wire you might say. Although quite where she gets some of her ideas I cannot imagine.'

I don't say nothing. I just sit there and look at Miss Cicely like I can't imagine either.

'Yes, she was full of invention, and games that frankly I sometimes had to put a stop to so as to enable the maids to get on with their work. Nevertheless, one could not help but grow fond of her and feel kindly towards her concern for those less fortunate. An admirable quality, I'm sure, despite her liking for that word "plight". One can only hope that her love for Father Kealey and the Catholic Church will help her to learn to express herself in more Christian terms.'

And then she stop and look at me. Right then Daphne step out on to the veranda and ask if she can come join us, so I say it alright with me and I look at Miss Cicely who just sorta raise her eyebrows and nod her head. So Daphne sit down and next thing Ethyl come out to see what Daphne want to drink and she say for Ethyl to bring her some of the sorrel they just finish making and then she say to me, 'Would you like some sorrel, Pao?' And I say yes but I notice how Miss Cicely pick up her embroidery and start sewing again like she was doing before I get there. For me the sorrel over sweet and it need more ginger. But it cool and refreshing so I drink it down.

I say to Daphne, 'Me and Miss Cicely just talking 'bout how the house now with the children gone.'

Daphne look at me like she wish she nuh bother sit down. 'Well of course, they were only here intermittently. Karl more often than Mui and he was a very quiet boy.'

'So it don't seem no different to you then?'

'It's difficult to say. Maybe after time passes without a visit. Maybe you come to notice their absence.'

Then Miss Cicely look up from her sewing and say, 'You surprise me, Daphne. I thought you and Karl were quite close.'

Daphne look like she dunno why Miss Cicely want to go say a thing like that. Like she think Miss Cicely done let out some big secret.

'Well I wouldn't say close exactly although we would talk together from time to time. He was here much more often than Mui, but then I have already said that.'

'Didn't you get some books so that you and he could find out all about England?'

Daphne spin her head 'round and look so fierce at Miss Cicely I didn't know she had that sorta fury in her. But Miss Cicely still concentrating on her needlework and she no pay Daphne no mind.

So I say to her, 'You do that?'

'Pao. You have to understand. Fay had made up her mind. I was just helping Karl to come to terms with it, trying to help him see it as a positive, a new experience, a new adventure if you like.'

I can feel my blood boiling but I don't say nothing. I just let her carry on and give myself a moment in case I go do something really bad in front of Miss Cicely.

'Something to look forward to rather than something to dread. It was going to happen. That was not in question. So it was a matter of what attitude he was going to have about it.'

'What attitude? And what attitude did he have?' Daphne nuh say nothing. So I say, 'What attitude did Mui have?'

'Mui didn't know anything about it. We thought it better to keep it that way with her.'

'We? You mean you and Fay? You and Fay that was busy plotting to take my children away from me?'

'It wasn't like that.'

'So what was it like?'

Then Miss Cicely say, 'I brought up the matter of the book because I did not want us to sit here talking in a way that turns a partial truth into a complete lie. It is true that the children were only here intermittently and also true that Karl was here more often than Mui. But it is not true to suggest that there was no engagement with them. And especially not true to suggest that there was no engagement with him.'

I sit there listening to Miss Cicely but I looking at Daphne because I can't believe she betray me like this. After everything I do, what with her meeting the Queen of England, and shopping in Miami, and how many hours I sit right here on this veranda and pass the time of day with her. After all of this she still go behind my back and help Fay take the children from me.

'Why you no come to me, Daphne, and tell me what Fay was planning?' But she don't have no answer. She just sit there with her eyes fix on the tile floor.

'You know how much it would mean to me that Fay take the

children away. You nuh care that Mui nuh seem like she want to get on no aeroplane to England? None of this matter to you?'

Miss Cicely say, 'What is done is done. We must believe that Daphne had her own reasons. Just like Fay had her own good reasons. The question is where do we go from here?'

I just sit there looking at Daphne and then I say, 'I come here today to ask you to give me Stanley's address in England so I can at least write a letter to my children.'

Before Daphne get a word out, Miss Cicely say, 'I am afraid I cannot help you with that, Philip. Stanley and I have never corresponded since the day he left to join the Queen's Royal Air Force. Not a whisper have I ever heard from him.'

I turn to Daphne and she say, 'I can't do that, Pao. I promised Fay I wouldn't do it.'

I have to control myself because all I want to do is get up and walk 'cross the veranda and give Daphne a box in the mouth. That is all I can see in my mind's eye. My arm swinging through the air and slapping her face and her head swivelling 'round to the side and her hair flying and the blood spurting from her nose and the split lip she got when her head swing back and me stepping back outta the way so the splash don't catch my shoes.

But I don't do none of that. I just sit there as still as I can and I say, 'Daphne, is not like I can even do anything. I don't know nobody in England to go cause no trouble. I not going risk a English jail to go try kidnap the children. I not going plague Fay to make her come back here. All I want to do is write a letter to my children. You can't understand that?'

She sit there but I know she not think nothing 'bout what I say to her. I know she only waiting for me to finish talking just so she can pause and say, 'I can't do it, Pao.'

When Ethyl come to see me the next week she tell me that Miss Cicely try to make Daphne tell me Stanley's address but she still won't do it.

'Miss Daphne say she understand how yu feel but she promise

her sister. That yu shouldn't feel so bad. Maybe Miss Fay not the best person for yu. Maybe yu realise yu better off without her. Maybe yu find somebody else that treat yu better and have some other children.'

So I say to her, 'Ethyl, all the time yu busy running to the post office with Miss Fay's letters to her brother did yu ever think to maybe make a note of the address?'

And she say, 'No, Mister Philip. It never dawn on me to go do a thing like that, but I know it in London somewhere.'

28

Resilience

When Judge Finley tell me that while I was busy trying to drink every drop of Appleton they got on the island Hampton and Desmond go find the two constables and give them a hiding I say to him, 'Yu serious? Yu mean them same two constables that help Fay take the children?'

'Yah, man.'

'They lose their mind? Wasn't it you and Clifton that sit right there and tell me there wasn't nothing we could do 'bout them two piece of shit?'

'We say yu couldn't go kill them like you want, but they could take a hiding so Desmond and Hampton go do it.'

'So how bad they hurt them?'

'It not too bad. They survive. They alright.'

'And what happen after that?'

'Nothing.'

'Nothing? Yu sure?' And Finley just nod him head. 'So how long ago they go do all that?'

'Six, maybe eight week.'

'And nothing happen?'

'Nothing.'

'And what Mutt and Jeff doing now?'

'They was off work a little while, but now they back in the police station just carry on like nothing happen. I reckon they know they do wrong and they take the punishment and now it done.'

Then George Morrison say Margaret want to go back to Scotland. So I ask him what she want to go do a thing like that for, and he say she not feel so comfortable here in Jamaica no more. There no place for her and her work.

'She says Jamaica is changing. She says that even though we have been here for so many years she will never be Jamaican. She will never be able to claim the dream of a truly independent and equal Jamaica. She will always be on the wrong side of that power divide. She says it is different for the white Jamaicans who were actually born here. They have birthright. She does not.'

'And what do you say, George?'

'Jamaica is my home and you are my family; Finley, Clifton, Hampton. I cannot even begin to imagine a life without you. There is nothing for me in Edinburgh except the dark winter and biting cold.'

'And yu son?'

'John is a child but a Jamaican. Half Chinese and half English, I know, but a Jamaican through and through. After all, which Jamaican does not have a little mix of this and that? But he is only five years old so he will have to go with Margaret.'

'So what you going to do, George?'

'I am conflicted. I came here over twenty-five years ago because it was what Margaret wanted and now she wants to go back I cannot find it in my heart to follow. Yet I know that she would be devastated to return to Scotland without me and I would miss her deeply. Well I can't even conceive of it. So I have agreed with her that we will go for a visit and explore the possibilities.'

So George getting ready to go back to Scotland and Finley decide that maybe George can go see if he can find where Stanley at, and Fay and the children. After all, Scotland only at the top of England. It seem like a good idea to me. He going that way anyway and then he can send back word to us 'bout what is happening.

189

But George not the only one going. They jumping on the plane by the dozen and they not looking back. And when I start take notice I see how things on the island getting real bad. Sure enough some people make a lot of money after Independence with all the development that was going on, but at the same time we had very high unemployment, and since we nuh got no welfare, the poor was just getting poorer, and the difference was really showing. Worse than anything we had before. Them with the money was affording the high life, mansions in Beverly Hills, Mercedes-Benz. They was busy buying up everything and hiring more help and jetting all over the place. The poor was just getting sick and tired and desperate.

The whole thing cause me a big problem as well because Chinatown was on the move. All these people I deal with all these years suddenly start take off for Canada or the US, and the ones that stay behind move uptown or go to Port Antonio, or Ocho Rios or Montego Bay like what Round One Chin do. Pretty soon, there was going to be nobody left in Chinatown to protect, because the people moving in didn't need or want no protection from me. They got that all sorted out themselves.

And as far as the gambling go nobody want do it. They too busy saving their hard-earn cash for the next flight to Miami. Plus with all this unemployment and poverty what happen was a big increase in street trade, which mean business really take a dive for the girls stuck in them East Kingston houses. So they start talking 'bout go working on the street, and no matter how much I try talk them out of it, they do it anyway because that is the only way they can see to beat the competition. All the time I just worry for them, because I remember how all them years back Gloria's sister get mash up by the American sailor bwoy and I think how I never want to see a sight like that again, or worse, that one of them go get killed.

The construction surplus, the goods off the dock, that all finish. Too much competition, too many people trying to make ends meet.

Finley say to me, 'Yu think George going stay in Scotland?'

And I say to him, 'Can you see George Morrison going back to regular doctoring in some cold, dingy hospital where he have to actually tend to the real sick and dying every day and at the end of the month they give him some little pay cheque that wouldn't last a afternoon at Caymanas Park racecourse, where the most exciting thing going happen to him is reading little John's school report and where he got to face the dark and the wind and the snow, and go back to being a church-going sober Presbyterian day in day out? Can you see that?'

And Finley look at me and just say, 'No.'

Well, whether or not he stay there, Morrison was going to Scotland so I reckon he could have a go anyway at looking for Stanley. But the truth was we didn't really have nothing to go on. Looking for Stanley Johnson was going to be like looking for a needle in a haystack, there was that many Jamaican ex-servicemen in London. Stanley and Fay could have been anywhere.

And when I was busy telling all of this to Michael him just look at me and say, 'I have the address, Pao.'

I can't believe my ears. After all this upset with Daphne and planning with Morrison, Michael sit down there as calm as you please and just say, 'I have the address.'

'Yu have the address? Stanley address?'

'Yes.'

'Where yu get it from?'

'Fay wrote to me.'

'Fay wrote to yu?' I talking so loud everybody in the fry-fish and bammy shack turn 'round and looking at me like maybe they think I going start a brawl. So I calm myself down and I say to him, 'Michael, how long you have the address? Yu nuh know I desperate to find where the children at?'

'It was a personal letter to me, Pao, about how she was finding life in England. It was the sort of letter one would write to one's priest.'

'Come on, Michael, we gone past that now. We both know that

any letter Fay write to you wasn't no letter that one would write to one's priest.' And I sorta mimic him because I was getting vex.

'Well I assure you that my reply was entirely the sort of response one might expect to receive from one's priest.'

And that much I believe is true. Michael already punish himself enough over Fay to go get catch up in a whole load of letter writing that going mash up him chances of making archbishop, because as well as everything else that Michael Kealey is, I discover over the years that him also ambitious. He know he get away with the Fay thing one time already and he not going chance it another time 'round.

'I received a letter from Mui as well.'

'And yu no say nothing to me? Jesus Christ, Michael, I can't believe yu. Honest to god. As if the secret catechism classes not enough, now yu have to go do this. Why yu nuh say nothing to me?'

'Pao.'

'Yes, I know. I sorry 'bout the blaspheming, but honestly, Michael.' And I calm down and I lower my voice and I see the rest of the customers resting a bit easier because after all Michael sitting there still wearing the little dog-collar thing.

'It only arrived yesterday and I knew I was seeing you today so I brought it with me.' And he take the envelope outta his pocket and hand it to me. When I turn it over I see it say 'Sealed and not to be opened by anyone except Father Michael'. I take out the piece of paper and start read.

Dear Father Michael,

I hope you are well. I am sorry not to have written to you before but I have been very busy settling into my new school, and I also know that Mama has been keeping you up to date with our news.

The lessons at school are the same – reading, writing and arithmetic – but not as much fun. The other children do not seem so friendly.

Uncle Stanley's house is small but he has made us welcome and

192

Mama says we should be grateful, which I am because otherwise we would not have anywhere else to live in England where it seems I must stay for the time being anyway.

I was not so happy about it at first which is partly why I did not write to you because Mama said you knew all about us coming to England so I was cross with you, and I only wrote to my papa instead. But I am not cross any more. England is not too bad. It seems OK. And since I miss you I thought I would write. Our parish priest is not like you. He is a very serious old man who I don't think likes children very much.

I have a favour to ask. Could you please ask my papa why he has not written back to me? Maybe he did not get my letter because I just wrote Yang Pao, Matthews Lane, Kingston, Jamaica because I did not know the post office box number.

I would be grateful if you could tell me his answer when you write back with all your news.
Love
Mui

I fold the letter and put it back in the envelope.

'I didn't know about her taking the children. Honestly, Pao. She asked me to go with her but there was no mention of the children and I never dreamed that she would do as she did. It was not in my reckoning. If Fay had mentioned it to me I would have counselled her to think again about the whole enterprise. You must believe me.'

'Is alright. I believe you, Michael. I know Fay taking the children hurt you almost as much as it hurt me. Maybe just as much, I don't know. Thank you for sharing this with me though.' And I hand the letter back to him. 'It means a lot to me to think that Mui write to me even if I never get the letter. But how come Fay let her write all of that to yu?'

'The envelope was sealed in the way you see and Fay simply enclosed it in her own letter to me.'

I think to myself so he get one letter from her and he reply and now he get another letter and god knows how many others in between. I take a deep breath but I don't say nothing 'bout it.

'So yu going give me Stanley's address so Morrison can go see what he can see?'

'I will, Pao, under two conditions. Firstly, that George Morrison does not make contact with anyone in Stanley's household including, obviously, Fay and the children. I do not want it exposed that I have given the address to you. Secondly, that you do not write to Mui at that address until we have worked out the best, most discreet way for you to communicate with them. I don't think that you writing to Stanley's address would be advisable.'

'So what return address yu think Mui give in the letter she send to me if it not Stanley's address?'

'I do not know, but neither do I understand why you have not received her letter. I would have thought that most postal workers in Kingston would have found the way she addressed it sufficient without need for a post office box number.'

I nuh understand what Michael is saying to me. And then I get it. He think the letter never get mailed. And when I think 'bout how angry Fay was with me and how she nuh want me to have nothing to do with the children I reckon maybe Michael got a point. Maybe Fay never send the letter. So I agree to him two conditions and him give me the address he already write on a piece of thin card him take outta him pocket.

Three weeks later Michael tell me that he been in touch with Fay and she agree for me to write to the children but she have a condition. She say I can write as many letters as I want but I must not say anything that criticise or undermine her. That I must not interfere with anything that she doing in England, especially if it involve the children, and I must not make any plan to take the children back to Jamaica. She bring the children to England for their safety and she don't want them taken back to no war zone like the way Jamaica is. And if she suspect that I doing any of them things, even if she get the slightest whiff, she going move house and I never hear from any of them again.

'That is some strong threat she making there,' I say to Michael. But him just sit there. Well, I negotiate enough deals to know that take-it-or-leave-it look on a man face. And the truth is I can't do nothing 'bout what Fay doing in England anyway, even though I reckon she must have do it illegally because I can't understand how she can take the children outta the country like that when she not got no divorce. Still, I reckon she doing what she think best for them so why would I want to criticise her for that? Jamaica is a war zone. The children safer in England, that is true. And as far as her threat 'bout moving house and disappearing go, the children getting older all the time so she can't enforce that even if she want to. Mui eleven now and Fay can't stop her. So the situation what it is. Like Miss Cicely say, 'What is done is done,' and the best thing I can do is try to take a positive view for the children sake.

So I say alright to Michael. I think the whole thing help Michael feel better 'bout himself that he able to fix something after all the guilt he have over Xiuquan and the telephone call and him too stupid not to ever think that Fay would take the children with her. I think he feel that he make amends now, and I think I feel it too.

The only problem I got is that George Morrison already leave for Scotland and the last thing I want now is for Fay to look outta some window and see Morrison standing there 'cross the street. That would make her convinced for sure that I was up to something. And worse, that I go break my word to her. But no matter how much I ring and ring the telephone number Morrison give me I can't get no answer. The days ticking by and I thinking any minute now this thing going turn into another calamity.

In between telephoning George I start wondering what I going write in this here letter. What can I tell them 'bout things because in truth everything here is a mess. Unemployment, poverty, shortages, violence. The foreigners own all of the bauxite and aluminium industry, more than half the sugar industry, well over half of the tourist industry and a big chunk of the new manufacturing industry. So no matter how hard the people work the

195

foreigners still taking out the profit and Jamaica not got no capital to invest in herself. She still the slave working to make the masa rich.

So I think to myself what future Mui and Xiuquan really got here? Next thing you know Xiuquan mix up with some bad element and him end up dead just like Kenneth Wong, because after all the commotion die down over the bow and arrow what I discover was that it wasn't the first time. Xiuquan been taking stuff from all over town without paying for it. That night was just the first time anybody catch him. And afterwards Ethyl tell me that when him up Lady Musgrave Road Xiuquan following after Kenneth any chance him get. So maybe he was heading that way.

And what 'bout Mui? What kinda life is waiting for her back here? When my brother leave Jamaica him tell me he wanted to be more than a Chinaman in Chinatown. And Mui deserve better than that too. She too smart to come back here and follow in my footsteps. So maybe Fay right after all. I sit down and I write.

Dear Mui,
My heart warmed when I heard from Father Michael that you had written to me even though I never received your letter. I am also glad to hear that you are well and school is good. Perhaps you should try harder to make friends with the other children. They may not be used to meeting such a very smart and loving Jamaican girl like you.

All is well here. Everybody misses you and send their love – Zhang, Ma, Hampton, Finley and everyone. And even though I am very sad that you are not here with me I think perhaps your mama is right that England is a better place for you right now so that you can grow up peacefully without all of this trouble we have down here.

And then I stop writing and I think should I be writing to the two of them? Or maybe I should write a separate letter to Xiuquan? But what play on my mind all the time is that he knew. He knew and he plan and plot with Fay so she could do what she done. He never even give me a chance to see if I could make it up with Fay and keep this family together. He just go ahead and let the three of them take off.

I think to myself I know two Yang Xiuquan, and both of them betray me. One with the tales him tell to Zhang, and the other one with the plotting he do with Fay. And both of them leave me. One to become a farmer in America and the other one to follow his mother to England. So maybe it was a mistake me naming the boy Xiuquan. Maybe Fay was right when she decide to just start call him Karl.

So I finish the letter.

I hope both your mama and Karl are well. Say hello to the both of them for me.
With much love
Papa

I put it on the side because I can't bring myself to mail it without knowing what going on with Morrison.

And then a couple days later I finally get through to him.

'Where the hell you been, man? I been ringing you for well over two weeks.'

'We've been in the Highlands visiting some of Margaret's family.'

'Visiting family? While I been going mad down here wondering what the hell you doing.'

'Is something wrong?'

'Never mind 'bout wrong. What yu do 'bout tracking down Stanley and Fay and the children?'

'Pao, I just got here and since we arrived we have had to visit every one of Margaret's sisters to introduce them to John.'

'So yu no go down to England yet?'

'No.'

'Good. Don't bother go down there. The problem solved.'

So I mail the letter and when I get Mui's reply she tell me all sort of things 'bout her school and what it like at Stanley's house. And how Fay got a job working in a office, which surprise the hell outta me because I never think Fay would ever do a thing like that. Get a job. So it make me realise how serious she is 'bout making a future for the children.

Mui write: 'You asked me to say hello to Mama and Karl, which I have done but I do not understand why you did not call him Xiuquan. Is there a reason?'

And when she finish send her love to everybody she say, 'I hope Gloria and Esther are well.' And she sign it with a PS. 'England is fine, Papa. But Jamaica is my home and that is where I want to be. I know that you will understand that.'

When I write back to her I just say, 'I decide to call him Karl as a way to maybe have a new beginning.'

29

Resourcefulness

Early in 1969 Norman Manley retire and him son, Michael, get elected as leader of the People's National Party, the PNP, which at the time was the opposition party in Parliament. The first time I hear Michael Manley it was on the Rediffusion and he was saying 'Better must come'.

So I start read 'bout the PNP's 'politics of participation', and them four basic commitments to create a Jamaican economy that was 'less dependent on foreign control, an egalitarian society based on equality and opportunity, a truly democratic society, and a society proud of its history and heritage'. It put me in mind of Sun Yat-sen and Mao Zedong and Zhang, and my own father, Yang Tzu. And it seem like maybe there was still a chance for us. Still a chance that Jamaica could hope for a better future. And when I go listen to Manley speak at one of him rallies he stand up there and say: 'We come too far, we're not turning back now. We come too far, we're not turning back now. We have a pride now. We have a place now. We have a mission now. And I say to you, my friends, together we are going to march forward under God's heaven building democratic socialism. Glory to socialism.'

And that was it. That was me and Michael Manley because this was how we was going to create a fair and just Jamaica. Just like how Zhang talk 'bout the right of the ordinary woman and man to live a decent life free from the tyranny of warlords and the domination of foreigners. This was the same thing, only now we wanted social justice and fair distribution of wealth, and we wanted to ease out from under so much foreign economic control.

When Michael Manley win the general election in 1972 I celebrate more than I done for Independence ten years earlier, because this time it really seem to mean something. It wasn't just that we going take over governing ourselves. It was like we really going do something. We really going make it different, like Manley say, we were going to 'walk through the world on our feet and not on our knees'.

Manley buy the public utilities, and take over all the foreign-owned sugar estates and a heap of the hotels. So instead of one man own one plantation, now we had workers' co-operatives, and small farmers working the land that nobody used to do nothing with. People was learning to read and write. There was day care and community centres. Plus the government bring out new labour legislation that replace the old Master and Servants Law and them introduce a minimum wage.

It was a new Jamaica. It was a new vision. It was new hope.

Judge Finley say to me, 'You all excited 'bout Michael Manley, but not everybody so happy with him.'

'What yu mean?'

'Yu nuh notice how many of them jumping on a flight to Miami since him introduce all these changes and especially since the property tax?'

'If yu going to redistribute you have to take from somebody to give to somebody else. That is how it work. Anyway, they can afford it.'

'Well, maybe they don't want to because them got five flights a day to Miami and every one of them getting fuller day by day.'

Finley was right. I just think to myself good riddance. If them don't want every woman and man to have a roof over them head, fair wages and equal opportunities, then let them go.

But what catch my attention was how all of them so busy trying to smuggle money off the island. They got US dollars stuff in them beehive hairdos, sew in the lining of them clothes and straw baskets, bury in cakes and little patties, stick to them leg and then put plaster over it like the leg broke. It was high adventure, that what it was. And every day in the newspaper there was more news 'bout people getting stop at the airport and where them got the US dollars hid.

But they carry on do it anyway, because they wasn't going leave them money behind. And they didn't seem to care nothing 'bout it being illegal under the Exchange Control regulations.

By the time we get to 1974 and 1975 things really getting bad because all we got is half the supermarket and wholesale business and although that going alright it not really enough to keep everybody going. The men getting restless. Sun Tzu say, '*When the troops continually gather in small groups and whisper together the general has lost the confidence of the army.*' So I start worry that I going lose some of them. Most likely Milton and Desmond. Me, Hampton and Finley been running together since we fourteen so I reckon we going stick together no matter what.

Sun Tzu say, '*A skilled commander seeks victory from the situation and does not demand it of his subordinates*', but I don't know how to make it mean anything. All I can think is there is some opportunity here if I can only figure out what.

When I write to Mui I say:

I know you want to come home but business is very bad down here. So it is better for you to stay in England for now. I sent Karl the money he asked me for to open up his nightclub so maybe you can help him with that. Why he want to call it the Opium Den I don't know. I suppose that is his business. But whatever you doing you need to study, because when the time come for you to come back it would be good to have a trade, like being a barrister like Norman Manley. That way you will really be able to help the people.

Then one day Margy telephone me. She finish her college course and move to New York where she do some other course and some other course, and now she working in a cosmetics company.

201

'What you do there?'

'I scout out new products and find ways to sell them.'

'You think you could do that for yourself if I set you in business?'

'Are you serious, Uncle?'

'Yah, man. But we need to have the company registered office in America, can be New York or anywhere you like, but New York is good. And we have to have a subsidiary here on the island.'

We set up Yang Cosmetics Company, which import raw materials and export locally enriched face creams, body lotions and other beauty products. The company registered in New York with business premises in Port Antonio. This is where Margy want to live when she on the island, because she think it truly beautiful over there.

The cosmetics company allow us all sorta currency exchange so now I am selling US dollars to all these rich Jamaicans in such a hurry to leave. We passing the US dollars through the cosmetics company and the Jamaican dollars through the supermarkets. And as these people getting to Canada and the US they helping me move more money through the imports and exports because they reckon they helping others like them to get their money out.

Everything turn out fine because I was selling US dollars at ten times the official exchange rate to people who would rather have US $100,000 in a American bank account than a million Jamaican dollars in Kingston. Especially since constant devaluation mean that the Jamaican dollar worth less and less even while it just sitting there in the bank. Plus, doing business with me mean that they nuh take no risk of getting caught at the airport and getting their money confiscated. Business was booming.

I make sure I put a good roll in the bishop's collection box because all the time now he got more and more projects for poor relief. And I stand by Michael Manley and his land and welfare reforms.

30

Wisdom

Zhang take sick. I call Morrison and tell him to come take a look because Morrison only last six month in Scotland before he tell Margaret he can't take it no more and she say she want John finish his education in Edinburgh and it alright with her if Morrison do what he got to, so he come back to Jamaica and breathe a big sigh of relief. When him come he say Zhang got pneumonia. Him say Zhang probably got more than that wrong with him but he would have to go to hospital to find out. But Zhang say him not going to no hospital. So that was that.

When Morrison ask Zhang how old he is him say he dunno. I dunno how old Zhang is and it turn out Ma dunno either. It seem like Morrison think Zhang just sick from old age, which don't surprise me none because when I come to Jamaica thirty-seven years ago Zhang was already a old man with grey on his head.

'I can treat the pneumonia but I suspect this is just a secondary infection. My guess is there is more to it, but if he won't come for tests I don't know what else we can do.'

When I tell Zhang what Morrison say, he say he not taking none of Morrison's medicine. He say him live this long time without a doctor and he going go to the herbalist and get something fix himself. But just as he try get up off the cot he fall back again. This make him vex so he just lay there and start mumbling and grumbling to himself.

Ma say it alright, she going go to the herbalist and sort it out. Zhang don't need no medicine from the imperialists. And she give Morrison a look and brush past him as she going up the yard with a bowl of red-wine broth for Zhang.

The day after that Ma tell me she going have Hampton move Zhang's cot into her room and I say no, she can put him in my room. It bigger and it got better light what with the two wooden doors that open out on to the little concrete square that catch the sun. When Hampton move the cot, Ma also get him move Zhang's rocking chair and she put it in the room with him and that is where she start sleep every night.

I move into the room next door that was Ma's room and every night I hear them talking and talking to one another till I fall asleep to the sound of it. And when I wake up next morning it still going on.

I can't get over how much they got to say to one another, because in all these years I can't remember ever seeing them talk to each other, not even once. It get so I start think that Zhang nuh talk to no women, because the only women I see him with is Ma and Tilly and he nuh speak to neither of them. It make me wonder what go on between the two of them all the time I not there. Maybe that is when they talk. But then I can't understand why they would do that. Why it would matter whether I see them talk to one another or not. Or maybe that not it. Maybe they just save it all up till now. Maybe they catching up on everything that happen since Zhang leave China in 1912.

Some nights I even lay there awake on purpose, just listening to them hushed voices. Just so I can marvel at it. Because even though I can't make out what they saying I can hear the tone of it, and I can hear them laugh. And that, the laughing, I never hear before, not from either one of them.

Ma got Zhang's cot in the middle of the room with his head lying eastward. She tend to everything he need, and three times a day she boil up the herbs and give it to him. On the days him well enough to sit up, Finley and Tartan Socks McKenzie come play dominoes. When him too weak, Ma read the Chinese newspaper to him, and on other days McKenzie read him the *Gleaner* and they talk 'bout politics just like they always do. McKenzie telling Zhang all 'bout what Manley doing and it seem to lighten his heart.

Ma go to temple while me or McKenzie sit with Zhang because she don't like leave him on his own. She tell me she praying to the Buddha for a peaceful passing for Zhang and enlightenment on him rebirth. She stop tell me that she praying for me to be a better man. She stop chastise me 'bout how I supporting the imperialists by doing business with them. She stop sniffing at me every time I go see Gloria or when anything get mentioned that connected to Gloria in any way whatsoever. All she concentrating on now is Zhang. Funny thing is it seem like she happy. There is a lightness in her spirit. Not that she happy Zhang sick, but that she happy she caring for him.

Zhang pass away one night in him sleep with Ma sitting there in the rocking chair still talking to him. Next morning she tell me I have to take care of things because I the eldest son. I dunno what to do because when they bring my father back from Shaji I was too young to know what was happening. So Ma show me and she help me. We lay Zhang's body on a mat on the floor and we cover it with a white muslin shroud. We place two Chinese coins in a large porcelain bowl and cover it with a cloth. And then we go outside and catch some water in another bowl and burn some candles and firecrackers and throw them into it. And this is the water that we pour into the other bowl on top of the coins to wash Zhang's body. Afterwards the whole house join in wailing.

We announce Zhang's passing by pasting a notice on the outside of the gate. And the evening before the funeral, when Zhang's body come back from the undertakers, the Chinatown merchants come 'round to pay their last respects.

I write a letter to my brother in America.

Dear Xiuquan,

Zhang died peacefully in his sleep. He missed you these past years. He tried to imagine your life in America but could not. Ma is well, although she also misses you, as do I.

Pao.

The reply I get from him vex me, so I didn't bother say nothing to Ma. I just pretend to her like I never hear nothing from him.

On the day of the funeral Ma have me place a pearl in Zhang's mouth and put a willow twig in his right hand to sweep away demons from his path, and a fan and handkerchief in his left. She put up the ancestral tablet bearing Zhang's name.

The funeral procession wind its way through the neighbourhood to the Chinese cemetery, with its white paper lanterns and banners and the musicians them playing some godawful twingtwang, because one thing the Chinese cannot do is make music. They can make food, so there was plentiful roast pig and fruit and cakes and such. But music, no. That was just a damn racket. The whole of Chinatown turn out including Merleen Chin, Clifton Brown, Finley and his wife, Hampton, Ethyl, Milton and Desmond.

The coffin completely covered with a silk pall, *kuan chao*, embroidered in a hundred colours that Chin get from China and bring with him when he come down from Montego Bay. And walking ahead of the coffin was Tartan Socks who scatter the road money to buy the goodwill of malicious spirits so they don't molest the wraith of Zhang on his way to the grave. Ma, she just walk behind Zhang coffin slow and quiet. Whatever she was thinking or feeling she was keeping to herself. Just the way she do her whole life when it come to her and Zhang. Madame Chin walk next to her thinking she was going to have to give some comfort. But it not so. Ma was straight and upright like it was a walking meditation she was doing, with peace in every step.

When it all done I sit down in my room and I read again the letter I get from Xiuquan.

My dear brother Pao,

I am deeply saddened to learn of the death of Zhang. Like you, I thought of him as a father, so I know how his passing must ache your heart. We have lost two fathers now, you and I, and I wonder to what purpose. China continues to be in turmoil, with the Communists showing, with their Cultural Revolution, that they can be just as cruel and merciless as the warlords and the foreigners they fought so hard to overthrow. And as for the violence in Jamaica, it makes me glad to be so far away. I have taken citizenship so I am an American now and no longer have to feel ashamed of being Chinese.

And then I take the letter out into the yard and I burn it.

Six month after Zhang's funeral Ma say she don't want make the fritters no more, or stuff the duck-feather pillows. She say she getting too old for it and I agree. Truth is I been trying to get her to stop for years, but now it her decision she happier with that.

Tilly still coming but she helping more 'round the place now, she doing more of the cooking and cleaning up and washing and such. All the time Ma just getting slower and slower. She stop play mah-jongg. She stop go to temple. She stop read the newspapers. Then one day she sit down in Zhang's rocking chair and she no get up.

I dunno what to do 'bout the washing and the funeral and everything so Madame Chin come back from Montego Bay to help me, and she make all the arrangements just like how Ma do it for Zhang. And when the day come she let me scatter the road money in front of the procession like McKenzie do for Zhang. We bury Ma right next to Zhang in the Chinese cemetery.

When I go back to Matthews Lane the place empty. Just me and Hampton sit down there look at each other. It seem like me and Hampton not got nothing to say.

Then him say to me, 'Me and Ethyl plan to go see her family in Oracabessa. You know, with the wedding coming up and all.'

'You already tell me.'

'And I was wanting to ask you if you would like it if me and Ethyl come live here with you after we married or if you would prefer to have the place to yourself?'

I look at Hampton and I say, 'Come on, Hampton, you must have plenty money to go get a place of your own.'

'That not what I saying. I saying maybe you prefer to have the company. Me and Ethyl already done talk 'bout it and she say she happy to come live here and help keep the place. She still going carry on work for Miss Cicely, but she going do it as a day help. She not going live up there no more. So she say if you want we come live with you here after the wedding.'

I look across the table at him and I remember that first day I meet him when Mr Chin tell him to carry the bags on the hand-cart, and then afterwards when him follow me 'round town all day and make a friend outta me even though I didn't want to pay him no mind.

And I say, 'Thank you, Hampton.'

'So what you going do for the few days while we gone to Oracabessa?'

'I go stay with Gloria.'

31

Wasteful Delay

In all the years me and Gloria been together we never had more than one night at a time. I was always running to go do something whether it was to make the next delivery or go sort out some problem or just get back to Matthews Lane in case Zhang and Ma getting vex with me for spending too much time with Gloria.

But these few days with her was like nothing I ever imagine. We just there in the house making tea and cooking up anything that grab our fancy, like we got all the time in the world, because although Esther still live there she out running the bank all day and busy 'bout her business at night. But Gloria want me and Esther come look with her for something nice to wear to Esther's wedding. So one day that is what we do. Esther marrying a Indian call Rajinder that she meet playing volleyball on the beach.

When we leaving the house Gloria put on the jade necklace and ring. Is the first time I ever see her out in them and she look good. Her dark skin just set off the gold. It really make it sparkle and I think to myself the jewellery look better on her than it would have look on Fay.

Another day we go take a picnic to the beach, which me and Gloria never done before, never. We never actually go anywhere in public together before.

It make me start think that maybe this is how it suppose to be with a man and a woman. Ordinary, just calm and regular. That maybe this is what it would have been like all these years if I just go marry Gloria in the first place. If I never let myself get distracted by what she was, and what everybody else think 'bout it. If I never set my sights on being married to Henry Wong's daughter like that was going lift me outta being a second-class citizen from Matthews Lane.

And then I start have a fancy 'bout what it would be like to be with Gloria like this all the time. What it would be like to live with her, permanent. The picture in my mind make me feel settled and content, but it not a picture of Matthews Lane. And it not a picture of this here house of Gloria's neither, because although the house nice, it small and quiet, and it all closed in with walls and doors and windows. And even though Matthews Lane little bit more than a concrete yard it got life. It got space and room to breathe. It feel more like it connected to the world, not this silent, cut-off feeling of Gloria's house.

When I get back to Matthews Lane Finley is waiting for me. I take one look at him and I know it was trouble. I sit down at the table opposite him and I say, 'OK, tell me what it is.'

'The two constables.' And right as soon as him say it I knew I was expecting it all along. I knew that this thing was never going go away. I knew it even that same night after them arrest Xiuquan and was sitting there and smiling at me and drinking my beer. All I was doing was hoping and holding my breath this long time.

'Yu mean Mutt and Jeff?'

'Them same two. They get kick outta the police force for drug dealing.'

'Drug dealing! Yu joking? Isn't every single one of them doing that same thing?'

'Well maybe not all of them. The thing with these two constables is they start take the drug business so serious they edging into the territory of some big police captain and this is what cause them the trouble.'

'So it a police turf war?'

'Something like that, and the upshot is the two constables outta work and looking to further their career as fully fledge drug dealers because they not even got no police pension now.'

I start to laugh. I can't believe Finley even bothering to tell me all of this like it have anything to do with us.

'Is only the two of them and without the uniform they need more muscle so they want to know if we want to go into business with them.'

And that is when I really laugh. I bust my gut.

'Into business with them! They mad? What on earth make them think I would go into business with them after what they do to me? I would sooner go marry Fay all over again and take all the grief she give me.'

'We not their first port of call. They been to DeFreitas but it seem them ruffle some feathers over there when they policemen and was busy ripping into DeFreitas's profit and him none too please with them. So now them think maybe yu will let bygones be bygones because yu recognise that them making yu a good business offer. After all them take the punishment way back when and never say nothing 'bout it. They put it behind them because they know them do yu wrong so maybe yu can just see yu way to say alright.'

'No, man. They may be desperate but we not reach that stage yet.'

'Yu want me fix up a meeting so yu can tell them?'

I think on it and I think what do I want to go meet them for? The two of them just a pair of good-for-nothing scoundrel who cross me once before and will do it again. And besides, what do I want to go get mix up in drug dealing for? That is some serious business, especially now that it not just a case of ganja, because this cocaine is bad and I still not forget yet what the British do to China over the opium.

I still sitting there thinking when Finley look at me and say, 'Yu not going meet with them?'

'Yu think I should go meet them?'

'Yu know you should. If yu no do it they will think yu disrespect them.'

So I go meet them and tell them my decision. But just like that night when they bring Xiuquan back to Matthews Lane and apologise for arresting him I can see that they angry inside. And even though I show the respect like Finley say, I don't think it wash no way with them and I can see that this thing still not done with yet.

Well I don't want to be no drug dealer but the money situation bad, because the whole ganja thing really getting outta hand. I reckon pretty soon it going to be the only business on the island and the only export Jamaica got to give the world.

Plus, the rise in oil prices is adding to everybody's troubles, including us, we using so much gas driving 'round from hotel to hotel with all the deliveries. Not that it going last much longer, because every week now the orders getting less and less what with the slump in the tourist trade that the American newspapers cause by telling them readers 'bout how bad the violence is in Jamaica.

Gloria think it good that Michael Manley got so much Cuban engineers here building schools and what not. But I say to her, 'Yu nuh see how much people worried we going get communism in Jamaica? Every day I open the newspaper, or step outta the yard or look 'pon a fence, somebody been busy scribbling their message 'bout what they think 'bout it. The other day I even see wall where somebody go paint on it "Manley is a traitor".'

'What you want from him? He trying to make a better Jamaica while everybody just worrying 'bout themself. They going lose their freedom. They going lose their money. We going lose democracy. What good did democracy ever do for poor people?'

I dunno what Gloria talking 'bout. Is like she so happy with how friendly Manley is with Castro she can't see how bad the situation is getting. Even just last week Milton take out a van full of groceries and have to leave it by the roadside and run for cover when him get caught in the middle of some big shootout. It costing me money. As well as now it seem like we risking life and limb just to go deliver some rice and flour 'cross town. Gloria don't seem to understand that the longer this go on the more people is talking 'bout how the USA going invade us like what happen in Cuba.

But every time I talk to her 'bout what going on all Gloria can say is, 'What you want from him?' Even after he go back up Castro for taking troops to Angola.

'The Angolan government ask Castro for Cuba's help to defend their country from the South African army invasion. Yu think he should have said no?'

'No. They ask for his help.'

'So yu think Manley should have go along with it when Henry Kissinger ask him to condemn the Cuban action?'

'No, Gloria. I think Manley do the right thing. A man got to stand up for what he believe in and stand by his friends.'

'So what yu want from him?'

'I don't know, Gloria, but now they cut off our US aid we practically bankrupt overnight, and now we going have to go borrow a whole ton of money. And paying that back with the interest them want is going kill us.'

Gloria don't say nothing because I think deep down inside, even though she so smitten with Cuba, she know Jamaica is in trouble.

When Manley go to the International Monetary Fund for help they agree to give us the money but in return they want a devaluation of the Jamaican dollar; a reduction in government spending; a increase in taxes; and tight wage controls.

What we get from all of that was unemployment and poverty, and no social welfare. And a bunch of people that think they got nothing left to lose except the miserable few streets in the neighbourhood they think is their territory. So if we think we see violence before we had no idea just how bad it could get. It was outright warfare. Right out there in the street. Shootouts, fires, bombings, rape, murder, everything. And all the time there was rumours that all of this was part of a CIA operation to destabilise the country because America didn't want another Cuba right there in their back yard.

So finally on 19 June 1976 they declare a State of Emergency, the second one since Independence.

Sun Tzu say, *'To win battles and take your objectives, but to fail to exploit these achievements is ominous and may be described as "wasteful delay".'*

I write to Mui:

> I know you finish your law degree now but things very bad down here in Jamaica. It so bad the government even introduce a new law to make illegal possession of a firearm a crime punishable by mandatory life sentence. They have set up a Gun Court to provide quick trials for those charged with gun offences. They have amnesties and they even using shock treatment on the gunmen. But life sentences and amnesties don't make jobs or put food on the table, so there is open gang warfare in the street. This is not the Jamaica you have in your mind. Not the Jamaica I want you to be coming home to. So you carry on studying for your barrister bar exam. Things will get better down here.

In December 1976 Michael Manley win a second term of office, but as time go on him social reforms was gradually grinding to a halt because we owe so much money in foreign debt and we had to concentrate on paying it off. Plus, we still losing skilled people. And it wasn't just the Chinese and it wasn't all over money. All sort of people was leaving, and for a lot of them it was because they just couldn't take the violence no more.

With all of this going on I never get to see Michael, he so busy trying to do something 'bout poor relief. And then I get a note from him.

> Pao,
> Please see the attached. It would mean such a lot to me if you decided to come.
> Michael.

The attached was a official invitation to attend at Holy Trinity Cathedral when the Right Reverend Bishop Kealey is to be installed as His Grace the Most Reverend Michael Kealey, Archbishop of Kingston.

32

Humility

I go see Michael become archbishop and I feel proud like he was my own brother. I sit there and I look at him in all his glory and I think we tread different paths me and Michael, but we travelled through this life together. Everything that I ever tell him stay with him. And everything that he tell me 'bout Fay and such stay with me. And even though him archbishop now, I know that Michael going always be there. We bonded to each other.

I never get a chance to talk to him that day but afterwards him tell me he see me sitting there in the cathedral, in the third pew back, and he think to himself maybe he got a brother after all, which I understand he mean me, because Michael an only child.

Then him laugh and say to me, 'Even if we have very different ways of communing with our Father.'

Three month later Esther get married. It seem to me that Gloria been planning this wedding for the past two years but maybe that not quite true. It just seem like it a long time in the making.

The morning I go up to the house it is a pandemonium. I dunno why Gloria tell me to get there so early. Maybe she reckon I going be late so she give me this early time. God knows what on her mind why she think I going be late for my own daughter's wedding, but it is two long hours she got me sitting there watching the dressmaker fuss 'round the place with a tape measure hang 'round her neck and I think well if she still sewing at this stage then the whole wedding in trouble.

The bridesmaid is two girls Esther know from St Andrew High School where all of them take their GCEs together. Cambridge Examination Board just like in England. These girls so thin I can't imagine any man managing to get hold of them. It must be like trying to pick up a glass but even after you completely close yu hand 'round it the glass still slipping through yu grasp. But both these girls already engaged so that just go to show what little I know 'bout it. They seem like they nice enough girls though, and them and Esther look like they close so that is good.

The make-up woman got a lot of tubs and tubes and bottles and jars that she spread out everywhere. She put a little cloth 'round every woman neck in case she go spill something on their chest and then she start rub little of this and that on the back of their hand so she can get the right colour and tone, so she say.

She say she going make them look perfect. That is her favourite word. Every time she finish do a little powder or rouge or whatever it is she do she stand back and she look at them and she say 'perfect'. And she do this with Gloria and Esther and the two bridesmaid till I start think that if I hear her say the word 'perfect' one more time I going get up and throw the woman outta the house.

The four of them just sit there and let her carry on perfecting 'round them while they hold out their hand because some other woman is busy at the side of them filing and shaping and painting on the finger varnish.

The hairdresser do a lot of oohing and ahhing. And he like to rest him hand flat on his cheek and swing him head from left to right. I suppose he trying to take in every angle of these creations that he busy concocting on top of the heads of these four women. He is standing there with one hand on his chin and the other one on his hip, and I am sitting there with one ankle resting on the other knee and my hands in my lap, and as he is studying them I am studying them. He is looking at the side and I am looking at the side. He is looking at the back and I am looking at the back. And then I start say things like 'Maybe it need straighten out a bit more' or 'Maybe you could sweep it up a little more at the side there.' And he stop and turn 'round and look at me and then turn back and look at the hair, and then maybe the chin and hip thing again, and then maybe he say, 'Yes, I think you are right.'

And then after a while I start to think to myself yu know maybe this not such a bad job. It artistic. You get to be with a woman and look at her. Really look. Really take her in. Most of the time a man don't do that. He look but he don't see nothing. But this way you get to make a woman feel cared for. Make her feel beautiful and good about herself. How many jobs is there where you get to do that? Yu get a chance to make somebody happy even if it only for a day.

When the wedding car finally turn up I feel relieved to be stepping out into the midday sun. Just as I get to the car I turn 'round and see Esther standing there on the veranda. She look beautiful, with the white frock just off the shoulder, flowing all the way down to the ground with the train that Gloria busy fetching up in case it drag over the dirty yard and the veil that Esther going pull down over her face. I never imagined I would feel so proud. I never imagined the day would come. It was almost like I never thought I would live long enough to witness a thing like this. Esther walk right up to me as I standing there holding open the car door and she say, 'Thank you, Daddy.'

And I think to myself that is the first time she ever call me that. All these years she always manage to say what she got to without calling me anything at all. Or sometime when I hear her talking to Gloria she say 'my father', and the way she say it didn't always sound too nice. So I look at her and I look at Gloria and then I look at Esther again and I think this girl really gorgeous, just like her mother.

We drive down to the Baptist church in Half Way Tree. The church not no Holy Trinity Cathedral, but it big and it beautiful with all the flowers that standing up there at the altar and hanging down the end of every pew.

This church not just no church, although it busy doing that as well, because Gloria tell me it got over eight hundred and fifty members. But the thing that Gloria like 'bout this church is that it a JAMAL adult education centre which Gloria tell me stand for Jamaican Movement for the Advancement of Literacy. It got all sorta thing going on there like a Christian education centre and a legal aid consultation service that Gloria think is a very good thing. Gloria tell me she been attending this church since 1968 when they start take an interest in social and welfare issues.

She surprise me. I just sit there in the car and look at her. I never figure Gloria for no church-going Christian. It don't really seem to go with everything else that she do.

She say to me, 'I used to be a regular church-goer as a child, yu know. Every Sunday morning my mother would make sure we scrub and dress and march us down the dirt road in all sorta frock with crinoline so we could go listen to the pastor pound that Bible.' And then she stop. And then she say, 'But it not God that I come here for. What I come here for is the chance to make a contribution and to help people change their lives.'

When me and Esther walking down the aisle I see Rajinder at the altar. And as I am getting close to him I realise that I never see a man look so happy. He look so happy it seem like him almost going to bust. Like him can't believe this woman is actually going to marry him. Like he is waiting there in that church surrounded by all his family and such and she is coming towards him and some dream he been having for god knows how long is finally going come true. So I start fret that the man going collapse before we get there, there is that much going on in his heart. But we make it, and the pastor say, 'Who gives this woman?' and I done my part.

I step to the side and all the time I am standing there I try to remember how I felt on my own wedding day. Well I know for sure that when Fay was coming down the aisle on Henry's arm I didn't look nothing like how Rajinder look. I think I was more worried than happy. Worried that any minute now she was going stop and just turn 'round and walk out the church and I would be there looking at her back like I done a hundred times before at Lady Musgrave Road. And even after she say 'I do', I still didn't believe it actually happen. That she actually marry me. The only time it seem real to me was when we was sitting in the car looking out at the cathedral and the crowd that was out there because I reckon all these people must have been bearing witness to something.

After they done with the praying and the singing and the signing we finally get to go sit down in New Kingston in the splendour of the Pegasus Hotel because Gloria take a liking to the fact that only last year the government acquire the controlling interest in the hotel and she very much in favour of the people taking over the tourist industry. But in truth there is not a lot of sitting. How much family this boy have is nobody's business because I am shaking hand after hand of this auntie and that uncle and the niece and the nephew and the brother-in-law and sister-in-law, and first cousin and second cousin and third cousin, which I don't know what kinda relation that is anyway, and the grandfather and grandmother and the mother and father and three brothers and six sisters. And all the time you doing it a whole army of little children running up and down the place like nobody got them under control.

I think my arm going drop off but Gloria say I must shut up complaining because it only the one chance I going get so I should enjoy it, which tell me that Gloria don't think Mui ever going come back to Jamaica, or if she do then it after she already married.

So now instead of standing there enjoying Esther's wedding I am thinking 'bout Mui and thinking that maybe Gloria right I never going see a day like this for her. And I think that is funny. Well it not really funny as such, because it was Mui that put me in mind of Esther in that first letter she send back to me after all that mix-up with Morrison going to look for Stanley. It was Mui that write 'I hope Gloria and Esther are well' and make me think I should go pay the child more mind. It was Mui remind me that I had another daughter.

All the way through the snapper and the chicken I am thinking what kinda child Esther was. And what I realise is that when she young Esther was like two completely different people. She quiet and careful with me, but when you read her school report it seem like she this carefree, long-jumping, volleyball-playing, drama-society, school-choir sorta girl. Yet never once did she ask me if I wanted to come watch her do her sport thing or see her school play or listen to the choir sing. And Gloria never mention none of this to me. Maybe she thought that after I read the school report I would ask for myself if I could go see something that Esther doing. Maybe she wanted me to make the first move. But it never dawn on me to do nothing. I just used to read the little report because Gloria give it to me and feel puzzled 'bout how come this nuh seem to be the same girl at all. Or after I read it and giving it back to Gloria I would say, 'She seem to be doing good.' And that would be it. In truth, a lot of the time it just felt like Gloria give it to me because she reckon I entitled to see it because I pay for it. Like I pay the school fees so I have a right to read the report. It was like that. And it didn't seem to me like I had any right to expect anything or ask for anything more than that.

It wasn't till Fay take the children that all of that change, maybe because Gloria think I only got the one child now so I can concentrate on her. So Esther only really become my daughter after Mui and Xiuquan was gone.

When it come to the speeches I already done tell Gloria that I didn't know what to say. What yu going say 'bout being the father of a woman you don't hardly know? And you busy giving her in marriage to some man you maybe meet two or three times. What yu going say? That for the first fourteen years of this woman's life you all but ignore her? You can't even remember how many times you see her and even when you did happen to come 'cross her you can't remember any conversation you ever had with her about anything at all. That in fourteen years you never read her a book in bed, or play a game with her, or take her to the beach, or help her with her pyjama party, or take her to the pictures, or eat ice cream with her, or watch her blow out any birthday candles. Yu can't even remember what present you ever buy her or what Gloria get for her and tell her it come from me. And then yu wife kidnap yu other two children and that is when you realise that you have another child. So it is only since the others gone that you start to get to know this woman and what you discover is that she is smart and funny and a caring person. Everything you would want yu child to be. Maybe everything you would wish you could be yourself but you are not. And on top of all of this, the very special thing about Esther is her forgiveness. That she had it in her heart to forgive me and just wait for the day that I would be there for her as her father who love her and feel pleased and proud that she is in this world.

Gloria look at me and say, 'That is fine. It honest.'

So when the moment come I get up and I say it. I tone down the first part a little bit and when I get to the part about being her father I say, 'Who she can call Daddy. Who love her and feel pleased and proud that she is in the world to be a daughter to me and Gloria, and a wife to Rajinder, but most of all to be a person to herself.'

I can hardly hear the clapping because right then I look at Esther and I see she got a sorta smile on her face but she crying. And then I feel something wet on my own face and I sit down and Gloria pass me a tissue to wipe away the tear.

After that when it come to the dancing Esther and Rajinder do what they have to and afterwards she walk straight over to where I am sitting and stand there with her hand held out to me for me to go dance with her.

I say to her, 'Esther, I can't dance.'

And she say, 'It doesn't matter.'

So I get up and I go on the dance floor with her, dressed in this black tuxedo and bow tie that Gloria say I got to wear. And as I am dancing with her I realise that the look on my face must be exactly that same one that Rajinder have when me and Esther was walking down the aisle towards him. Like a dream I didn't even know I had had just come true. And when I look over to Gloria still sitting there at the table, I see the dream had come true for her as well.

33

Marches

Mui pass the Bar exam. She send me a copy of *The Times* newspaper from England that got her name in it – 'Called to the Bar at Lincoln's Inn.'

But even while I was busy showing the paper to everybody I know and telling them what a brilliant daughter I have there was trouble brewing. And after a lot of talk and telephone call and this and that Finley say we have to go meet this man, but we have to go to Negril because he tell Finley he not going to no Blue Lagoon. He say he is a Miami man. A man for blue sea and blue sky not some dark dingy Kingston bar.

Finley tell me him name Ian Maynard Fitzgerald and I say, 'What? What kinda name that is?'

'I think it the sorta name that got history and a whole heap of family with big connections. Otherwise, why would you bother yourself with a mouthful like that? Not unless you think you impressing somebody. I wouldn't be surprised to hear that him great-granddaddy fight with General Custer.' And me and Finley laugh. 'Anyway,' Finley say, 'seem him got a nickname, Sam.'

'So where that nickname come from?' And Finley just shrug him shoulders.

Sam got himself a hotel in Negril right on a nice piece of that seven mile of white sandy beach they always advertising in the tourist brochure. The hotel big, it impressive, it classy. Sam tell us it got all the American and German newspaper for sale right there in the lobby shop. It got the beach, two swimming pool and five restaurant serving every kinda food that the tourist want to eat. It got helicopter trips to the Blue Lagoon, by which he mean the big blue water hole over Port Antonio way, not my favourite bar in Kingston. It got waterskiing and every beach sport you can think of. It got entertainment day and night. It got babysitting and kindergarten club. And the best thing? It all inclusive. The guests never have to step foot outside the place, and to keep everybody safe and sound they lock up the big gates every night at seven o'clock, half hour before nightfall, and they don't bother tell the people that they not no street violence in Negril, that all the trouble in Kingston. No, they just like to keep it simple with all the tourist lock up inside there being all inclusive while the local shops and bars and restaurants going to hell because they not got no customers. And the all-inclusive profit going straight back to America because Sam is a Miami man.

So me and Finley sitting down on this here veranda with Sam while the little waitress is running backward and forward with the rum punch and shrimp salad and Sam is leaning his big white self back in the chair admiring his own handiwork with his poolside Greek temples, and stone lions with water spouting out their mouth, and artificial waterfall like Jamaica not got enough natural beauty without Sam bringing all this concrete in here.

Well Sam hotel got everything, except one thing. It not got no paying guests because the American media so busy frightening all of them good US citizens with they stories of robbery and rape and murder and violence and mayhem in Jamaica that none of them want to set foot down here no more. Even though in truth the whole thing local and don't involve no tourist anyway, and certainly not in Negril or Ocho Rios which is where all the tourist traffic at.

When Sam finally get round to telling us what he want, he say, 'Merleen Chin,' in this smooth, silky voice like him making a commercial for some chocolate bar. But that didn't fool me none.

I knew right away what he was after, because when we finish with the Charles Meacham business and baby John getting born, Merleen finish school and go study tourism in America and now she back she get a good job in a big European vacation company booking people into hotels and what not, and that is good for us what with all the hotel contracts we busy negotiating all the while.

'Merleen can't full up your hotel with guests just like that.'

Sam smile like he sweet. Like he think he some handsome Prince Charming, even though he got little chests like a woman and he flabby 'round the middle. Sitting there in some seersucker shirt and white slacks and shoes, but no socks. What kinda man go 'round the place and no wear no socks?

'Well if she can't we'll have to think real hard about what you're proposing to do right here.' And he look at me and then at Finley and back at me again. Then he smile and say, 'Come on, guys, we're all grown men. You know the score and I know for sure that you two have a lot more experience at this kind of conversation than I do. Right?'

We don't say nothing to him, so he just carry on.

'I tell you what, how about I just say these three little things I have in mind and you see how that hangs with you. First, Merleen Chin. Wouldn't it be great if she could get some guests placed right here in this little piece of wonderland? Maybe get us up to what, and I want to be fair with you guys, so let's say eighty-five per cent occupancy. I'm sure she can do that. Second, Margy Lopez and that cute little cosmetics company. Yeah. All that importing, and for the supermarkets too. I could source all of that for you. Really. I spend a lot of time Stateside. It wouldn't be any problem at all. Third, good staff, so hard to come by, don't you think? And the wage bill, man, what can I tell you? I would so like to dampen down with that. Know what I mean? But heck, they'll just run off or go to the unions. So maybe you can figure out how to get all that to work?'

'We don't have nothing to do with no unions.'

'Ah yes, but your friend Mr DeFreitas does, doesn't he?'

We just sit there and look at him.

'I know yu think yu got us over a barrel and that is why we going do all of this for you.'

'Barrel?' and him lean forward. 'You want me to spell it out? Illegal gambling, extortion, prostitution, stolen goods, money laundering, and that's to say nothing about perverting the course of justice, you know, little girls flying off to Miami when they should be here facing a double murder rap. You get my drift?'

I take my hand and just rest a finger against my lips in case I go say something that I regret. Sun Tzu say, '*When an advancing enemy crosses water do not meet him at the water's edge.*'

Then in a real friendly voice him say, 'Hey, you probably need some time to think about all of this. You know, figure out how you're gonna get this shit together.' He reach into the top pocket of his shirt and pull out a business card and hand it to me.

'Why don't you call me when you are ready?' And he get up and walk off, stopping at the door to tell the waiter to put the drinks and such down as business entertainment. Then he turn 'round and come back to the table and lean across it and say to me, almost in a whisper, 'And let's not forget about the archbishop. An affair with the gang boss's wife?' He sorta raise his eyebrows both together. 'What would Rome say?' And he knock on the table a couple of times with him knuckles and say, 'Don't keep me waiting.'

When we leaving the hotel me and Finley see the two constables standing up in the lobby dress in some nice, neat, press security-guard uniform.

Sun Tzu say, '*Those who do not know the conditions of mountains and forests, hazardous defiles, marshes and swamps, cannot conduct the march of an army.*' So I tell Clifton to go find out what happen and it turn out that Mutt and Jeff so mad with me for turning down their drug deal, especially after they take the hiding and nuh say nothing, that they decide to go dig up everything they could find out about me and anybody that have anything to do with me. And all of this information they decide to go give to Ian Maynard

Fitzgerald because they can see that he got money. And since they more interested in the money than bringing me to justice they run off to Negril with the news because Sam got the wherewithal to take advantage of everything they got to tell him. Plus it seem like maybe Sam in the drug business with them now so the three of them busy living it up in Miami when they not here guarding over Sam's wonderland.

And who is Ian Maynard Fitzgerald? Some old boyfriend of Clifton's. That is how Mutt and Jeff come 'cross him in the first place, tailing Clifton to Negril and Miami where he leading this double life.

So I say to Clifton, 'This man, he nuh supposed to be a friend of yours?'

And him say, 'I used to think so.'

I can see Clifton already feel bad 'bout it so I don't say nothing more, especially since it not Clifton fault anyway, it mine for refusing to join the constables in their drug dealing. But that was never going to be, so it was always a calamity just waiting to happen. And in truth it been sitting there waiting a long time, not from the drug dealing, not even from the hiding they take, but from the moment the two of them decide to go help Fay take the children from me.

34

Control

The telephone ring and when I pick it up it is Mui. She say she ready to come home.

'Mui, yu know that is what everybody want. That is what yu been working so hard for all these years, but honestly this is not a good moment.'

'Papa, it's Jamaica. Is there ever going to be a good moment?'

'Maybe not, but there will be a better moment than this one. Trust me on that. Anyway, has something happened? Yu nuh sound so good. Yu sound like maybe yu just done crying.' She quiet at the other end of the phone. 'Something happen then?'

'I met a woman at one of the dinners. She is a head of chambers at Lincoln's Inn.'

'Yes.'

'And I happened to mention that I am Jamaican and she remarked that she had been to Jamaica many years ago. Anyway, she seemed quite friendly. She asked me my name, which it seemed like she already knew. And then she asked me who my father was, and when I told her she completely changed towards me. She became very dismissive, almost hostile. It was such a sudden transformation I started to wonder if I was imagining it, and then afterwards I thought perhaps she had some kind of personality problem because someone told me that she actually asked to be seated next to me.'

'What this woman called?'

'Her name is Helena Meacham. If you know her it may be under a different name. I know she has been married and divorced and I'm not sure if Meacham is her married name.'

'No, that is her name from when she was down here. But so what? What so important 'bout this that it make you cry?'

'Well, since I met her some horrible things have been happening around me. First of all I seem to be getting less work from the chambers' clerk. Less work, less well paid, less interesting. Second, people who used to be quite friendly have stopped speaking to me, and a few have been quite rude or nasty. I am beginning to feel completely ostracised.'

I think to myself 'ostracised', what kinda word is this? But then I know Mui smart enough to make her way in England so now she got all sorta English word and she even sound like she English as well.

'Yu nuh think maybe yu taking it all too serious?'

'No, Papa, it's really horrible.'

'And yu think this Helena saying things to people to make them start treat yu this way?'

'I can't say for sure. I haven't even seen her again since the dinner, but it does seem uncanny in its timing.'

Uncanny? I think she completely outta my league now.

'But how do you know her anyway?'

'I help her and her father fix a couple problems they had down here.'

'Then surely she should be pleased to have met me.'

'It wasn't . . .' and then I run outta words but it no matter. Mui cut straight 'cross me.

'This thing with her happened a few months ago and my life has been unbearable since then. I don't see how I can carry on like this so I thought the best thing to do is just to come home. That is what I have been wanting to do all along anyway.'

'Mui, yu not that long qualified. Don't yu think yu should stay there a while and get yourself some experience?'

'You don't understand, Papa. I hate what I am doing. I hate having to get up every day and go to work to face people who have become so cold towards me, who can barely bring themselves to look at me, who walk out of rooms when I enter them. It takes the pleasure out of everything. Everything. At least if I come home I can feel that I am doing some good.'

'Calm yourself down. Yu getting yourself all irate over some stupid woman. What yu mother say about it anyway?'

'I haven't said anything to her about it.'

'Yu nuh tell your mother 'bout it? Mui, yu got to talk to her. She right there with yu. Not like me four thousand mile away on a telephone. Anyway, how can people change just like that? They nuh know yu long before all of this happen? How can one woman make them turn like that?'

'Power, Papa. She has it and I don't. Besides, like you always used to say, white people stick together and that is as true in England as it is in Jamaica.'

I think to myself Mui need to simmer down and take it steady. Everything got its edge. You just have to find it. Sun Tzu say, *'The general must rely on his ability to control the situation to his advantage as opportunity dictates.'*

35

The Burning of Personnel

I reckon that getting out from under Ian Maynard *Sam* Fitzgerald was going to take a bigger authority than me. And what with the phone call with Mui and Gloria pointing out to me that Margy Lopez didn't kill nobody, it put me in mind of Charles Meacham and the thing I realise is that Meacham stop paying me. Him just stop, just like that. Years back. And me so busy feeling bad 'bout Fay taking the children, and Zhang and Ma, and all the excitement with Manley and everything I never even notice. And then I think well, that sorta rude of him. So now I think it time to catch up with Meacham and that murdering daughter of his, Helena.

I call Clifton and say to him let's go get a drink over the Blue Lagoon. And I ring George Morrison and tell him the same thing.

When we meet up I say to Morrison that I glad to hear John finish him training to be a doctor now and that he and Margaret coming home after this long while. And I congratulate Clifton on him big promotion. 'You almost at the top of the tree now, Clifton, eh? Chief of police going be your next stop.' And we clink our glass and drink, and then I tell the two of them what I want them to do.

'Charles Meacham! We nuh finish with him yet?'

'I reckon him still owe us one.' But George and Clifton not so sure, so I say, 'Come on, George, you know all 'bout England. And, Clifton, you know all 'bout policing. I reckon between the two of you we can find Meacham. I even give you a head start because Helena Meacham a barrister with chambers in Lincoln's Inn in London.'

The two of them just sit there and look at me. Then George start waving him arm at the bartender to bring him another Appleton, and Clifton say, 'Yu joking? Yu can't be serious. A barrister? For real?'

'For real.'

Him think on it a little while and then him say, 'Well, they say hide in plain view. So maybe that what she doing. No safer place than right there in the lion's den. But yu know this a serious business. You playing with fire if yu going take these two on.'

'Trust me.'

When Clifton ring me a few days later him say him got news and when I go meet him over the Blue Lagoon him tell me.

'Charles Meacham rise up the ranks to become a major in the British army but now him retired and living in Winchester. The daughter, Helena, go study law at Oxford University and then she go to the Inns of Court School of Law. She called to the Bar in 1968 and now, like yu say, she have her own chambers in Lincoln's Inn specialising in family and criminal law for women.'

When Clifton finish reading from him little notebook I tell him to give me the address of Helena Meacham chambers in London, and when I get back to Matthews Lane I get on the telephone and order up a big bouquet from one of them international flower people and I send them to her with a note.

Helena,
So good to have caught up with you after all these years.
Warm regards,
Winston Morgan and Aubrey Williams (Club Havana)

When Meacham telephone me the next day I just say to him, 'Charles, how you doing?'

'My daughter received your flowers. What silly little game are you playing now, Yang?'

'Game, Charles? I not playing no game. Is this a game to you? Is that why you just decide to ignore me and hope I wouldn't notice?'

'That was years ago. I decided that enough was enough.'

'True. But I just need one more favour from you. I have a little problem down here that I think you can help me with.'

Meacham quiet at the other end of the telephone so I tell him what I want, and I tell him the name of the culprit and him two henchmen.

'I couldn't possibly do something like that! What do you think I am?'

'Well before you hang up the telephone let me just say, which I sure you know anyway, there not no statute of limitations for murder. Plus, with everything I hear tell 'bout the new-fangled things they doing with this here DNA, I sure pretty soon they will be able to do something with this knife I still got from the last time I meet your daughter. But anyway, Helena doing so well with her lawyer work and everything I reckon she must know 'bout all of that as well.'

Meacham still quiet so I say, 'And then when that is done you can rest easy and just ignore me because you right, fair is fair and enough is enough. You won't hear nothing from me after that.' I catch my breath, and then I say, 'Tell Helena to give my daughter a rest as well. She will know what I mean.'

Meacham just hang up the telephone. But two weeks later Finley come tell me that Sam Fitzgerald and the two constables disappear. It seem the three of them up in Miami having themself a good time and they just disappear. Just like that, not a trace, and the authorities think it probably drug related.

I think to myself yes sir, the British army is good. I think they must be as good as the CIA, maybe even better, they get their business done so fast.

A couple days later Mui ring me and she seem happier. She say everybody alright with her again. She getting work like she used to. People talking to her just like nothing ever happen. She like her job again. She going stay in England but I mustn't forget, she still want to come home when the time right in Jamaica, and I just say, 'Yah, man.'

36

Precautionary Measures

But the whole thing unsettle me, and I start think 'bout what would happen if I should end up marking off the days on the wall of some Kingston jail cell and mopping the floor in the penitentiary. I think well the boys alright, they been making good money all these years, but Merleen only got her little job at the vacation company and Margy nothing more than an employee at Yang Cosmetics.

I tell Merleen to come have lunch with me up in a hotel in New Kingston. The restaurant quiet so I choose a table in the far corner behind some tall potted bamboo.

'I was very young, and he seemed so mature.' And then she laugh. 'Well, I suppose he would seem that way, being old enough to be my father.'

I just smile. Merleen turn into a fine woman. She gracious, and composed.

'I thought he knew everything there was to know. I thought I was going to be cared for, protected, educated, groomed if you like. I thought he would make something of me.' She stop while the waitress put down the teriyaki chicken and rice in front of us.

'I felt sort of honoured. Foolish, wasn't it?' And then she laugh again.

'That wasn't foolish. Yu was a child. And he was a grown man.'

'A grown man who came here and captured something young

and innocent, something in its infancy, and he took what he wanted from it and when he was done he left us to fend for ourselves, John and me. Independent if you like.' And she smile. 'Rather like an English Pinkerton and Chinese Butterfly.'

Well now she completely lose me, but I get her drift because she and me both know she not just talking 'bout her and Meacham, she talking 'bout the British and Jamaica.

When we finish eat and deal with our business I walk with her down the stairs into the lobby and through the side door, past the empty swimming-pool loungers that the tourists should be sunning themself in and the empty chair under the almond tree where they should be reading their book, and we make our way past the rubber trees and coconut palms, and along the path following the pale blue flowers on the plumbago hedge into the hotel car park. The air still damp from the morning rain.

Next day I ring Margy and tell her that I going take a trip to see her next time she in Port Antonio. Then Finley decide we all going go because Port Antonio is really beautiful.

The day before we supposed to go Milton tell me that all the rain we been having the past two weeks cause so much flooding the government declare five parishes disaster areas and they busy evacuating people from them homes.

'Communications is down and the road system not looking so good under the strain. Plus the *Gleaner* say we facing huge agricultural loss and all sorta health hazards from dead livestock, and damage to water supplies and sanitation.'

Milton talking just like he quoting the newspaper to me.

'So yu think we should call it off? Yu want me fix another time to go see Margy?'

Him stick his thumb in him belt that he always wear now ever since that thing with Clifton Brown, and say to me, 'No, man. I just telling yu, that's all. We still going drive over to Port Antonio tomorrow. No problem.'

Me, Finley, Hampton and Milton set off the next day, Milton driving. The water in the road so bad that when we coming down

Mountain View Avenue a motorcycle stall in front of us and when the rider put down his foot the water come over his ankle.

Once we outta the city we come face to face with this rural mass that is still Jamaica. The donkey carts; the roadside higglers with them wooden carvings and conch shells; roasted sweetcorn for sale, or three wet fish on a string; multicoloured timber huts in blues and pinks and yellows with them rickety makeshift roof, or some piece of rusting corrugated-zinc sheet; fruit trees growing wild – mango, avocado, ackee, breadfruit, jackfruit, pawpaw, nase-berry, soursop, bananas; pineapples laying on top; yams and sweet potatoes in the ground; the banana plantations stretching out on both sides of the road, with them little blue plastic bags that they wrap 'round the bananas to protect them from disease.

Plus with the road not so good anyway and with all this rain, the thing turn treacherous. Potholes full of water and covered in a sorta white slime that wash off the grit and hardcore they scatter down in a effort to patch everything up.

And I think to myself how is progress and prosperity going catch up with a place like this? Especially when every time we take one step forward the rain or the hurricane come to drive us ten steps back.

When we get to Poor Man's Corner the River Yallahs completely take over the road, gushing fast from left to right and plunging down a steep embankment in this muddy reddish-brown waterfall. Milton stop the car. When the big station wagon behind us over-take and slowly power its way through the water, the spray reach up above the top of the windows.

Milton decide to take a chance. He nudge the car forward trying to keep a steady speed so the engine don't stall, but when we hit the deepest part halfway across, him slow down and it worry me. We make it alright though, and when we reach the other side Milton laugh and say, 'Man, even I was sweating then.'

At Green Wall a dead cow lay in a bus stop, all brown and bloated, and frothing at the mouth.

At Morant Bay I ask Milton to drive up to the courthouse where

Paul Bogle and his followers stage the demonstration in 1865, and where the volunteer militia fire on the crowd and spark the uprising. What amaze me wasn't just that the building still standing there, with its red brick and whitewashed stone, but it still functioning as a courthouse. So as I climb up the semi-circular stairway to the upper balcony I begin to hear voices and realise that a trial is actually in motion. And even in this heat the barristers still dress up in them wigs and gowns just like they do it in England.

Above me the round white turret perch on the top of the roof. Below me the statue of Paul Bogle, machete in hand, and the commemoration plaque which read:

> Here in the front of this courthouse on 11 October 1865, Paul Bogle of Stony Gut led his people in a protest at the injustices to the poor in the courts presided over by the planter-magistrates. It was the start of what became known as the Morant Bay Rebellion. Paul Bogle, George William Gordon and hundreds more were brutally slain. Behind this building is buried the remains of many of these patriots whose sacrifices paved the way to the independence of Jamaica. We honour them.

It was early afternoon by the time we reach Port Antonio, the blue sea on one side and the lush green hills on the other. The Blue Mountains in the distance and yet so close I could almost smell the coffee. We climb the hill to San San. When we get to Margy's house, Milton ease the car down the steep driveway into the carport. Margy's housekeeper come to the door to greet us.

We follow her through the dim, cool house and step out on to the rear terrace into the brilliant, dazzling sunshine. The deep blue of the Caribbean stretch out before us, the abundant green of the surrounding hillside, the white sand beach of San San Bay, with the twin harbours of Port Antonio and Navy Island in the distance. I could feel the sea breeze on my face and taste the slight salt in the air. And somewhere in my own head I hear Harry Belafonte singing 'Island in the Sun'.

Margy come up from the lower garden, standing on the top step with her short thick wavy hair trembling on the breeze.

'Let's go straight to the factory, I want to show you something. It won't take long and we can have lunch when we get back.' She reverse out a big four-by-four and we all pile in.

Margy excited 'bout everything she showing us and how she change this and improve that, and reduce the waste and increase the product line. She talking fast and she pleased with herself. It don't mean nothing to me except, when I look at the accounts, I know the business doing good.

When we get back to the house she say, 'I hope you like marlin. Port Antonio is famed for deep-sea fishing, marlin, tuna and kingfish especially.'

The fish pan-fried and simmered in a light curried coconut sauce. It really delicious.

'This here is a long way from a airport,' I say to her, 'what with your constant hopping between here and New York.'

'There is a helicopter shuttle service between Ken Jones Aerodrome and Kingston. The road from Kingston is so bad now the whole town is just relying on the cruise ships for its livelihood. What's going to happen when the wharf falls down I don't know because it isn't looking too good and they don't have the money to rebuild it.'

After coffee, I ask Margy to come walk with me in the garden. We go down the stone steps and follow the path past a load of fruit trees, and a huge crepe myrtle with its lilac flowers and dark green leaves. Then we pass hedges of poinsettia, deep magenta and pink bougainvillaea, and red and yellow hibiscus. We come to a stop at her poolside pergola that covered in wild orchids in pinks and whites and purples.

'You really have a beautiful place here, Margy. I can see why you running back from New York every chance you get.'

'I love it. I don't think I could live without it. You know Errol Flynn once said he had never met a woman as beautiful as Port Antonio. And that's saying something, isn't it, coming from him?

I don't know how any Jamaican can live without Jamaica or the promise of it.'

When we sit down on the little bench I turn and I say to her, 'I want to talk to yu 'bout the business. It doing good, very good, and all that down to your hard work and how yu so smart with all this cosmetics thing. I have lunch with Merleen, maybe you already know?'

'Yes, she told me on the phone.'

'Merleen going have her own vacation company now. And I want to do the same thing with Yang Cosmetics. I want yu stop being a employee and become a full partner so if anything happen to me yu going be alright.'

Margy look at me like she half surprised and half relieved because she must have guessed it from what Merleen tell her.

'Thank you, Uncle.'

'But you not going get your name come first like Merleen. Chin Yang Vacations don't sound too bad, even though I still think Yang Chin would have sound better. But Lopez Yang don't work. I think it got to be Yang Lopez Cosmetics.'

'But it isn't just cosmetics we do now. We have a whole range of bathroom and kitchen products as well that we retail out of our own stores not just outlets in department stores like we used to. That is what I was telling you and showing you earlier this afternoon.'

'So what yu want call it?'

'Plain and simple, Yang Lopez.' She hesitate, and then she say, 'Do you mean a fifty-fifty partner like you did with Merleen?'

And I say, 'Yes. Fifty-fifty. The papers all drawn up, except for the name, and I going have the accountants sort it out and bring them over next week so you can sign them.'

'So fast?'

'No reason to wait.'

When we go back up to the house Margy go inside and come out with a parcel. It beautifully wrapped in a heavy stripe paper of green and brown and blue.

'I got this for you in New York but I feel a little embarrassed giving it to you now after that conversation. Please believe that this was for you anyway.' And then she hand the package to me and I take it from her and unwrap it.

She say to me, 'The Flor de Farach was manufactured in 1958 and shipped to Tampa prior to the 1962 Cuban embargo. The shop's proprietor bought the entire consignment and now he is selling them in this wonderful shop on the corner of Fifth and East 46th Street. When I bought them he said I wasn't just buying a box of cigars, I was buying a piece of history.'

When I open the box it got layers of packets of little Farachitos. I lift out a packet of five and sorta look it over.

'I know you get Cuban cigars here all the time but these were so tiny and cute I thought even Gloria might approve.' Then Margy look at me all expectant and say, 'Try one.'

So I take one out and unwrap it. When I smell it, it got a sweet nutty aroma. I light it and I take a puff. Margy look at me like as to say how is it?

Well, I think Margy good enough to go buy me a present so I not going say nothing 'bout the Americans and their Cuban embargo. I say, 'It taste like the beginning of something new. Something sweet and adventurous. It taste like freedom.' And she pleased with that.

When we leave Margy's I just say to Milton, 'Let's go to Ken Jones Aerodrome and jump on a helicopter back to Kingston, and you can come pick up the car some other time.'

37

Contestable Ground

In 1980 Manley lose the election and Edward Seaga become prime minister when the Jamaica Labour Party take power. They say that seven hundred and fifty people get killed in the months running up to that election, and they reckon that whereas up to 1976 the gangs was using sidearms, mostly the .365 Magnum, by 1980 they was using rapid-fire M16 rifles.

By the next year we break off diplomatic relations with Cuba and we get back the US aid and foreign investments start flooding back again.

But even though the foreign investment good, it mean we not really in charge of our own destiny. Is the foreigners in charge of our destiny, because is them telling us what to do, and them deciding what going get cultivated or developed, and them deciding the time frame, and them deciding how much investment them putting in for how much profit them taking out.

Every day the street filling up with more advertisement for Pepsi and Sprite and Coca-Cola, and IBM and Citibank and Cable & Wireless, and Nestlé, and KFC and Burger King and Esso and Texaco. And all I can hear is Zhang in my head saying 'you back in the grip of the foreigners'. And I think yes, but this situation completely different. Because in the old days everybody could see that it was the British that was responsible for the slavery, whereas now it seem like we are the ones responsible for this mess we in.

Nowadays it hard to see how we being controlled by foreign powers because this new kind of imperialism come wrapped in a cloak that look like help.

The other thing that strike me 'bout the way Jamaica changing is how everybody start talking 'bout Africa. Is like we 'Out of Many', but the 'One People' seem to be just the Africans. Is Africa this and Africa that. Marcus Garvey and Haile Selassie. And ever since the world discover Bob Marley, everything turn to Rasta and reggae. It like they think the only true Jamaican is a African. Like they forget that the original Jamaican was the Arawak Indian and after the Spanish and British get through murdering all of them we was all imports. Every last one of us. But it no matter, all I see and hear every day now is how we got to get back to Africa.

You can hardly see a Chinese man on the street these days. Their feet don't even hit the sidewalk between the Mercedes and the tennis court, or the golf course, or the airport tarmac on them way to their next vacation. And that's the ones that still here, the ones that didn't leave Chinatown to go jump on a plane and never come back. I reckon I must be the only Chinaman left in Chinatown, because even though the signs still here – Chin's Bakery, Chen's Groceries, Hoo's Cleaners, Lee's Hardware, the Golden Dragon, Panda House, Bamboo Garden – the Chinese have long gone. And now, when I step outta the yard at Matthews Lane, all I see is a mass of black faces looking at me and wondering what the hell I am still doing here.

Still, I reckon things good enough for Mui to come home if she still want to, so I write to her and tell her that. But it seem she too busy. She all excited with some big case that taking all her time and she want finish with it before she come. So I say alright. When yu ready then.

38

All-under-Heaven

'I going move to Beverly Hills.'

'California?'

'No, over Long Mountain. Don't fool with me, Gloria. Yu know what I mean.'

Gloria turn 'round where she standing at the stove and she look at me. And then she drop one shoulder and raise one eyebrow and stick a hand on her hip all in one smooth move.

'You going move to Beverly Hills?'

'I going buy a house and move outta Matthews Lane and move to Beverly Hills. I think it time.'

'So what bring this on?'

'The whole thing gone to hell, Gloria. Ever since we come here, ever since I was a boy, we reckon we was going to make a better Jamaica. A Jamaica where we was all brothers. We was going to drive out the foreign imperialists and we was going to shake off the yoke of colonialism and oppression. And now since Manley lose the election it all gone to hell.'

'All that talk 'bout imperialists was Zhang. It was Zhang that was always talking 'bout the right of the ordinary woman and man to live a decent life while you was busy robbing the US navy and driving chickens all over town. And you still busy making money now even though *it all gone to hell*.'

I nuh like the way she mimic me like that.

'That not fair, Gloria.'

She look at me a minute, and then she soften and she say to me, 'Alright, OK. Tell me what you do to make a better Jamaica. What you actually do to help the people.'

'I give Michael Kealey all that money all these years for his poor relief and such. And I support the government social reforms.'

'And where you get all that money from?'

'What it matter where I get it?'

'No. Tell me where you get it.'

'You know where I get it. And you also know that I never hurt nobody that didn't have it coming, and I didn't take no money off of nobody who didn't enter into business with me of their own free will.' Gloria making me vex now and I can hear my voice raising up.

'So you spend your whole life making all this money outta people through their own free will and now you going come tell me that you all dejected because the revolution lost and you going go exile yourself in Beverly Hills?'

And then she sort of ease back, like she just rest all her weight on the back leg there, and get herself comfortable. And I know I was in for it.

'You want talk 'bout revolution, but this was never your revolution. You never been poor, not so poor you hungry; you never had to find yourself a job or put a roof over your head. You never needed to get yourself an education. You were never made to feel degraded or ignorant or worthless because of the colour of your skin, and have to stand there like a damn fool while them shut every door in your face, and while you watch even the most stupid white people moving up instead of you. You didn't have to feel the shame of what been done to your people, and witness how that shame sit on your mother and father and brother and sister, and neighbour and acquaintance. No, you live in Chinatown all this long time because you was comfortable, and now you not so comfortable you have the choice and the money to go move to a mansion in Beverly Hills.'

245

I can't believe she just say all of that to me. I say to her, 'So it alright for me to carry on my bad ways when I can come in handy to fix this and that?'

'I never said nothing to you 'bout your ways. If you remember right, that is how you and me meet when I come to ask you to help me with the thing with Marcia. That was how you and me start. And I never had no feeling 'bout how you put that sailor boy in the hospital. I not talking 'bout what you do, because at least that have a kind of honesty to it. I'm talking about how you talk.' She pause a bit and then she say, 'There not going to be no revolution here, Pao. This is not China. It is Jamaica. And that is not how Jamaica is.'

I just say to her, 'So I take it you not going come live with me in Beverly Hills then, which is what I come here to ask you.' And she just look at me like she reckon she already say enough.

I go away and I think about it, and I can see Gloria got a point. It true I never had to go get no education or job or any of the things Gloria talking 'bout, but then I dunno what she expect from me. After all, what she expect one man to do? Isn't it the masses that got to rise up? Isn't it the masses that got to seize their ideal and take back their land? Isn't it the masses that got to shake off the yoke of oppression?

And I supported that. I give Michael Kealey all that money and I support Manley. So fair enough, a lot of US dollars leave the country illegally, but that would have happen anyway, with or without me. And for my part I give back a good chunk of that money.

And if she think I should have done something more than pass over the money then it because she just choosing to forget. Like she don't know how many PNP supporters was getting shot in their bed after somebody kick down their door in the middle of the night; and how they stab the Peruvian ambassador to death in his own house, and gun down national security minister Roy McGann, and the PNP candidate Ferdie Neita in broad daylight; and how they shoot Bob Marley in his own back yard because they think the Smile Jamaica concert was him supporting Michael

Manley. And that was way before him get Manley and Seaga to join hands on stage at the National Stadium that night. And all the time we saying 'Better must come', every political rally end up in a shootout or confrontation like what happen at Old Harbour, or the night me and Hampton get pinned down by gunfire on the road coming through Spanish Town after we go listen to Michael Manley address a meeting. It because she choose to forget what happen to Kenneth Wong, and because she nuh seem to realise that the only involvement yu could have was to either run for government or pick up a gun. And I wasn't about to do neither.

So I go buy the house anyway, from a Chinese man that was heading for Canada. It right up the top of the mountain, with a front gate guarded by two stone Chinese lions and a winding drive-way, and five round white columns running from ground to roof on the far side of the semi-circular carport. The front door was a double door, wide and red, and above it the Chinaman already paint the Tai Chi surrounded by the eight diagrams of the Pa Kua for good luck and prosperity. The garden set to lawn, with shrubs, mahoe trees, mango, calabash, tamarind, and a single lignum vitae that stand all alone at the far end. The white of the house look good with the red roof, and the red awning that shade the terrace 'round the back where the swimming pool at. I pleased with it. It big and bright, and it catch the sun, but it cool on the inside.

Hampton and Ethyl move with me, and Finley and him wife, and Milton and Tartan Socks because McKenzie not got no family and he got nowhere to go anyway. I sorta turn the place into Yang Compound. Sun Tzu say, '*When you conquer territory, divide the profits.*'

I hire up some boys to make the place secure because I didn't want nobody coming in here and shooting me the way they waltz in and shoot Bob Marley just for organising a concert. I reckon the gunmen would really fix me if they ever find out how much money I give to the PNP.

When I leaving Matthews Lane I have to go fetch out the knife Meacham daughter use to murder them boys down at Club Havana, but when I go take it outta the safe I find it not the only thing in there. There a little notebook as well. So I open it and start to read.

Today
Merleen Chin: Crying as she is leaving Papa's shop. What makes a young girl cry so much?

The little book turn out to be some kinda diary thing that Mui been keeping all them years back. She got everything note down in it. Mama kneeling down in the confessional one side of Father Michael while they got a chain drape 'cross the curtain of the compartment the other side of him so that nobody can go in there. Merleen Chin crying as she coming outta the shop that afternoon. Mrs Samuels in such a state Hampton got to drive her home. Papa and Mama fighting and Mama leaving Matthews Lane. Father Michael visiting Lady Musgrave Road and Mama and Grandma Wong arguing. The sad policemen that arrest Karl. The ugly grey English car park outside the shop with the young girl sitting in it that Karl say is a Rover 100 four-door saloon that belong to the English army man. Uncle Kenneth and fingernail man standing on the corner of King Street and no matter how much we shout and wave at him he just ignore us and carry on pointing and yelling at some big group of men across the street.

But I didn't see no fox's head all I saw was the shiny silver top of the walking stick and him, fingernail man, sitting on a orange crate at the bottom of King Street with his chin resting on his hands leaning on the top of the stick. But Karl say it was a fox's head and he say that the English chase the foxes down on horseback with a pack of dogs that tear them apart. And then the hunters smear the fox's blood on their own face and cut off the fox's tail to keep for a trophy.

I nuh read the whole thing but I start think that if she so smart taking all of this in, and writing it down like this, and using the safe for her own personal hiding place, then maybe she deserve to have the knife as well. Maybe I shouldn't go throw it in the sea like I planned. Maybe I should just keep it for her and the little book as well in case one day, who knows, she might find some use for them.

That first night in Beverly Hills I take my cot and put it out on my bedroom balcony and I go to sleep under the clear Jamaican sky. I smell the freshness of the eucalyptus and I listen to the silence, which my heart welcome after all them years of sound systems booming out the ska and rocksteady and reggae that drift across town on the evening breeze. And I think to myself maybe I finally find some peace. Maybe I finally find myself a place to put down my head and call home.

Sun Tzu say, '*Your aim must be to take All-under-Heaven intact.*'

39

Desolate Ground

I pick up the telephone and ring Daphne Wong the minute Ethyl tell me Miss Cicely take a turn for the worse.

'How she doing?'

'Well you know, they've been trying to control the situation with drugs, but right now it seem like we fighting a losing battle.'

'How she doing in herself?'

'She comes and goes. Some days she is better than others.'

Miss Cicely start take sick a few month before we move from Matthews Lane. So just as we thinking that Ethyl going stop working for the Wongs it turn out that she travelling down the hill to go maid for Miss Cicely every day because she can't stand, after all these years, to go let Miss Cicely down when she need her most. So whereas the main traffic in domestics is travelling to Beverly Hills, Ethyl is busy doing the journey the other way 'round in this little Toyota that Hampton buy for her even though I don't think Ethyl got no driving licence and the only lessons she get is driving 'round the garden with Hampton at her side. Still, Ethyl just like half the drivers in Jamaica and the car is a automatic so that can't cause too much trouble.

When I go see Miss Cicely she in a bad way. She so weak she can't get up and she can barely open her eyes. Not that it matter because Daphne tell me that her sight failing so bad she can hardly see nothing anyway. She pleased me come to see her though and she hold out her hand and I take it as I sit down in the chair next to the bed.

'Philip. How is Philip?'

'I am good, thank you, Miss Cicely. But I come here to see how you doing.'

'Well, all I can say is the good Lord is taking his own time getting ready for me to come and join him. Least I pray that is the direction I am heading in. Who knows, He may be thinking about the other place for me.' And she give a little chuckle and I laugh with her.

'I don't think you need to be fretting yourself over that.'

'Oh, Philip, you always had such faith in me. But in all honesty, I was not the best of mothers. I wasn't good to Fay. I know everyone tired of listening to her complain about how badly I treated her, but it doesn't mean it wasn't true. And I had no time for Daphne. Not really. I was too busy arguing with Fay to even notice what Daphne was doing. I just expected her to carry on without me. And as for Kenneth, well you know all about that. I didn't have one idea in my head about what to do with Kenneth.'

I interrupt her and I say, 'You sure you want to be telling me all of this, Miss Cicely? You sure this is what you want to be talking about right now?'

She turn her head to the side a little, her eyes still shut.

'You know, Philip, I think it is. Who else can an old woman tell? And I feel I need to tell someone before I go to meet my Maker, just so I can acknowledge to Him that I know the mistakes I have made. Well, some of them at least. Silent prayer is a wonderful thing, but it is also very healing to have someone to talk to. That is where the Catholics have the advantage with their confessions. But is it alright with you, Philip, that is the question?'

'Whatever you want to do is fine with me, Miss Cicely.'

'You know that when Fay went to England she went to stay with her brother, Stanley. Stanley was my firstborn, but Mr Henry was not his father.'

Miss Cicely stop and I look at her wondering if she expecting me to say something. I can't think what to say. Still, I reckon I should try, but just as I go open my mouth, not even knowing what going come outta it, she start up again.

'Stanley was born out of sin. The worst sort of sin you can have between a father and daughter.' And she pause, and then she say it again. 'The worst sort.'

I so surprised she telling me all this, I feel like my body gone into shock. It cold but it clammy at the same time. It feel like my joints seize up rigid. It feel like I going get stuck in this position leaning forward on the chair with her hand in mine.

'It has taken a whole lifetime to try to wash off the shame of what Mr Johnson did to me. Because even though I was only a child, it felt somehow like it was my doing. Especially since Mr Johnson didn't seem to have any shame himself about what happened. And then Henry had the good grace to marry me.'

She stop, and I breathe. And then she say to me, 'Philip, take a look for me and see if that window is still open. It is so hot in here and I can't feel the slightest bit of breeze.'

I look over and I see the window wide open. Then my eye catch a fan resting on the side table, a Chinese paper fan, so I walk over and pick it up and when I come back, I sit down and start fan her with it.

'Oh that is good. Thank you. I just can't stand the noise of that ceiling fan.'

We silent for a little while and then she say, 'Did I ever tell you the story about how Henry and I met and how we happen to get married?'

'No, Miss Cicely, you never did.'

'Henry came to Jamaica in 1903, the year the great hurricane destroyed most of the north-east of the island. His Chinese name was Hong Zilong, so the British immigration officer turned that into Henry Wong. And of course, the same thing happened to you. Anyway, Mr Johnson had gone to Kingston to get somebody to help out, not to work in the fields, you understand, but somebody who could do washing and cooking and things like that.

And when Mr Johnson came back to Ocho Rios to the banana plantation we lived on, and where he was the foreman, he brought Henry with him.

'Henry was just a boy, and his mother had put him on the boat from China with a fine collection of hampers of preserved food, crystallised fruit and pickled vegetables. Needless to say, by the time he had made the sea journey and arrived at the plantation he had nothing left. Not because he had eaten it all, but because he had been robbed every inch of the way. What Henry did have, though, were his clothes, into the lining of which his mother had sewn pieces of gold.

'Henry ran a cookhouse for the plantation workers because Mr Johnson thought it was more economical and time-efficient if the workers shared communal food rather than everybody cooking for themself. So Henry made his money from that, and he earned some extra doing laundry that they brought down from the great house. He also ran errands for Mr Johnson taking messages here and there, going to fetch and carry, and sometimes cooking some special dinner for one of Mr Johnson's women friends, of which he had plenty.

'When Henry finally left he bought himself a grocery store in Ocho Rios, with the money he saved on the plantation and the gold from his mother.'

By this time I starting to feel the heat myself and my arm getting tired like it going drop off. Ethyl must have read my mind from the kitchen because right then the door open and she come in with a jug of ice-cold lemonade. I rest down the fan and I pour out two glass for me and Miss Cicely. Then Ethyl start point to the tray that the jug and the glasses sitting on, and I see a drinking straw laying there. She carry on pointing but I dunno what she mean, so eventually she just lean over and pick up the straw and stick it in the glass. So when I hold out the glass to Miss Cicely, and she reach out with her hand and steady it, I just hold the straw firm so she can find it with her mouth and suck. Next thing I hear is the click of the door as Ethyl close it behind her.

'My mother ran off to Panama with another man and left me with him, my father, Mr Johnson. That's how come I was there with him. Then along came Henry, and he showed me the first bit of kindness I experienced in my life. Henry Wong was the sweetest, gentlest man. A kinder man you could never meet. So when Mr Johnson told Henry that I was pregnant and I needed someone to care for me Henry just said yes. In truth, Mr Johnson talked him into it. He told Henry that now he had his shop doing so well he needed a wife. And pretty soon, because of my condition, he would have a whole family, and that was good for him. And when Henry asked him why he wasn't going to be looking after me any more Mr Johnson said, "I don't want a life with no baby running under my feet." And when Henry asked him who the father of the baby was Mr Johnson just said, "Don't you be worrying yourself 'bout that. I know the man concerned and he won't be bothering you none." Actually, I think Henry just felt sorry for me and thought that since he wasn't planning on marrying anybody else he might as well marry me. I think that is how it was. Years later he got a woman in Ocho Rios. He thought I didn't know, but I did. I just chose not to say anything about it, that was all.'

And then I think Miss Cicely start to cry even though I didn't see no tears. It was just something 'bout how her mood change, how it sort of dip down. Or maybe she just start to cry inside.

'When the baby came I decided to give him the same name as Mr Johnson, Stanley. So every time Mr Johnson came to sit at our table, he would look at Stanley and be reminded of the terrible thing he had done to me.'

I see a few beads of sweat appear on Miss Cicely's forehead so I pick up the fan again and start make some breeze 'round her.

'I suppose I worried that Stanley and Kenneth would turn out to be like him, Mr Johnson, even though Henry is Kenneth's father. I worried that they had bad blood from him, through me, and they would turn out to be bad men. But more than that, they would turn out to be bad black men, and they would end up

254

proving white people right, because that is the other thing a mother always has to be mindful of. So I was always on the lookout for any sign of Mr Johnson's badness. I watched out for it. I warned Stanley and Kenneth against it. I tried to make up for it with my afternoon tea and Victoria sponge. And I called on Almighty God when I got frightened that we were going to give white people any reason to believe that they were right about us being wicked heathens. And that applied to the girls as well, that is why I spent so much time fighting with Fay. I can see that now.'

Miss Cicely's funeral surprise me. Not because the church was so full, I sorta expected that, but because people had come from all over the island to pay their last respects.

There was people from Ocho Rios, who remember Miss Cicely from when Henry open his first shop and she used to spend Saturday mornings giving away food to the poor. There was people from Port Maria, where Miss Cicely's mother come from, that she used to write letters to and, from time to time, send money to help ease their way. There was people from Montego Bay and Port Antonio that she meet through her various church gatherings and there was a whole load of Methodist ministers from all over the island.

Plus, there was the people I expected to see, the well-off of Kingston, or what was left of them anyway.

Fay didn't come though. But that didn't surprise me none, since there was no love lost between the two of them. Karl I knew for sure wouldn't bother with it, but I sorta half fancy that maybe Mui would make the journey. But she didn't.

A few days after the funeral Daphne call me to say she want to see me 'bout Miss Cicely's will. When I go up to Lady Musgrave Road she sitting on the veranda with a bottle of Appleton by her side. When I walk up to her, she pour me a drink, but it look like she not drinking nothing herself. She tell me that Miss Cicely leave me all the supermarkets and wholesalers and wine merchants. And that she leave the house and contents, and a pile of money in the bank, to split between her and Fay.

I look at Daphne how tired she seem. Like her whole body sagging. Not that she big, because she is a trim woman. It more like the weight of her misery dragging her down. And then I think to myself that in all the years I know her, I never actually take her in before. But now I see she got a kind face. It sad, but it gentle and it sorta caring. Daphne would be the one to look after yu, even if every day yu would want to say to her 'lively up yourself nuh'.

'I feel honoured that Miss Cicely think so highly of me.'

'It didn't surprise me. She was always very fond of you, Pao, you must have known that. And in any case, you are the one who has been working so hard all of these years to make those businesses a success. It is only fair after all.'

I didn't say nothing. I just wait because she look like maybe there was something else she want to say. Or maybe something she want me to say to her. A kind of wish that she was holding her breath for. But I wasn't saying nothing. I still not forgive her for the business over Stanley's address.

Daphne start up again, 'I have no problem with any of that. My problem is that all of the money is in Jamaican dollars, and even if I manage to get a good price for this house there will be sizeable taxes and difficulties in getting the money off the island.'

'What yu mean off the island?'

'I want to go to England to be with Fay.'

She surprise me but then I think, well she not got nothing here anyway. So I say OK and I arrange to take the house off Daphne and have all the money change into US dollars. And then Margy move it to London and convert it to sterling. I give Daphne a good rate as well, better than the bank, and I didn't keep no commission for myself. I reckon it was the least I could do for Fay.

Daphne so happy when she get to London and look in her bank account she ring me straight away to say thank you. Just before she hang up the telephone I say, 'Say hello to Fay for me.'

It wasn't till after Daphne leave Jamaica that Ethyl tell me that the first time I go visit Miss Cicely after she take sick, Daphne had the whole house in a state of excitement. She had the maids dusting and sweeping, and washing and scrubbing every inch of every ornament, every lamp and shade, every table, chair, sideboard, bedstead, wardrobe, dressing table, windowsill, skirting board, window shutter, wooden floor. Every toilet, sink and bathtub. Every cupboard door, glass pane, veranda rail and balustrade. Every doorknob and hinge. Every photo frame, picture and wall hanging. There was that much to do.

Daphne had Edmond clear and spruce up the garden. Trim the lawn and tennis court. Cut back the bougainvillaea. Weed the rose beds. Sweep up the mangoes from under the tree. Cut hibiscus and red ginger for the vases in the house.

She had Ethyl throw open every window to give the house a good airing, and position two wicker armchairs next to each other on the veranda with one of them occasional table in between. And she had Ethyl place a ashtray and box of matches next to the cigars that she instruct Edmond to buy for her the day before.

She had them shop for oysters and she get them make fresh hot red-pepper sauce. She even have Edmond wash and polish the Wong maroon Mercedes so that it could stand proud and gleaming in the driveway.

Then she sit on the veranda, in Miss Cicely's favourite chair, and wait. Ethyl tell me that Daphne wait there till the midday sun pass over. She wait till the afternoon shower come and gone. She wait till the smell of cool rain on hot grass fade and the sound of crickets begin to threaten. That was when I finally show up and the whole house breathe a mighty sigh of relief.

'You don't remember nothing 'bout it?'

'No, Ethyl, I don't. I remember I was later than I wanted to be, and I remember standing on the veranda steps with her asking me if I wanted to take some sorrel with her. But my arms was full of chocolates and grapenut ice cream for Miss Cicely and I didn't want to stop. I just tell her I want to go straight through and she step aside so I could go into the house.'

And then with Ethyl telling me all of this, I cast my mind back to the morning I go take Daphne to the airport, and how she hug me so long and close I thought she wasn't going let me go.

I sell the Wong house to a property developer who turn it into a nice little hotel with the swimming pool and tennis court and everything, even though they rip up the grass and put down a hard court because they didn't want the expense of having to water it and tend it all the time in that heat.

I ask Gloria if she want the house before I sell it and she say no. And then she say to me, 'What I would like is a little place on the north coast. Back off the road, in one of them little coves outside Ocho Rios where Esther can bring our grandchildren and we can be together and relax like a family.'

When we go up to Ochie to look for a house it turn out Gloria already know the place she want. It in a little cove, just like she describe it, with a private beach and a nice veranda looking out to sea. It small but it nice and fresh with the breeze blowing through it. And not only does Gloria know the exact house but the caretaker know her by name. It turn out that the house belong to Henry Wong. It still in his name even though him been dead all these years because nobody in Kingston don't know nothing 'bout him owning it. So the sale complicated, but it Jamaica, so I pay the realtor and him fix things just fine. When I go sign the papers my mind reflect back to when Henry was laying sick in the Chinese Sanatorium and how Hampton tell me one day that he think him see Gloria up there and when I ask him who she visiting him say him dunno because him only see her in the car park. But I didn't say nothing to Gloria because it seem to me that whatever happen between them was all a long time ago. And anyway, like Sun Tzu say, 'Do not linger in desolate ground.'

40

Terrain

I get a phone call from Gloria. Esther have the baby and it a girl. 'We have a beautiful granddaughter,' she tell me.

When I go see Esther and the baby, Gloria is there and she look proud and beautiful. She look more beautiful than the baby, because in truth I never seen a beautiful baby. Them always look sorta wrinkled to me. Not that I seen that many babies, but anyway.

Esther look happy laying up there in the bed with the baby in her arms. And she ask me if I want to hold it, but I say no.

So she say, 'Go on. Just hold her a little minute. She not going bite you.'

'Bite me! What she going bite me with? No, man, I worried I going hurt her, she so little and frail.'

Then Gloria say, 'She little but she not so frail. You ever think what she just done go through?' And everybody laugh.

So Gloria sit me down, and take the baby off Esther and put her in my arms, and she arrange me so I got the baby safe and secure.

'What you going call her?' I ask.

Esther say, 'Sunita.'

'Sunita. Sunita.' I repeat it to myself. And I look at this tiny little African, Chinese, Indian baby and I think to myself, Sunita, you are Jamaica. Out of the many, you are the one. And you won't have no need to go back to Africa, or China, or India because this is where you belong, with your own identity and dignity. And I remember what Michael Manley say all them years ago, 'We come too far, we're not turning back now. We have a pride now. We have a place now. We have a mission now.'

While Esther and Gloria still inside, Rajinder take me out on the veranda and give me a cigar. And just as I taking my second puff him say to me, 'There was something that I wanted to talk with you about.'

I look at him sorta quizzical, because all the time they been married me and him never had that much conversation to speak of. Rajinder is a university-educated man, we not got that much in common.

'I'm sure you know from Esther that I got this job down at the docks some six months ago. It's a good job, a good middle-management position. But the trouble is I have a problem with some of the dock workers.' Him pause and look at me.

'What kind of problem?'

He look behind him inside the house like him worried 'bout who going hear. Then him sorta whisper, 'I talked to Esther about this and asked her if she thought you might be able to help but she wasn't that keen.'

'What kind of problem?'

'There is a small group of dock workers who don't ever seem to do any work. They are on the payroll, but actually they spend the whole day playing dominoes, and sending out for food and chatting with each other. That is when they are there, because half the time they don't come. They just don't turn up, but they are still paid as if they are there every day putting in a full day's work. This means that the others have to carry their workload, but they accept it because they are afraid.'

'I know what this is.'

'I've tried talking to them but it doesn't seem to do any good. I mean, obviously there are procedures for dealing with underperforming staff except I don't think they would be that receptive. And then three weeks ago one of them physically threatened me with a knife.'

'So you 'fraid for your life?'

'I am afraid, yes. But I also think it is a bad situation and I don't know what to do about it. And well, I guess I am just going on hearsay and reputation when I think that you might be able to help.'

Right then Gloria step out on to the veranda so I just say quietly to him, 'Leave it with me.'

'Is there something you can do about this? Esther is very reluctant about me even asking you. She thinks we should be able to handle it ourselves without getting you involved.'

I look at Rajinder and then at Gloria and she say to me, 'Rajinder already talk to me 'bout this. Is me tell him that it OK to ask you.'

Next day I ask Finley to go find out what going on down the dock and when he come back it turn out to be just what I expect. It a little gang thing, the same way Kenneth Wong was drawing his wage from the supermarket all the time he was running errands for Louis DeFreitas. It a kind of double-income arrangement that work good for having something to declare on your tax return. And if the boss don't like it, him suddenly find himself with a lot of union trouble.

'But,' Finley say to me, 'this is the bit you going like. The little ringleader named DeFreitas.'

'DeFreitas?'

'Yah, man. Anthony, they call him Tony for short.'

'So who would he be?'

'Louis DeFreitas's nephew.'

I give this a lot of thought before I go do anything. I think about what Zhang would say to me if he was still here. I think about what Zhang must have said to Mr Chin all that long time the two of them sit up the top of the yard at Matthews Lane talking 'bout Merleen and the baby. I think about Sun Tzu, and what he would have to say about a situation like this. And I decide that both Zhang and Sun Tzu would say, *The general who in advancing does not seek personal fame, and in withdrawing is not concerned with avoiding punishment, but whose only purpose is to protect the people and promote the best interests of his sovereign, is the precious jewel of the state.'*

And then I think to myself sure enough Sun Tzu right 'bout all these things, but maybe life not just a matter of strategy. Maybe it about something more than that, or something different anyway; something different from just ducking and weaving and manoeuvring; something that got more to do with what Zhang say 'bout benevolence and sincerity, humanity and courage.

And then I think 'bout the time I had with Gloria when Hampton and Ethyl go up to Oracabessa. And when I was listening to Zhang and Ma talking into all hours of the night. And all the time I have with Michael. And I start think that maybe there is something an individual can do that make a difference.

I ring Louis DeFreitas and ask him to come meet me at the fried-fish and bammy shack over Port Royal that Michael love so much. It is a place of peace to me, a place of calm beauty, and reasonableness. It is a place where men can talk from their hearts and not have to strike a pose or take a position.

When Louis come over there he look relieved to be catching a bit of cool breeze instead of being trapped in the still heat of West Kingston like he is used to. His face look pale and puffy. And he got his thinning hair slick back. Maybe he even look a little like he stooping. Not straight and upright like he was in the old days. And he been losing weight as well.

I say, 'I want to thank you for coming.' Him just look at me and nod his head. The waitress put down the food in front of us and rush back inside to the air conditioning.

'I have a little problem, Louis, and I think you can help me with it.'

DeFreitas look at me, but him still no say nothing. He just fix on the fish and start to eat.

'We did a lot of things and we said a lot of things in our youth. And I don't know 'bout you, but there was some of them I wish I hadn't done. I wish I had thought better of. But look at us now, we old men you and me.'

DeFreitas look at me for the first time like maybe he just start listen to me.

'I got no fight with you, Louis. You use Samuels to sell your guns in my neighbourhood and I didn't say nothing. I give you back the guns and I even give you Samuels.'

'And you get to keep Chinatown in a fair exchange.'

'Yes. I get to keep Chinatown and I not grumbling 'bout that.' DeFreitas ease back.

'Then what happen to Samuels happen to him. And I didn't say nothing. I didn't say nothing even after you send Mrs Samuels to me to look out for. Even though you and I both know that was really your responsibility what with Samuels being your man at the time.'

DeFreitas start pay attention to me now like him wondering where I am going with all of this. Him back stiffen a little and he grab on to the walking stick with the silver fox head for some sorta comfort even though him still sitting down. And right then I see that him done cut off the long fingernail on his little finger.

'That whole thing with Samuels cause me a lot of trouble with my wife and her leaving me and such. But I not blaming you for that. That was my own stupid fault. Just like it was a stupid thing for me to go hire up Kenneth Wong. Hampton warn me against it and I didn't pay him no mind. But then that is one of the things I do in my youth that I regret. Not that anything can be done about that now. But Kenneth getting killed really turn Fay against me and that is when she decide to run off to England with my children. And I can't tell you how that grieve me.'

DeFreitas start to look at me like maybe he understand what I talking 'bout. Like maybe he got some regrets of his own.

'And even though I know this whole thing with Kenneth had something to do with you, I didn't say nothing. Well now I got a problem with a situation involving my son-in-law. Your nephew, Anthony, giving him hell down the dock. My son-in-law can't get nothing done because Anthony got the usual little gang thing going on down there. I don't know if he working for you or if it just a freelance thing, but then a while ago somebody go threaten my son-in-law with a knife and now him 'fraid for his life.'

I stop and I look at DeFreitas. He look at me like maybe there is something 'bout this that he care about.

'I know you a father and grandfather yourself, Louis. Me, I only got the one grandchild, and I would like to see her grow up with a father as well as a mother.' I take a pause. 'I never ask you for nothing before. In fact I never ask nobody for nothing my whole life, but I asking you this. Get Anthony off the dock. Get him go take his gang and run his scam somewhere else. And get him leave my son-in-law in peace and good health. Do me this one favour.'

DeFreitas don't say nothing. He just rest up the walking stick and carry on eating his food.

Then him say, 'You right. This fish and bammy really good.' And then him pause and I just wait. 'I will talk to Tony for you, but I not making yu no promise, yu understand.'

41

Disposition

After Edward Seaga get elected in 1980 things get better, but his government couldn't grow the economy enough for people's liking so by 1989 Michael Manley was back in power. But him older now, more circumspect, and I think the fire had gone.

Then I start to think that maybe it wasn't just from Manley that the fire had gone. It was gone outta me as well. And maybe it was gone outta Jamaica. It was almost like the whole island move into a different phase of life. We live through our turbulent youth and come out the other side. And that other side was a place of acceptance. Not a place of contentment, it didn't feel as happy or as comfortable as that. Maybe it was a place of resignation. We become resigned to how things was, and we just decide to try do our best with that.

It wasn't a bad place to be. We had a kinda truce now that put a stop to the violence, and encourage back the foreign investors and the tourists. There was less talk of Africa and the Rasta revolution, less prophesising 'bout how Babylon was going to fall. Some said that instead of hope there was surrender. Me I just think that maybe we miss our chance, and I remember how many times Zhang say to me that people were against communism because they pronounce the word wrong, that if they pronounce it right they would feel better about it. He would say, 'Emphasis not at beginning like comm-unism. Emphasis in middle, commune-ism.'

And even though we still struggling to sort ourselves out after the English come here three hundred years ago and set everything up so careful and tidy – Africans on the bottom, the Indians, the Chinese, English on top – I think we doing OK. But I wonder to myself how many other countries there are like Jamaica? How many other countries been through what we been through? How many of them still going through it like us? All because some long time back somebody decide to pick themselves up and sail halfway 'round the world to come colonise us. And it not just about the English and the slaves. It about the Americans and the money.

So one Sunday I go take a drive to see Michael and I stop off at Holy Trinity on the way. I park the car under the shade of a mango tree and go inside. The church practically empty. It surprise me. Every other time I been there the place was busting at the seams, all the pews packed and a whole heap of people standing, some of them all cram together at the back. The sun shining down on the altar, and hanging on the wall behind it a life-size carving of Christ on the cross and, above that, a stain-glass window of the same thing in blue and red and yellow.

But this Sunday there was just a few young people getting them First Communion, in a heavy heat because the ceiling fans wasn't doing a thing to help. So people was sitting there fanning themselves and listening to the priest tell the young people that now they received the body of Christ, Christ was inside them and they should behave like Christ. That people interpret everything from within the worldview they have, and therefore they cannot understand another perspective unless they suspend their own past experience and what they think they know, and seek to understand what they see. And that Christ would help them to do that, like a uncle or godfather.

Afterwards, when I see Michael, I give him the envelope I bring for him. He take it and look at me and say, 'What is this?'

'That is the arrangements for my funeral.'

'Your funeral!'

'I reckon it time I sort a few things out. I not going live for ever.'

When he go to open it I stop him. 'There will be plenty of time for that when it happen. You can let the glue rest till then.'

Him look at me sorta quizzical so I say, 'I feel like I come to a new place what with Zhang and Ma and Henry and Cicely gone. And then a while back I had to go ask a man for a favour. A man that I distrusted my whole life. And I discover that maybe my life don't have to be all ducking and weaving and manoeuvring. Maybe I could afford to take my foot off the gas, especially after I get a fright about how all of this could end, and manage to make it through OK. So I think it time for me to count my blessings and stop reaching after something that maybe was nothing more than a idea I had about myself. Maybe it time I just be who I am and settle for something that is real.' And then I laugh and say, 'That is till the time when the Almighty make up his mind to come for me.'

Michael just sit there and look at me kindly like him taking confession. And then I say, 'I get a letter from Mui. She going come home. She done with all the excitement of them big important cases that keeping her busy this last little while and she say it time she come home and make herself useful. After all these years, eh? Anyway, I thought you would want to know if she not already tell you herself, that is.'

And right then I think to myself I glad I keep the knife and little notebook for her. Maybe when she come home she can decide what she want to do 'bout Helena Meacham.

42

Weaknesses and Strengths

Sun Tzu say, '*Of the five elements, none is always predominant; of the four seasons, none lasts for ever; of the days, some are long and some are short; and the moon waxes and wanes.*'

Gloria decide she going have a party for the baby. It nuh make no sense to me but she say, 'So what, we can't have a party to celebrate our granddaughter's birthday?' And I just agree to go along with it even though I can't see how a little thing like that going know the party for her, and we going have all these grown people just standing 'round the place with a piece of cake and bowl of ice cream in their hand. But that is what Gloria want. And maybe I feel like I have something to celebrate as well because since Miss Cicely go leave us the supermarkets and wholesalers and such, and since we get the vacation and cosmetics business on a right footing, we legal now. We completely legitimate. No more driving chickens and cigarettes 'round town. In fact I can't even remember the last time I go over the Blue Lagoon.

We have the party up in the house in Ocho Rios and in truth I don't think Gloria is celebrating the baby at all. I think she celebrating a new life. A new life for me and her. Maybe the life we should have had all along.

Everybody come up to the coast. Finley and his wife, Hampton and Ethyl, Clifton, Merleen Chin and John Morrison, George and Margaret, Milton, Marcia and the two other girls from Gloria's

East Kingston house. Even Margy Lopez show up with some woman we none of us ever see before. And then we have the guests of honour, Esther, Rajinder and baby Sunita. It was family.

I stand on the veranda and look out at the calm, blue Caribbean and I think how glad I was that I manage to sort out that wharf thing with DeFreitas and how only last week I tell Gloria 'bout the arrangements I make for her and Esther if anything should happen to me, and she just laugh and slap me on the arm and say, 'What going happen to you?'

And then I realise that I wouldn't complain if I happen to drop down dead right there. I start picture the whole thing, how they take me to the hospital and start go through my pockets. A pocket-knife with two blades and a bottle opener, a cigar packet with three Flor de Farach Farachitos, two wads of notes – Jamaican dollars and US dollars – some wooden toothpicks in a silver container, and a black leather photo wallet with the figure of a crane under a pine tree engrave on it, and inside a photograph of Mui in her barrister wig and gown and opposite it one of me sitting down holding baby Mui, and Xiuquan standing next to the chair.

I think about my life and how hard I tried to find something to believe in. Something that would mean something to me, like how Zhang had his stories of China and the masses throwing out the foreigners and making a life of their own. Like how Mr Manley say, Jamaicans had to make an identity, and dignity and destiny for ourselves. But it wasn't the same for everybody. Like Gloria was always telling me, not everybody had their sights set on building a nation. Some people just wanted to put food on the table. And I suppose that was me as well because even though I talk Zhang's high ideals I was still busy just making money and fixing any problem that anybody wanted to bring to me. I try hard to believe that out of many we could be one people, but when the shooting start I couldn't make up my mind to go get myself killed over it. Not like my father did in China.

But like Zhang was always telling me, everything got consequences. Everything you do or don't do is connected to everything

269

else. So any time you do something you making another thing that will be waiting for you 'round the corner. And then I start wonder if Michael is right 'bout God and all of that, and how the Almighty is fixing to punish me for all the things I done.

Gloria come out on the veranda and stand next to me and we listen to the gentle lap of the Caribbean on the shore. She got a smile of contentment on her face. And then she reach out and take my hand and look off into the distance where she tell me, on a clear day, she can see Cuba. I think well, out of the many Sunita is the one so maybe I make a contribution after all. I can hear a commotion inside and Michael's voice greeting everybody.

And then I think 'bout Mui coming home after this long time. And I think if I drop down dead right now that is the only thing it would grieve me to miss. And then I think no, I would miss that I never find a way to have nothing with Karl even though him and me exchange a few lines from time to time. And I would miss the possibility that me and Fay ever cross paths again.

That is when I realise that I not dead yet, so maybe it not all lost. And I remember how Zhang rest his palm flat on my chest one time and say to me, 'Everything is in your own heart.'

Author's Note

Han Suyin once wrote that we Chinese are history-minded. And as the world knows, we Jamaicans are politics-minded. Perhaps it is no surprise, therefore, that this book, my first work of fiction, should turn out to be a political history. Not only because every story has a context, but also because context creates the possibilities of what might be, fashioning the circumstances of people's lives so that they decide to do one thing rather than another, making their story unfold in this way rather than that.

So whilst Pao's story is completely fictional, I have tried my best to get the context right. This has involved a huge amount of research including books, films, the internet, as well as several trips to Jamaica and endless questions and queries to my mother and other members of my family. The key documentary sources are listed on page 275.

In the end though, in true Taoist style, *Pao* is a book about Jamaica's history, and it is not a book about Jamaica's history. It is a book about Jamaican people and it is not a book about Jamaican people. What it is, is a book about the world, and the universe and the ten thousand things.

Kerry Young, June 2010

Acknowledgements

When this book was submitted to Bloomsbury, Helen Garnons-Williams remarked that it had the potential to be truly wonderful. If it has achieved that potential, it is because of her. Thanks also to Sarah-Jane Forder for her meticulous and sensitive work. I had no idea copy-editing would be so much fun. Erica Jarnes for taking charge of the things I found scary and for keeping me on track through the process. My agent, Susan Yearwood, without whom Pao would not have found his way to Helen. And to Amanda and Charlie, and all those who helped to make the impossible possible, and who cheered me on over the years, thank you.

Key Sources

Black, Stephanie, *Life and Debt in Jamaica*, Tuff Gong Pictures, 2001

Chen, Ray, *The Shopkeepers: Commemorating 150 years of the Chinese in Jamaica 1854–2004*, Periwinkle Publishers (Jamaica) Ltd, 2005

Han, Suyin, *The Crippled Tree*, Panther Books Ltd, 1972

Jian Bozan, Shao Xunzheng and Hu Hua, *A Concise History of China*, Foreign Languages Press, 1986

Manley, Beverley, *The Manley Memoirs*, Ian Randle Publishers, 2008

Manley, Michael, *Jamaica: Struggle in the Periphery*, Third World Media Ltd in association with Writers and Readers Publishing Co-operative Society Ltd, 1982

Nhat Hanh, Thich, *The Heart of the Buddha's Teaching*, Broadway Books, 1999

Nhat Hanh, Thich, *The Art of Power*, HarperOne, 2008

Pan, Lynn, *Sons of the Yellow Emperor: A History of the Chinese Diaspora*, Kodansha America, Inc., 1994

Powell, Patricia, *The Pagoda*, Harcourt Brace & Company, 1999

Rogozinski, Jan, *A Brief History of the Caribbean*, Meridian, 1994

Salaria, Fatima, *Blood and Fire*, screened Sunday 4 August 2002 on BBC 2

Sherlock, Philip and Bennett, Hazel, *The Story of the Jamaican People*, Ian Randle Publishers, 1998

Sun Tzu, *The Art of War*, translated by Samuel B. Griffith, Oxford University Press, 1971

The Gleaner, *Geography & History of Jamaica* (23rd edition), The Gleaner Company, 1995

Van De Wetering, Janwillem, *The Empty Mirror*, Arkana, 1987

Williams, C.A.S., *Outlines of Chinese Symbolism and Art Forms* (3rd revised edition), Dover Publications, Inc., 1976

Pao
by Kerry Young

These discussion questions are designed to enhance your group's conversation about *Pao*, a sweeping historical saga about a young Chinese man in Jamaica who rises to become the "godfather" of Kingston's Chinatown.

About this book
Pao is about to marry the wrong woman. Seven years after he immigrates to Jamaica from China, he meets Gloria, a beautiful Jamaican prostitute who steals his heart. But Pao's beloved mentor, Zhang, from whom he inherited the Chinatown "family business," does not approve of Gloria. So Pao decides to marry Fay Wong, the elegant daughter of one of Kingston's richest Chinese men. Suddenly Pao is running not only the Chinatown underworld, but also many legitimate businesses too, thanks to his profitable marriage.

But Fay is miserable in Chinatown; she plots an escape to England, taking her two children with her. Although Pao is devastated to lose his family, he realizes that his children are safer far away from Kingston—after Jamaica gains independence from England, all hopes of unity and brotherhood soon dissolve into violence. As chaos overtakes the streets of Kingston, Pao must face his part in Jamaica's struggle to overcome its great divides: between Chinese and African, capitalist and communist, wealthy and poor.

For discussion

1. The novel begins in 1945, when Pao first meets Gloria, then flashes back to his immigration to Jamaica seven years earlier. Why does the novel open with the love triangle of Pao, Gloria, and Fay, instead of at the beginning of Pao's life in Kingston?

2. *Pao* is written in dialect, with words spelled as Pao pronounces them. What is the effect of reading the novel in Pao's voice? What would the novel be like without Pao's distinctive voice as narrator?

3. Consider Pao's first impressions of Jamaica as he arrives from China by boat. How does the city of Kingston look to Pao? How does he quickly make Kingston his home?

4. When Pao falls in love with Gloria, Judge Finley tells him, "Marriage is not for celebrating. It is something you do to give your children a name" (6). Why does Pao choose to marry Fay Wong, and what price does he pay for his choice? How does he eventually reconnect with Gloria's daughter, Esther, even though he has not given her his name?

5. Compare the two Yang brothers, Pao and Xiuquan. How are the brothers similar and how are they different? Xiuquan declares, "I want something better. Something better than being a Chinaman in Chinatown" (45). Does Pao, too, want something better? Explain.

6. Consider Pao's inheritance from Zhang. What does Pao learn from the older man? Pao hopes that "maybe one day I become like him, a man that believe in something. A man that is loyal to a cause. A man that people can count on" (51). How does Pao grow up to become like Zhang, and how does he remain different from his mentor?

7. Discuss the impact of Sun Tzu's *The Art of War* on Pao's decision making. How does he put Sun Tzu's strategies to action? At the end of the novel, Pao realizes, "And then I think to myself sure enough Sun Tzu right 'bout all these things, but maybe life not just a matter of strategy . . . Something that got more to do with what Zhang say 'bout

benevolence and sincerity, humanity and courage" (262). How does Pao strike a balance between Sun Tzu's teachings and Zhang's principles?

8. According to Zhang, "the Jamaicans same as the Chinese, poor and exploited and oppressed" (30). If the Jamaicans and Chinese are "brothers in arms," as Zhang believes, why are there tensions between these two groups? How does Pao strive to overcome the ethnic tensions of Kingston, and when does he fail?

9. Discuss the ongoing conflict between Fay and her mother, Miss Cicely. How does Miss Cicely treat her daughter? Why does Fay rebel against her mother, even as an adult? What are the origins of their dispute, and why are they unable to resolve it?

10. Pao narrates, "When Michael Manley win the general election in 1972 I celebrate more than I done for Independence ten years earlier, because this time it really seem to mean something" (200). Why is Pao skeptical of the 1962 celebrations of independence from England? Why is he more interested in politics in the 1970s? Does Pao do his part to improve the living conditions of all Jamaicans? Why or why not?

11. Discuss Father Michael's involvement in Pao's life. What is the basis of the friendship between these very different men? What attracts Father Michael to Fay, and what price does Father Michael pay for his temptation?

12. Consider Fay's escape to England. How does Pao react to his family's disappearance? What steps does he take to get his children back, and how does he realize that they are better off in England than in Jamaica?

13. When Pao arrives from China as a boy, he becomes Philip Young; when his son Xiuquan settles in England, Pao agrees to call him Karl. What is the significance of these name changes?

14. Consider the long rivalry between Pao and Louis DeFreitas, the gangster who controls West Kingston. How do these two powerful men conduct business differently? How do Samuels and Kenneth Wong fall victim to the gang war? How do Pao and DeFreitas finally resolve their rivalry?

15. Kerry Young, the author of *Pao*, moved from Jamaica to England in 1965, much like Pao's daughter Mui. How does Young portray Mui in the novel? Why does Mui remain attached to her father and to Jamaica, even as a barrister in England? The novel ends just before Mui's homecoming to Jamaica. How does this ending feel?

Suggested reading
Cristina García, *Monkey Hunting*; Ha Jin, *Waiting*; Anchee Min, *Pearl of China*; Jean Kwok, *Girl in Translation*; Edwidge Danticat, *The Dew Breaker*; Junot Díaz, *The Brief Wondrous Life of Oscar Wao*; Jamaica Kincaid, *Annie John*; Julia Alvarez, *In the Time of Butterflies*; Lisa See, *Shanghai Girls*; Henry Chang, *Chinatown Beat*; Beverley Manley, *The Manley Memoirs*; Sun Tzu, *The Art of War*

Kerry Young was born in Kingston, Jamaica, to a Chinese-African mother and a Chinese father, a businessman in Kingston's shadow economy who provided inspiration for Pao. Young moved to England in 1965 at the age of ten. She earned her MA in creative writing at Nottingham Trent University. This is her first novel.